PULLING UP THE WEEDS

PULLING UP THE WEEDS

Caroline Ashton

ABOUT THE AUTHOR

Caroline was born in Durham City but has lived in many different parts of the country before finally settling in Norfolk. Aged eleven, she began writing stories for the school magazine and has continued whenever work, marriage and raising three children have allowed. She started writing (almost) full time during a creative writing degree with the Open University. Caroline's favourite activity, other than writing, is walking with her husband and two cocker spaniels.

ACKNOWLEDGEMENTS

Once upon a time, in 2006 to be exact, a group of disparate people set out on the first presentation of the Open University's creative writing course. Nine months later some of them had become a close group of friends known as the Snugglers. To them my grateful thanks for their continuous support, advice, criticism and affection.

To my husband my thanks for his support and for valiantly ignoring the dust that gathers on every horizontal surface while I write.

DEDICATION

To my mother who would have loved to read this.
To my daughter who may yet do so.

CHAPTER ONE

If there was one thing Virginia Lesage hated more than walking uphill away from the GP's surgery it was walking downhill towards it. The days of sweeping up the drive to Hardingham Hall Consulting Rooms in George's Mercedes to see one of his fellow consultants were long gone. As indeed were George and the Mercedes. At seventy-two, Virginia thought, life should be getting more comfortable not less. Not that dropping dead of a heart attack on the fifteenth tee would have been particularly comfortable for George. But at least he wasn't now left with a house that was too big, bills that were too high and a pension that was, thank you very much George, too small. These facts angered and puzzled her in equal, daily measure, particularly on a sunny May morning such as this one.

Virginia pushed open the surgery door. The antiseptic foam dispenser greeted her beside the hi-tech log in screen on the left-hand wall. This was ridiculous; all she wanted was a renewed prescription for the occasional sleeping pill. There was really no need to have to trail down here and sit amongst a lot of sick people. She punched in her sex and birthday. Yellow letters on the bright blue screen told her she had been recognised. Not by the receptionists, she thought. No need for them even to look up from telephones that never stopped ringing.

Virginia cast a quick look at the available seats. One was next to a young mother inadequately controlling a toddler while her baby wailed in its pushchair. Another near an elderly man with a hacking

1

cough. The one beside the early-middle-aged Mrs Someone she'd occasionally seen at the WI market on a Friday morning looked the safest. She sat down next to her and nodded.

Mrs Someone nodded back. 'Good morning.'

'Indeed.' Virginia could have sworn the woman had sat up straighter. Not that it made her as tall or as straight as Virginia's stick-thin figure. She chanced a second look. The woman's face was flushed across the nose. Her cheeks and eyes were red. Drink, Virginia thought. She had heard something to that effect after Mr ... er, Capstowe, that was it, Anthony Capstowe, had died a couple of months before George. She felt a quick stab of envy for anyone who could escape into a haze of rosé. Even the briefest encounter with alcohol gave her a massive headache. Nor would drink solve her shortness of cash or ease the constant penny-watching. Only make it worse.

A high-pitched beep sounded above the coughs and wails. A band of red letters marched across a narrow screen above the archway to the consulting rooms. *Andrea Capstowe to Doctor Frank room 6.* Andrea stood up, nodded to Virginia then disappeared under the arch.

Thankfully left to her own company, Virginia picked up a copy of the surgery newsletter from the low table beside her chair. A list of clinics - antenatal, diabetic, autumn flu jabs – filled the bottom right-hand corner beneath a photo of a smiling young woman in a nurse's uniform. Christine, the text said, was joining the practice and was looking for a temporary room until she could arrange her own accommodation. For a moment Virginia was tempted. Then, no. Straightened finances or not, she really did not want anyone else fidgeting around her house, large as it was.

She dropped the newsletter onto the table and picked up the parish magazine instead. Adverts and announcements filled the pages. The upcoming summer fête, the junior school sports day, An Inspector Calls performed by the local amateur dramatic group for one week only, tickets still available. The back page had a list of all the local groups. Half way down were the contact details of Facing It Together. Virginia shuddered. Never. Not in a million years.

The screen beeped. This time the marching letters said *Virginia Lesage to Doctor Mellows room 4.* Virginia rose and went to ask for more sleeping pills.

Home from the surgery, Andrea Capstowe switched on the CD player in her lounge. Pachelbel's Fugue in C Major bounced joyfully into the lounge. She bent down and skipped a couple tracks to the Chaconne in D Minor. The mournful sounds lasted for ten seconds before she snapped them off.

'For God's sake,' she muttered. She dragged a hand though her mousey hair. 'I've got to get out of this mess.'

Mess it was. Not in the material sense. These days the house was tidier than it had ever been. Tidier than when Anthony had scattered his sheets of music across the dining table beside his violin. Tidier than when he had sat in the third bedroom making fragile, melon-bodied lutes and music stands. She never went in there now. Never dusted the light bulbous frames or the spindly stands. To her, Anthony's scent still lingered and his presence still filled every corner. She could almost hear his voice calling her to come and hear his latest composition.

The mess, such as it was, was all in her head. The succession of counsellors she had seen had filled it with words like 'letting go', 'new chapter', 'moving on'. 'Coming to terms' and 'blessed release' had washed round her ears until she'd decided to stop consulting people and start consulting the vin du pays instead. Now she'd have to abandon that too, given Doctor Frank's frank description of liver damage this morning. Definitely Frank by name and frank by nature. Not beyond repair, apparently. At present, apparently. Apparently. The words had struck her like a major chord. Doctor Frank was encouraging, supportive, everything a concerned GP should be. And she was grateful. Really she was.

She walked back into the hall. The morning's post lay on the floor, pushed aside by the opening door. One double-glazing promo envelope, one electoral roll 'Important Information' envelope, and one flyer advertising the local estate agent. Perhaps that was the answer. A 'new chapter' in a new house. Moving out and 'moving on'. A glimmer flared in the corner of her mind. Perhaps she should sell this place. She looked around. The carpets were decent; the walls were unassuming shades of white and cream. She and Anthony had painted them all three years ago. That final happy year before he'd been diagnosed. Neither of them liked vivid colours that went out of date in six months. No, the house was OK. It just needed a little brightening up. A little ... what was the word the TV designers used? Juzzing. Well, an indoor plant or two from the garden centre should juzz it up enough.

She picked her car keys out of the slim dish on the hall radiator cover. The mirror above it shot an image of flushed cheeks and reddened eyes back at her. Not good. Her teeth clenched onto her bottom lip. Yesterday would have been their twenty-sixth wedding anniversary. She'd celebrated, if that was the word, every minute of it. Every second from when she'd woken at eighteen minutes past three in the morning until the last one ticked away past midnight. Her companions for the celebration were still in the kitchen. Three of them, tall, slim and dark. All of them with Côte du Rhone in flourishing letters on the labels stuck across their middles.

The car keys tinkled back into the dish. The pot plants would have to wait.

The change from April's excessive showers into the sort of early summer morning that sometimes graces England had the Old Oak Garden Centre heaving with retired couples and young mothers. Rosie Reynolds sallied through the glass doors in full sail, moving rather faster than would normally be expected for a lady of her years and width. The tall green racks of colourful seed packets trembled at her approach, as well they might. They stood close together. Every time the floating scarves, loose sleeves and gathered skirt on Rosie's wide figure drifted close to them they threatened to topple to the floor like felled dominoes.

Rosie's hand gravitated towards the vibrant packets as if of its own volition. It started at the As (angelica for improving circulation and immune system), skipped to the Fs (feverfew to ease migraines) then to the Ls (lemon balm to counter depression). One by one the packets dropped into the green plastic basket on her arm. She swept round the far end of a rack towards bright packets of marigolds and valerian.

Satisfied, she headed for the checkouts. Only one was open. A queue of six people and four blossoming trolleys trailed from it. The last trolley contained two trays of red and white striped petunias. Clutching rather tightly onto it was a short, plump, elderly woman in a beige dress and jacket.

Rosie peered at the flowers. 'They're pretty,' she said. 'Look lovely in a hanging basket.'

Gwendolyn Fellowes looked from the plants to Rosie and back again. 'Oh dear. I don't want them in a basket. I thought I'd put them in the border by the front door.'

Rosie tutted and sucked air through her front teeth. 'Is it a sunny spot?'

'Oh yes. Arthur always put petunias in there.' She frowned. 'At least I think they were petunias.'

Rosie shifted her basket from one ample hip to the other. 'These'll straggle all over the place.' She took hold of the trolley. 'Come on, let's go and find some better ones.'

At the word 'better', the checkout girl paused her hammering of the till keys but Rosie had turned away and missed the sharp glance flashed in her direction.

Gwen trotted along beside her as fast as her arthritic hip allowed. 'Arthur was so particular about the garden. I don't like to see it looking uncared for.'

Rosie circumnavigated a woman with a toddler in her trolley. The child was pulling leaves off a purple-flowered hebe.

'Your husband?' Rosie asked.

Gwen nodded. 'I buried him in January.'

For a fleeting moment Rosie had visions of the late gentleman happily ensconced six feet under the front border. She banished it. 'I've seen you in the post office haven't I? Aren't you Mrs Fellowes?'

Gwen nodded. 'Gwen – well Gwendolyn really, but only Arthur ever called me that.' She sighed.

'I'm Rosie Reynolds. I do herbal remedies. And reiki massage. You should try it. Does wonders for the peace of mind.'

'Oh I don't think I could. Caroline would never approve.'

'Who's Caroline?'

'My daughter. She wants me to sell up and move into a sheltered flat but ...' Another sigh.

Rosie slid to a halt beside the bench of potted geraniums. She peered at Gwen's face. 'You don't sound keen.'

'I'm not. I've lived there more than forty years. I like it.' Her face drooped. 'Caroline keeps saying I don't need five bedrooms any more. Not now.' She sighed. 'It's all so difficult. And all the bills.'

'Ah – left you a bit short, did he?'

The wrinkles on Gwen's round face lifted into a smile. 'Oh no. Arthur was most particular. He had everything arranged properly. It's just that ... well, he did all the money things. Accounts and such. It's all been a bit confusing since he went.'

Rosie patted her hand. 'You just tell them you're staying put, dear.' She set off again, swerving between the tables of massed hebes and grasses.

Gwen bobbed along behind her like a dinghy after a yacht. Catching up, she said. 'I wish I could. But it's so difficult with Caroline.'

'I think you could do with a centaury remedy.'

'A century? But I'm only eighty-two.'

Rosie laughed a deep-throated laugh that shook her wide bosom and sent her scarves fluttering. 'Not century. Centaury. It's a plant. Pretty thing. Little star shaped flowers. If you take a tincture of it, it boosts your courage. I've some at home. We'll get you some when we've finished here.'

'Oh, I don't ... I mean, I don't know. I've never done anything like that before. Arthur always said –'

Rosie dismissed the late Arthur with a flick of her hand. 'Now's the time to start. You want to be able to say No to your daughter, don't you?'

Gwen rather looked as if she wanted to say No right now. Instead she took refuge in, 'I don't want to put you to any trouble.'

Rosie heaved the trolley to a halt beside a bench covered with trays of double petunias. 'How did you get here? Have you a car? I walked. It's only about a mile. You could give me a lift home.'

'Oh dear.' Gwen clutched her hands together. 'Will there be enough room? There's the plants and Miffy.'

Rosie had visions of another disapproving daughter lurking in the boot of Gwen's car. 'Who's Miffy?'

'My little dog. She always sits on the back seat. She has her own cushion.'

'Well, I shall be in the front with you so that'll be fine. Now ...' Rosie peered at the petunias. 'Let's get your flowers sorted.'

CHAPTER TWO

Rosie's home was pretty much like her. Wide, low, colourful, slightly outmoded and comfortably disordered. It seemed entirely suitable that a gentle sun shone on it and the plants thronging both sides of the straight gravel path to the front door. In the sitting room, with the bundle of snow-white fluff that was Miffy hugged to her chest, Gwen could see the back garden was much the same. No lawn, only narrow grass paths between clouds of perennials, shrubs and herbs.

'Oh,' she said. 'It's lovely. So full of flowers. Arthur always put ours in borders round the lawn.' She sighed. 'He kept a lovely lawn.'

'I love flowers. I'd have more if I could. And a bigger garden.' She steered Gwen towards a sagging chintz-covered armchair. 'Sit yourself down and I'll make some camomile tea. Then we'll sort you out. Camomile tea is good for the nerves.'

Gwen felt a great and urgent need of something that was good for the nerves. She held onto the dog with one hand. With the other she twisted the lock of grey hair beside her ear round and round her finger until it would twist no more. Sounds of tea-making echoed from the kitchen. Gwen sighed.

By the time Rosie had finished with her, she had a small bag of herbal remedies and a leaflet on reiki massage (twenty pounds a forty-five minute session). She was also five minutes late for her hair appointment at Ellie's Hairem. She teetered out to her car - well, the late Arthur's Audi to be exact. Miffy, dumped onto her back seat cushion, indicated her intense disapproval. Gwen shushed her and drove at a geriatric snail's pace round to the small parade of shops. She never drove anywhere other than from her house to the village shops. The car was too big and she hated parking it. Visits to Waitrose's supermarket, or indeed anywhere else, required the services of Abbey Cars. Mr Alex James was always delighted to oblige a frequent customer.

Gwen peered over the top of the steering wheel. All the parking spaces outside the shops were taken. With a sigh that was fast becoming a permanent feature of her day, she slid the wheel through her ten-to-two hands and parked outside a bungalow three doors away. The car was rather less than parallel to the kerb.

Gwen wound the back windows halfway down and left Miffy snoring in the locked car. She crossed the road to the salon causing a delivery van coming up behind her to break more than the driver had intended. The salon looked empty. No-one stood or walked around inside. No-one sat in the three padded chairs in front of the mirrors. No spotlights illuminated them. Gwen reached the door. A sheet of A4 paper announced that Ellie's Hairem was unexpectedly closed for the day for 'Family Reasons'.

'Oh dear,' Gwen's hand half covered her mouth. 'I'd forgotten.' She hurried back to her car as fast as her twinging hip allowed.

Eleanor Duncan sat in the back of the long black Bentley that was creeping along Barton Road behind her husband's hearse. Why, she wondered, do undertakers call cars carriages? It was ridiculously old fashioned. Victorian, even. Carriages had horses with tall, black feathers nodding on their heads, not low, throbbing diesel engines. The car bumped over the speed table at the crossroad with Church Lane. Ellie clutched at the plaited strap hanging beside the window and looked out. Tall beech trees reaching across the road turned it into a dappled green tunnel. A pair of young women pushed their infants along the footpath in large-wheeled pushchairs. A gentleman well into his fifties walked a small cocker spaniel towards them. It all looked perfectly normal. Was perfectly normal. Ellie didn't feel perfectly normal. She didn't know how she felt. Shocked? Yes. Sad? Well ... no, not really. More ... she hated to admit it ... but lodged in the bottom corner of her mind was a minute splinter of relief.

Kenneth hadn't turned out to be her idea of a perfect husband. Probably not anyone's really. Not unless they liked having curses from an overworked, obsessive chef rattling round their ears at one in the morning when the not-so-dearly-beloved arrived home from his restaurant. The shouting almost made having her mistakes turned into jokes at the golf club something of a relief. Ellie remembered how he'd basked in the uproarious guffaws while she'd had to endure sympathetic glances from the other wives. Glances that had knotted the breath in her throat and made it almost impossible to plaster an aren't-men-silly smile onto her face. On the whole, she'd been grateful he'd found so little time to attend. There'd be no more of that now. Nor of his fanatical insistence on knowing everything she spent, every penny of Hairem's profit. Nor of –

The Bentley lurched. It turned through the church gates and scrunched up the pebbled drive. Ahead, the hearse glided to a halt at the porch door. The carriage pulled up behind it. The undertaker-in-chief slid out of the hearse. He held a black, crêpe-swathed top hat in the crook of his arm. Its long tails fluttered in the breeze and very nearly caught in the door when it swung shut. Stony-faced, he clicked her door open and handed her out as if she were seventy-two, not forty. Ellie straightened her black skirt, new, and tugged down her black jacket, also new. The slim suit might be appropriate but black really wasn't her colour despite her blonde hair. She decided she'd never wear it again.

She followed the coffin and the vicar's careful enunciation of 'We brought nothing into this world and it is sure we can take nothing out' up the aisle. Strange, she thought, how a few seconds could delete a whole person. Make them into something that had almost never been. Kenneth had driven out of the golf club into Elmtree

Avenue hundreds of times without hitting the tall tree opposite. What was so different about last week? Had he skidded? Had something got in his way? A dog perhaps? Was he thinking about the restaurant as usual, and not about driving? Ellie would never know. She wondered when reality would hit and she'd start to miss him. If it ever did.

Back at the house – her house now – she handed round plates of nibbles. Most of Kenneth's golfing buddies had turned up, bringing their wives. The men were drinking their way through Kenneth's single malt, transferring, when that ran out, to a bottle of Bristol Cream bought many Christmases ago. The wives, as designated drivers, stood together, sipping orange juice and staring at the décor.

Virginia Lesage held up her hand against the proffered plate of mini sausage rolls.

'No thank you.' A brief flash of sympathy washed across her face. 'I'm so sorry, Eleanor.'

Ellie's mouth turned down briefly. 'Thank you.'

A small silence developed.

Virginia laid a hand on Ellie's arm. 'It will get better you know.'

Ellie glanced up. 'What? Oh, yes, of course. Thank you.'

Virginia smiled charmingly and excused herself. Shock, she thought. It's always a shock.

Ellie drifted away from her guests, through the conservatory and into the garden. Someone in a voluminous dark blue skirt was bending almost double beside the shed in the far corner.

'Hello,' Ellie called.

Rosie, face upside-down with her hair descending slowly earthwards, peered under her outstretched arm and smiled. 'Mrs Duncan.' She straightened up. 'What a lovely patch of burdock. May I have some? Very good for detoxing, you know.'

Ellie didn't know. She looked at the clump of thistle-like plants with long frilly leaves like curly kale. 'Yes, if you want to. They're only weeds. Kenneth wasn't a gardener. Nor am I.'

A smile puffed Rosie's cheeks up to her eyes. 'Oh thank you. It's very difficult to find any burdock these days. Have you a spade?'

Ellie blinked. She pointed. 'There might be one in the shed.'

Rosie rattled the door. 'It's locked.' Enthusiasm gave way to reality. 'Oh, I'm so sorry. How selfish of me. You won't want me bothering you today. I'll comeback tomorrow, shall I? With my spade?'

'I don't mind. You can do it now if you'd like. I'll see if I can find the key.'

When Kenneth's wake had died a death, the burdock roots reclined on the garden path in three of Sainsbury's orange plastic bags. Rosie and Ellie sat in the conservatory looking at the white clouds that were turning an unpromising shade of grey. Cups of camomile tea sat on the round wicker table between them.

Rosie gave a half cough. 'I always carry a few T-bags with me.' She waved at her embroidered tote. 'Good for the nerves.' When Ellie did not answer, she went on. 'It must have been a great shock for you. So sudden. And you so young.' She tutted. 'Not like poor Mrs Capstowe. Sad, slow way to go that was.' She peered at Ellie. 'In some ways a quick exit is something to be grateful for.'

Ellie wondered if Kenneth's last milliseconds had any grateful aspect to them. She rather thought not. Probably more of an obscenities aspect.

Rosie plumped herself back in the padded rattan chair. 'So what'll you do now?'

Ellie shrugged. 'I'm not sure.' She sipped the insipid liquid in her cup, wrinkled her nose at the taste, and considered. 'What I'd really like,' she said after a few moments. 'Is to open a second salon.'

'Excellent.' Rosie almost clapped her hands. 'A new chapter. New beginning.'

Ellie gazed round the conservatory and back into the lounge. 'If I found myself a smaller place, I'd have the equity from here to pay the rent on another salon. Just until it got going.'

Rosie sipped her tea without grimacing. 'So you're not senti-
mentally attached to this place then?'

'Oh no. This was Kenneth's choice even though it was mostly
mum's money. I've never really taken to it.'

'Well, that's good. Now you can move. Go somewhere you'd
like.' Rosie smiled. 'You're being very sensible, doing what you
want.' A quick sigh. 'If only all the bereaved saw it like that. There's
poor Mrs Lesage rattling around in that great house in Merland
Crescent which I'm sure she can't afford.'

'Poor? Mrs Lesage? Surely not.'

'Oh, I think so. She always used to look so smart. So well turned
out. How long is it since she came to you for a haircut?'

Ellie tilted her head. 'Now you mention it, she's not been in for
a while.'

'I thought not.' A pause. 'There's been something of a rash of
deaths this past year.'

'Has there?'

'Oh yes. I always read the Hatch, Match and Despatch in the
local rag.' Another sip of tea drained her cup. 'My dear Malcolm's
been gone for ... oh, it must be fifteen years now.'

'Really?' Ellie's eyes opened wider. 'How ... er, how did you
manage for the first few weeks?'

'Oh, it wasn't too bad. Dear Malcolm didn't care to have me
going on about herbs and healing all the time. When he went, I read
everything I could about them. Went on courses, did some training.
Then I dug up the lawn and planted flowers and shrubs instead. It
all kept me busy.'

Ellie thought Dear Malcolm didn't sound particularly dear
at all. At least Kenneth hadn't made her give up her salon.
Useful financial top-up, he'd always said. Not that she'd ever
let him have all of the profits. Only some of them. Keeping her
self-assessment tax form away from him had become something
of an art.

Rosie was still talking. 'Now's your chance. Sell this place. Move on.' She waved the empty cup around wildly. 'Get yourself that new salon.'

She stopped talking, cup suspended mid-air. Her eyebrows drew together. After a moment, she put the cup back on the saucer and stared at it. The pause lengthened. At last her face lifted and her eyes brightened.

'Is something wrong?'

'Oh no.' Rosie shook her head. Two hairpins tumbled out of her pepper and salt hair. 'Nothing at all. Just a little thought crossed my mind.'

CHAPTER THREE

On Wednesday morning four pink envelopes dropped onto four different doormats. Virginia picked hers up immediately, relieved to see it wasn't another bill. She slid her ebony letter-opener under the flap. The fold slit open with satisfying neatness.

A pink card trimmed round the edge with narrow ribbon and stuck with two long lavender flowerheads fell out. Gold felt tip script said:

Rosie Reynolds
invites
Mrs V Lesage
to tea at 4.00 pm on Tuesday 6th May at
Laburnum Cottage
Old Church Lane
RSVP   01374 416782

Scrawled across the bottom in pencil was:

PS I'm not selling anything

Virginia looked at it. Why on earth would Rosie Reynolds be inviting her to tea? She frowned. She tapped the corner of the card against her long front teeth. Should she? Well, tea would be one less meal to prepare. Or pay for. Easing the card back into its envelope, Virginia Lesage prepared to send her thanks.

By Thursday afternoon Rosie had four RSVP's of thanks. She hadn't expected them any earlier. One day to allow for surprise and curiosity; one night to sleep on it; and one morning to think 'Well, why not?'.

She had tidied all the trappings of card-making and patchwork out of her sitting room. Vases of flowers cut from the garden that morning stood on every available surface except for the cut down and painted dining table in front of the sofa. On that were a small white cloth and a tray of mismatched, flower-patterned cups and saucers. The only odd note in the room was the cheval mirror near the television. Several large sheets of wallpaper were clipped to the top with straining clothespegs. At three fifty-five Rosie carried a plate of sandwiches and three-tier stand of fairy cakes out of the kitchen and put them beside the tray. A minute later she switched the kettle on again.

After the smiles and hello's and thank you's, the women were all seated in the lounge. No-one spoke while Rosie poured the tea. Four pairs of eyes focussed on the emerging liquid. It was gratifyingly tan. Four women sat back against the chintz with relieved smiles.

Tea, plates, sandwiches and cakes safely distributed, Rosie too sat back, holding her tea and smiling. Her plate stayed on the table.

'I expect you're wondering why I asked you here.' A few murmurs answered her. 'Well, I've been thinking. We're all widows - most of us fairly recent - and I think we can all help each other.'

Virginia opened her mouth. Rosie held up her free hand. 'No, let me finish. I've been a widow for fifteen years. I know it's a sad time at first and a lonely time after. No matter how good the family is - if you've got one - there's a lot of lonely evenings. After my Malcolm went I could go a whole day without speaking to another living soul. A whole week sometimes if the postie hadn't been and it wasn't one for paying the milkman.'

'I know,' Gwen said. 'It's just like that for me.'

Andrea's eyes turned a little pinker. She stared down at her cucumber sandwich and perfect fairy cake.

'And money doesn't go so far these days,' Rosie went on. 'Everything's more expensive and the Council's just put the tax up again. As for the gas ... well ... I had to sit down when I saw my last bill.'

'I'll agree with you there,' Ellie said. 'The one for my salon's bordering on exorbitant.'

Gwen sighed so heavily ripples appeared on the top of her tea. 'That's what Caroline keeps telling me.'

'We're agreed then, bills are getting bigger.' She put down her tea and picked up her plate, directing her eyes to Virginia. 'Mrs Lesage?'

Virginia pushed her shoulders back. 'If you say so.'

'Where's this leading?' Ellie asked.

'To The Big Idea.' Rosie took a bite of fairy cake. Half of it disappeared. Four women watched her chomp it happily. A thin line of icing sugar transferred itself from a sponge fairy wing to her top lip.

'Rosie!' Ellie said. 'What is it?'

Rosie swallowed. Her fingers clenched on the half-eaten fairy cake. The second wing fell off unheeded. She took a deep breath. 'What about selling our houses and buying a big one to share so the bills'd be smaller and we wouldn't be lonely and someone'd be there if we got the flu and couldn't get out to the shops?' She slid to a halt, panting and slightly flushed.

The four women stared at her.

No-one spoke.

After a moment Ellie said, 'Share?'

'Yes.'

'All of us?'

'Yes. Well, those who'd want to. Be cheaper if we all did it.'

'Live together?' Virginia said. 'You mean like in a ... a commune?'

'Not exactly,' Rosie said. 'We don't have to have chickens or anything.'

'I've always fancied chickens,' Gwen said. 'I love eggs but they're high cholesterol. Arthur had to give them up with his heart.' Her voice trailed away.

'But one or two a week is safe,' Rosie said.

Ellie put her plate down. 'Can we stop talking about eggs and get back to this idea?'

'It's impossible,' Virginia said. 'We can't possibly live together.'

Rosie swung round so fast the remaining cake crumbs trembled on the edge of her plate. 'Why not?'

'Well ... we just can't. We're ... we're all too different.' Virginia's words were forced out as if she had developed sudden, verbal constipation.

'Does that matter?' Ellie asked.

'Of course it does. I couldn't live with someone who was ... well, not my sort of person.'

'Really?' Ellie's eyes brightened.

Andrea relaxed into her chair. She propped her elbows on the arms and laced her fingers under her chin. She stared at Virginia. 'Well you don't have to, of course. Not if it wouldn't suit you.'

'Oh dear,' Gwen said. 'I hope we aren't going to fall out.'

'We won't fall out,' Rosie told her. 'We're all grown up, and I bet we're all just as lonely as each other.'

'I don't agree,' Virginia said. 'I have many interests.'

'Such as?' Andrea unfolded her arms.

'Well ... there's reading. I enjoy puzzles. And BBC4 programs. And there's my garden of course.'

'So - which one of those do you do with other people?'

Virginia came as close to glaring at another person as she had ever managed. 'I'm really not answerable to you, Mrs Capstowe.'

'No, you're not. Perhaps you aren't lonely then. Perhaps you have children who visit.'

Virginia's face shut down like a planet-wide power cut. 'George and I were never blessed.'

Ellie put her cup on the table. 'I'm so sorry,' she said. 'Neither was I. There was always something Kenneth wanted to do first.'

Virginia shrank into the chintz chair. 'It wasn't that. It just ...
never happened. I -' She broke off. A degree of haughtiness returned
to her face, mostly due to her long nose. Her spine stiffened. 'It's of
no consequence now.'

Rosie smacked the chintz-covered arm of her chair. 'The main
point is bills.' She frowned. 'Then the company.'

'I was telling Rosie only last week that I've always wanted to
open another salon,' Ellie said. 'I could if -'

'And there's cruises.' Gwen sat up. Her arthritic hip twinged
unnoticed. 'Arthur said it wasn't sensible to spend money just to
look at the sea.'

Andrea took a sip of the tepid tea. 'I've always wanted to spend
time in the south of France.'

'Right.' Rosie put down her plate and picked up a black magic
marker. Standing, she drew a squeaky line down the centre of the
wrong-way-round wallpaper looped over the mirror. 'Fors,' she said,
writing the word on the top left. 'Againsts.' The marker squeaked
again at the top right.

'Holidays,' Gwen said.

'Lower bills.' Rosie wrote down it then put Holidays underneath. After five minutes the ideas dried up. On the paper were
twenty-six words.

Fors	Againsts
Lower bills	Bigger bills
Holidays	More upkeep
Spare money	Council tax
Company	No privacy
Help	Guests?
Bigger garden	Pets
Grow own stuff	Hard work

'What about the legal side?' Ellie asked. 'Deeds and stuff. And what happens if one of us dies?'

'I'm glad to see common sense is asserting itself,' Virginia said. 'You'd have to sell to cover whoever's estate it was.'

'Oh that's true. I know my Caroline would want the money.'

Rosie carried on, undaunted. 'There must be a way around it.'

'We could all make a will and leave it to the others,' Gwen said, looking round brightly.

'So the last one alive gets everything?' Virginia said. 'That's not fair.'

Gwen's face slumped.

'Well you can't take it with you.' Andrea's lips folded into a narrow line. 'Unless you've found a way, Mrs Lesage.'

Virginia moved her plate with the crumbs of three sandwiches and two cakes onto the cut-down dining table. She rose. 'You'll have to excuse me. This really isn't my kind of thing.'

'That's a pity, but if that's how you feel ...' Rosie let the sentence fade into the air. Virginia did not respond. Rosie sighed. 'I'll show you out.'

The pair left the room. Ellie and Andrea's glances collided. Both looked quickly away.

Ellie cleared her throat. 'It's not a bad idea. Now.'

'I think it's a good one, dear.' Gwen helped herself to another fairy cake. 'I'd rather live like that than in a ... a housing shelter. Or with my Caroline. I'd never have a moment's peace in her house.' She pulled one cake wing off and ate it. 'She and Christopher took me to Something Court once. Assisted living they called it. Cramped, I'd say. The whole flat was tinier than my sitting room.' The other wing disappeared. 'And at least if Mrs Lesage isn't there, she can't complain about Miffy.'

'Miffy?' Ellie asked.

'My little Bichon Frise.' Gwen smiled. 'She's lovely. Such good company.'

Ellie looked at Andrea. 'What do you think?'

Andrea turned pink. 'I don't know. I'm sorry. It's just ... I find it a bit hard to think of things at the moment.'

'Oh, I'm sorry. How thoughtless of me. You'll need time to ... um, think.'

Andrea turned pinker. She blinked hard but a tear still escaped. 'I don't think I want time to think. I've done too much of that.' She brushed her cheek. 'Anyway, you're much more ... well, it was his funeral last week, wasn't it?'

Ellie nodded. 'Yes, but our house was Kenneth's choice. I never quite liked it so I don't mind leaving it. In fact I'd be glad to.'

'I don't think I could leave mine,' Andrea said. 'Anthony still seems to be in every room.'

'Then perhaps you should leave.' Rosie came in through the door. 'Perhaps you need to leave to start afresh.' She pulled the top off her felt tip marker. Flipping the first sheet of wallpaper over the back of the mirror, she said. 'Now, let's make a list of what we'd want in a new place.'

Ellie's eyes brightened. 'En-suite bathrooms for everyone. Absolute must.'

Rosie wrote Musts at the top of the blank sheet and underlined it twice.

CHAPTER FOUR

Discussion of the Musts took until early evening. Andrea left the others holding out their hands and looking skywards on Rosie's doorstep and walked along Old Church Lane trying to see through her tears. Trying to think through the continuous refrain of pros/cons, pros/cons, pros/cons that was pounding in her brain. Pros? What were the pros? Like Ellie said, not living in a house with Anthony's presence in every room. Not walking past the closed door to the room where he'd died. Not avoiding their bedroom. Not feeling so alone. Not feeling … anything.

Cons? There had to be cons. Cons were leaving her hiding hole, her refuge. Her last link with their happy married life. Living with three other women who were barely acquaintances was a definite con. That was something she hadn't done since university. She remembered the tiffs, the arguments, the plain bitchiness that could flare up over some trivial something. Thank goodness Virginia Lesage had said 'No' straight out. She'd be certain to bitch. The way she looked down her nose at everyone more or less guaranteed it. No woman that superior was going to live in … what did she call it? A commune?

And the others? What about them? Ellie was OK. As a person, of course. She'd be weepy now with whatsisname just gone. Not that she'd looked it but at least she'd understand how Andrea felt. Perhaps they all would. Apart from little Gwen Fellowes. She didn't look as if she understood very much at all. And that raised the biggest con. Never mind about one of them dying, what if one of them developed Alzheimer's. Or Parkinson's. Or something equally unpleasant. What then? Andrea knew she couldn't stand to watch another slow descent into death.

She reached her house on High Oak Road as the first heavy thunder drops splashed onto the front path. Her key turned in the lock. She took a deep breath, and walked back into Anthony's company.

The next morning, Marian Bowler had three phone calls in quick succession before she had time to put her sandwiches in the office fridge. Mrs Reynolds wanted her to value Laburnum Cottage (formerly 3 Old Church Lane). Ellie Duncan wanted the same for 32 Francis Glebe Court. Mrs Fellowes would very much like her, please, to tell her how much Ashton House might fetch if she ever decided to sell it. Perhaps.

'What on earth's happening,' Marian asked David Trisk. 'There's a mass exodus of widows going on.'

David Trisk of Quickmove Estate Agents, established 1998, said, 'I don't care. If they want to move, we'll gladly help them. This quarter's sales figures aren't so good. When do we see them?'

Marian eyed Trisk's smart suit and slick hair. 'I think I'd better do it. What with them all being widows ... and Ellie Duncan only just. I didn't think she'd move so quickly.'

He shrugged. OK. When?'

'They were all very eager. It's Laburnum Cottage in about twenty minutes and Francis Glebe Court in the lunch hour. Ellie can't close the salon until then. And ...' She consulted the diary. 'Ashton House later, but not before half past three. The daughter's visiting, apparently. I don't think Mrs Fellowes wants her to know.'

'Really?'

'That's the impression I got. She said she'd phone if there was a problem so I think the daughter's it.'

Marian parked outside Laburnum Cottage and switched off her windscreen wipers. She climbed out and, holding her clipboard over her head, fumbled with the latch on the gate. Rain began to darken the shoulders of her navy jacket. The gate suddenly cooperated, flying open then swinging back against her knees. Muttering, she hurried up the path and raised her hand to knock on the green door. It flew open.

'Come in, come in.' Rosie beamed at her. 'I've had a quick tidy round so you can see it at its best.

Marian scanned the hall. An untidy pile of magazines on a narrow table left almost no room for the telephone. A pair of slippers with drooping green bows was shoved underneath it. Two - no, three coats and a mac hung on a bent-wood coat-stand, complete with draped red scarf and what looked to be a large, turquoise, paisley shawl. If this was Laburnum Cottage at its best, Marian didn't want to see it at its worst.

She took a photograph, trying to angle it so the coat-stand failed to intrude. She managed to eliminate more gardening magazines and books, and a Culpeper's Complete Herbal from the sitting room by putting them on the floor behind the sofa. The kitchen was her biggest challenge but she'd been an estate agent for twelve years and knew what she was about. A few minutes of 'I'll just line these up a little' and 'Isn't this china chicken sweet beside the egg stand?' turned a mess into an airy, country-style room that glowed despite the gloom outside.

By the time she had all of the photographs she wanted, the house on the camera's memory card looked far neater than it actually was. In the garden, Rosie pointed out every variety of rose and perennial by its botanical name until Marian was in danger of being late for her appointment with Ellie.

'I'll pop you a summary through the door tomorrow,' she said.

'Can't you tell me how much it would be now?' The sparkle left Rosie's eyes.

'We always like to get things properly formatted.' Marian backed out of the front door. 'I'll be as quick as I can.' She managed to get three steps down the path.

'Not even a general idea?'

'I'll be as quick as I can,' she repeated, and fled.

Ellie's house was completely different. It stood in a row of similar houses, all with precise, unfenced patches of grass at the front. A few had flowering shrubs along the front edge, separating private from the public worlds. Ellie's private world was tidy, clean and hollow-sounding in its neatness. Small and soulless, Marian thought, until the kitchen had her gasping on the threshold.

'Bloody h-. I mean goodness me.'

'Kenneth was a chef,' Ellie explained. 'Everything had to be just so. Even here.'

Here was a spread of stainless steel worktops, two separate ovens in wall units, a hob with eight burners, an American fridge that would probably count as a small bedroom in one of the new houses they were building at King's Meadow and an island unit with a double sink.

'Goodness,' Marian said again. She took eleven photographs.

Ashton House was one of the older houses that stood respectably aloof on Merland Crescent, seven houses down from Virginia Lesage's Old Vicarage. It stared out of its tall windows at Marian Bowler struggling with another uncooperative front gate latch. 'What is it with these gates,' she muttered.

At the top of the path, Gwen Fellowes opened the front door. Despite her head barely reaching Marian's chin, she practically dragged her inside and peered up and down the road like a nervous bird before she shut the door.

'I'm so glad you came,' she said. 'I don't know that I am going to sell ... I just thought I might. If I wanted to.'

'It's quite all right, Mrs Fellowes.' Marian tried to push Miffy's front paws off her navy skirt and away from her tights without appearing to do so. 'A lot of clients like to test the water first.'

'Water? There's nothing wrong with the water, is there?'

Marian's fingers tightened on her clipboard. 'I mean some people like an estimate of possible selling price to help them decide what to do.'

'Ah. Yes.' The worried frown left Gwen's face. 'That's what I want. Then I can make up my mind.'

Marian had grave doubts that Gwen was going to make up her mind about anything this side of Christmas. And it was only May now.

In Quickmove Estate Agents' bright office, David Trisk swung round in his manager's chair, weaving his Parker ballpoint backwards and forwards through his fingers. 'Well? How did it go?'

'Hmm. Middling. I'm not sure about Glebe Court. The husband was a chef and the kitchen's far above the usual. If we get someone who likes cooking, it could go for two hundred. One nine five at least.' Marian dumped her bag and clipboard onto her desk by the columns of house details hanging in the window.

Trisk sniffed. 'Not bad. What about Laburnum Cottage?'

'I think it would probably fetch two ten to two thirty ... if she tidies it up.'

'Better.'

'Ashton House is best of all. It would be, on that road. Not had much done to it for years but nothing that a few coats of magnolia couldn't fix. Probably fetch ...' She shrugged. 'Three two? Three fifteen for sure.'

Pound signs clicked through Trisk's eyes. 'That's seven fifty k in all. Say seven twenty to seven thirty for all three at completion. That's ... fifteen k if they go for our fixed fee, just over twenty-one if they don't.' He tilted his chair back on its swivel stand. 'Not bad.

Not bad at all.' The ballpoint rapped a triumphant tattoo on his desk.

Alone in her house, Andrea wandered from room to room and into the kitchen. Day dwindled into evening beyond the undrawn curtains. She opened the back door. The air brushed cool against her hot, teary face. She grabbed the handle of the grey wheelie bin beside the gate. The bin tipped backwards onto its two wheels. She swung it round the gatepost, hitting the recycling box on the way. A tinkling waterfall of shifting glass sounded. Andrea let go of the wheelie bin. Inside the box she counted fourteen wine bottles.

'Damn this,' she said. 'Damn this to hell and back. Anthony wouldn't want this.' She dragged the wheelie bin down the short drive, cursing when it rammed into her Achilles tendon.

Back in her dining room she attacked her laptop, prodding the keys until it showed her a nationwide property website. She hammered Chevelling Market into Location, twenty into Search Radius and waited. The site told her, rather tersely she thought, that there were over five hundred properties for sale and would she refine her search parameters. She told it to look for four-bedroomed detached houses within fifteen miles. This time it told her there were sixty-three properties for sale. She paged through them until she found one that looked similar to hers. Same age, same size and more or less the same condition, to judge by the décor. The main difference was the one on the screen had no conservatory and hers did. It had cost them twelve thousand so she added an extra ten to the other house's asking price. Two hundred and eighty thousand pounds.

'There'll be charges and moving costs off that,' she said to the pc. A few more prods and it answered that agent's fees could vary between nought point seven five to two point five percent. Or they could be fixed. Andrea knocked the ten thousand off again.

She leant back in the chair, sucking the nail of her left index finger and staring at the screen. Ten miles, she thought. Maximum.

Any further and I'd lose all my private pupils. And four - no five bedrooms. Four for us and one extra for a guest. And a decent garden. Rosie wants a decent garden. A few seconds later the website showed her all the houses that met her new criteria. The second looked a distinct possibility. I wonder what the others would make of that one, she thought, switching on her printer.

CHAPTER FIVE

The morning was unseasonably cold. Virginia switched on her central heating for the twenty minutes she allowed herself for washing and dressing. Twenty minutes raised the bathroom temperature enough to stop the crêpey skin on her arms and chest puckering into goose bumps. This morning the boiler flared then emitted a pitiful 'plop'. The hiss of burning stopped.

'What are you doing now?' she demanded of it, jabbing the switch again.

The boiler failed to respond. It failed to respond to any of the several subsequent jabs. Virginia put a hand to her forehead. Memories of the cost of having the previous boiler replaced nineteen years ago sent a cold shiver down her spine. Memories of her last bank statement sent an even colder one back up it.

'How could you, George? How could you leave me in such a mess?' She remembered all the social events she'd had to attend. All the people she'd smiled graciously at to further his climb up the private medicine ladder. All the photographs in the County Journal. All the admiring junior doctors and adoring nurses. George had been quite keen on photographs with adoring nurses. And now here she was with one hundred and seventy five pounds, twenty-three pence in her bank account, no savings and a pension that was paltry considering his former income.

'I wish I'd had a job now,' she told the boiler. 'At least that Ellie Duncan has something to fall back on. Not that she needs it. Not with her husband's restaurant. It must be a little goldmine if the prices were anything to go by.'

The boiler door slammed shut with a metallic rattle. Virginia washed her hands and face in the kitchen sink with water boiled in the kettle. Then she telephoned GasServe. They could, would, come out this afternoon at about three-thirty, seeing as she was an elderly - sorry - vulnerable customer. Virginia, wearing two cardigans and an eiderdown over her knees, spent the intervening time shuffling papers on her dining table, wondering where she could possibly cut down on her expenses. The answer eluded her.

The boiler man shut the front cover. 'I'm sorry, Mrs Lesage, it's had it. They aren't making replacement parts any more. And if they were there's no guarantee that something else wouldn't go shortly after.'

'It doesn't mean a new one, does it?'

'Yes. Sorry. They're not cheap. You're looking at anything from fourteen hundred pounds upwards.'

Virginia thought the floor was coming up to meet her.

The man put out a hand to steady her. 'This is a big place, ma'am. It needs a big boiler.'

'Is there nothing you can do to keep it going just a little while longer?'

He scratched his head. The way Virginia's sparse grey hair was pulled back into a thin bun reminded him of his Gran. 'Well, I could try to find a part second-hand. We're not supposed to, but I could. Might be one on eBay.'

'I'd be so grateful,' she said. 'I just need it to keep going while I, er ... sell the house.'

The man patted her arm. 'I'll see what I can do.'

'You will give me the cost first, won't you?'

'I will. I'll let you know tomorrow or Friday.'

Virginia let him out of the kitchen door. She made herself a cup of tea and stirred three sugars into it instead of her usual half spoon.

She didn't have a thousand pounds, let alone fourteen hundred. The scrimping and saving of the past couple of years knotted itself into her throat. It forced tears into her eyes. She could feel her heart beginning to thud until she realised she was holding her breath. It burst out of her on a sob. Another sob joined it. The sobs became a barrage. She folded her thin arms onto the table, lowered her head onto the sleeves of her two cardigans and cried.

Thirty minutes later with her face rinsed in cold water she walked down to the short parade of shops in the centre of the village. Quickmove Estate Agents stood on the opposite side of the Post Office to Ellie's Hairem. The vicar's wife was chatting to Doreen McPherson at the Post Office door. Virginia walked past, nodding to them. She grasped the long pink handle on Hairem's glass door and pushed.

Ellie excused herself from gelling a girl's humbug-streaked hair into spikes.

'Good morning, Mrs Lesage. Would you like an appointment?'

Virginia shook her head. She pitched her voice lower than the pan pipes music filling the salon. 'I just wanted to ask you if that … er, idea of Rosie's was going ahead.'

'Yes, I think so. At least Gwen and I are going for it with her.'

'Ah.' Virginia folded her lips. She stared at the floor.

Ellie turned her back to the salon. 'Are you perhaps thinking of joining us after all?'

Virginia straightened her spine. 'It might be worth rather more consideration than I gave it at the time.'

'I see. Well, it's your decision, of course.'

'Indeed.'

Ellie tried, and failed, to think of something positive to say. She smothered a sigh. 'Why don't you pop into Quickmove and see what they say?'

'Oh, I couldn't do that. Er …, someone might see.'

Ellie summoned up a trace of charity. 'Come on. You can use the phone in the back.'

Five minutes later Marian Bowler replaced the handset.

'You'll never guess what,' she said to David Trisk.

Friday night at the Quickmove estate agency was a happy time. On their books they now had five more houses with a total asking price of one million, three hundred and forty-five thousand pounds.

Friday night at Andrea's house was more hysterically excited than happy. Admittedly one of the last two bottles of Merlot in the kitchen cupboard had been broached. Consequentially, a few tongues and inhibitions had been loosened. The lists of MUST HAVES and WOULD LIKES and MUST NOTS had grown considerably. Four women and one small dog crowded round Andrea and her laptop. She typed in Chevelling Market and selected a ten mile radius and five bedrooms. They would have liked six but five was as high as the parameters went.

'What about the price?' Andrea asked.

'Well,' Ellie said. 'If we all put in the same amount that would be the fairest way.' Four pairs of eyes turned on Rosie.

'They said I might get two hundred and thirty - if I was lucky.'

'You'd have to take fees off that - say two twenty. Then you'd like a little to spare I assume,' Andrea said. 'How about two hundred?'

Rosie nodded. 'That'd be fine. I'd have enough for lots of flowers.'

'Oh, I think flowers and plants for the garden should come out of a kitty, dear,' Gwen said. 'It's not fair to let Rosie buy them all when all of us would get to see them.'

'But -' Virginia began.

'Let's worry about that later,' Andrea said. 'First we've got to see if there's anywhere we like that's suitable.' She left-clicked on the Price max box and scrolled down to £1,000,000.

'That's too much for me,' Ellie said. 'They thought I'd probably get one nine five. Two hundred at most.'

'Really?' Virginia said. 'I thought the restaurant was a little ... er, doing well.'

'It was but Kenneth wanted to put as much equity into it as possible so he got a smaller house. Thank God we'd barely any mortgage on it.'

Andrea scrolled back up to £900,000 and tapped 'enter'.

'Oh dear,' Gwen said, looking at the 1000+ properties note that appeared. 'We don't need to see that many, do we?' She clutched Miffy a little too tightly. Miffy urged her not to.

'Oops.' Andrea selected £700,000 for the minimum price and they only had seventy-six properties to look at.

After ruling out those anyone considered too ugly, of which there were quite a few; a minimalist modern house Andrea adored but no-one else did; three farmhouses - with farms; four barn conversions - too costly to heat; any in a town centre - council tax too high; and those with a small garden or too much traffic noise, there were only seven possibles left. While the printer churned out five copies of each set of particulars, the widows applied themselves to the second bottle of wine. Miffy jumped disgustedly down from Gwen's lap, curled up on a spare cushion that had fallen from the sofa and began to snore gently.

Beresford House looked marvellous but it had bedrooms on three floors and only one en-suite. Maltcrofts Hall and Cottage looked equally marvellous until you noticed the Hall's west wall was rather too bowed for comfort. Lychgate House proved to have four good-sized bedrooms but one that was little more than a box room. Mastringsett Hall looked great until they realised there was no possibility of adding extra bathrooms. Four of the eight bedrooms at Crentwell Lodge turned out to be in an annex set up for B&Bs. Five copies of all four houses were screwed up and dropped into Andrea's waste paper bin. Harford Manor, however, took their united breath away. Arts and Crafts style, seven bedrooms (four en-suite) plus one on the ground floor and six - six! - acres of garden, plus swimming pool. Orchard House only had three en-suite bath-rooms but the floor plan showed there was an easy way to add two more. Everyone slid their copies of Harford Manor and Orchard House into the named, manila folders Andrea had prepared. Last was a very modern house in Woodman's Lane. It had four bedrooms on the first floor, all with adjacent bathrooms, and the study on the ground floor was conveniently next to a shower room. Its particulars joined the other two.

'Are we all going to go and see them together?' Gwen asked.

'How about we go in pairs?' Rosie said. 'That way it won't look so much like a coach party. If one's any good, we can all go a second time.'

Virginia smiled. 'What a good idea. I can go anytime.'

'Shouldn't we wait until we've sold our own places first?' Ellie said. 'That way we won't see something we all love and then lose it because we haven't the money.'

Andrea slumped back against her chair. 'I suppose that's more sensible.'

'Not such fun though.' Rosie picked up her glass. 'We could go anyway - just to get an idea.'

'That's a bit unfair on the owners,' Ellie insisted. 'They'd think they'd a chance of a sale. And they wouldn't have really.'

A depressed silence filled the room.

Rosie swigged another mouthful of Merlot. 'I know what we can do. We'll wait until one of us has a sale then we can say perfectly truly that we're on the way to getting the money.'

Nods and smiles appeared. Happy murmurs bounced over wine glasses.

'Good.' Rosie raised her glass. 'Here's to us. Here's to Widows United.'

Everyone cheered and gulped their wine. 'Widows United.' Virginia developed a dark red Salvador Dali moustache.

Saturday evening was fading into twilight. The Hairem had stayed open late to allow the maximum number of over-excited girls to have their hair styled for the middle school prom. After the last trio had departed in clouds of giggles and shrieks, Ellie sat at the pale cream console table that served as Hairem's desk and started copying the values of the day's cheques onto a paying in slip. After each entry she glanced at the progress Tracy, the current Saturday girl, was making round the salon with the broom and dustpan.

Tracy heaved all three swivel chairs away from the mirrors and slid the broom purposefully along the angle of cream flooring and skirting board. The last vestiges of hair trimmings drifted upwards. She applied herself enthusiastically. Her current ambition was to be a beautician with her own salon, just like Mrs Duncan. Tracy's mother considered this extremely unlikely. Tracy consistently failed to address her GCSEs with anything like the diligence she exhibited with the broom or with hanging out with her friends. Tracy's mother had pointed this failing out to her several times. *Only washing hangs out, not girls who want to get on* had become her mantra.

Joanne, the second stylist, emerged from the back room where they left their coats and ate their packed lunches.

'So you're really moving, then?' She lined up her brush and tail comb on the mirror's narrow shelf at her preferred chair.

'Yep.' Ellie stopped noting down the cheques. 'All agreed.'

'Wow. Brave of you.' Joanne pushed her arms into a chunky, multi-coloured cardigan. She lifted her bag off the chair. Tracy hurried over to straighten it up in front of the mirror. 'Mightn't it be a bit soon?'

'I don't see why. Gather ye rosebuds and all that.'

Joanne slid a quick sideways glance at her. 'As long as you're happy with it.'

'I am.' Ellie wrote 32.50 on the slip's next empty line. 'Definitely.'

'Right then.' Joanne peered in the mirror to tweak an errant strand of hair back into place. 'That's me done.' She slung the bag over her shoulder. 'Bye. See you Tuesday.' She pulled open the plate glass door and disappeared into the bright evening.

Tracy hovered by Joanne's chair with both hands gripped round the broom handle. 'Ellie?'

'Yes?'

Tracy advanced. With broom. 'Mum says is it convenient to miss the second and third Saturdays in August? Only they want to go to Corfu then.'

'Of course it is. It'll be nice to have a holiday all together.'

Tracy's face said quite clearly that a holiday with parents and two younger brothers was not the average sixteen-year-old's idea of nice.

'I'll put it in the book.' Ellie flipped the pages over to August. A golf club flyer flapped onto the floor. She picked it up. Summer Ball, it said. £50 per person. Black Tie. 'Oh, I'll have to get that wine stain off the front of my -'

Her breath froze.

She stared at the flyer.

It shook in her hand.

Breath came again in a huge gulp, followed by others of increasing rapidity. Her face coloured. Tears streamed down her face. She pressed her fingers over her mouth, gasping for breath. Under Tracy's horrified eyes, she buried her face in her hands and sobbed.

Tracy stood transfixed, knuckles white on the broom handle. She bit her lip. She looked around, pointlessly since she had seen Joanne leave. Suddenly a mother's presence did not seem such a bad idea after all.

CHAPTER SIX

Ellie's house had the greatest number of viewings. She was the first to receive an offer. Or three to be precise, which did not surprise her after hearing the gasps that had emanated from almost every woman, chef or not, who had entered the kitchen. The highest offer was from buyers who were renting. They were eager for a speedy completion, preferably before their notice ran out. Ellie didn't mind that at all.

She called Andrea who hurried round to celebrate the news. In the triumphant kitchen, the square Senseo coffee machine by the kettle hissed and disgorged dark aromatic liquid into two bright mugs. Elie stirred milk into it and put one on the kitchen table in front of Andrea. The paperwork from Quickmove lay between them. Ellie pointed her mug at it.

'Look at this stuff Marian gave me. What am I going to do about completion date? I can't wait until everyone's sold. I might lose the sale.'

'Easy. You stay with me. Then you can complete whenever they want.'

'Won't you mind?'

'It'll be fine. As long as you don't mind my music.'

'No, not at all. But you'll have to let me give you some rent.'

Andrea shook her head. 'Just buy your food. It'll be nice to have someone else in the house.' She fished a sweetener tube from her bag. Two miniscule white tablets plopped into the mug. 'I'll empty the wardrobe in the big bedroom for you. It's still full of Anthony's things.' She stirred the coffee slowly. 'I left them in there when I moved into the other room. Couldn't bear to sleep in ours any more. Couldn't bear to throw them away.' She picked up her cup and sipped. 'Would you like me to give you a hand with Kenneth's?'

Ellie shook her head. 'No thanks. They're all gone. I took them to Oxfam last week.'

'Oh ... that was quick. Too many memories I suppose.'

'No, not really. Ken wasn't ... well, I wasn't very happy to tell you the truth.' She propped her elbows on the table, hands clasped round her yellow mug sitting there. 'Not for ages.'

'I'm sorry. I thought you were OK. Everything seemed ... OK. Your business was fine and ...' Her voice drifted into silence.

Ellie shrugged. 'It was only the salon that kept me sane.'

'Oh.' Andrea sucked the nail of her left index finger briefly. 'You never thought of leaving? You're younger than me, aren't you? Forty? Forty-one? Young enough to start again'

Ellie rotated her arms upwards without lifting her elbows from the table. The mug was close enough to sip the coffee. 'Forty-two next November.' A sip. 'I thought about leaving quite often. Never did though. I suppose I always hoped he'd go back to how he used to be.' Another sip. 'It's odd but I feel as if my life's been on hold for years. Now it feels as if I'm starting again. My life, I mean. The one I wanted. Expected. Not the one I got. The one other people made me live.' She stared into the mug. 'This last couple of weeks I've sometimes wondered if I could manage on my own.' She swirled the last of the coffee. 'Kenneth always said I couldn't. Said it was all too much of a big bad world out there and me with too little sense.'

'But your salon? You do that OK. There's always plenty of customers.' Puzzlement mixed with indignation coloured Andrea's voice. 'It can't be easy doing all the VAT and stuff either. Or ordering things. And you hire out chairs to the other girls. That's not something everyone could do. I couldn't.'

'Oh, that's not difficult.' Ellie prodded the forms on the table. 'These look a lot worse. How do I know if any drains to next door cross my property?' She picked up the Fixtures, Fittings and Contents form. 'Do people really take the light switches with them?'

Andrea held out her hand. 'Let's have a look. We'll all have to do these.' She scanned the page. 'Good grief. Cutlery rack. Toothbrush holder. Clothes line.' She tossed the form down. 'I can just see Gwen filling one of those in. We'll have to help her.'

'Gwen's fine. She's a sweetie but I'm not so sure about helping Virginia. Not sure she'd let us.'

'She is a bit … distant. Comes of having had a consultant for a husband I suppose. Lots of money and cagey with it.' She picked up the Property Information form, scanned it and tossed it down too. 'I see what you mean about the drains. What about your deeds? Have you got them?'

'The building society has. I've got to close the mortgage. Thank god it's not much.' She scowled. 'Kenneth wanted to use mum's money to update the restaurant kitchen but I wouldn't let him. I wanted my home safe.'

'Good for you,' she grinned. 'See? You can manage when you want to.'

Before the next weekend, when she wasn't cutting, colouring or perming hair, Ellie had selected everything in her house that was Kenneth's rather than hers and phoned every charity she could think of.

'You'll never believe it,' she told Andrea. 'Apparently people who go to charity shops 'cos they can't afford furniture don't want teak dining chairs. Or tables. Or anything else. They just want designer stuff.'

'They should be so lucky. When Anthony and I started out we had a bed, a cooker and a fridge.'

By the time Ellie had disposed of all the furniture she didn't want, courtesy of the local council – sixteen pounds for every three items collected - she had trouble finding a removal firm that was not demanding a small fortune to move what was left. With just one day to go to completion, everything she did want to keep was in an air-conditioned room at The Big Box Company and she was in Andrea's master bedroom. So far her presence had not been a problem with the half dozen viewers who had come to look round. The only real problem was Andrea herself. She was packing everything in her house, regardless of whether she would need, or want it later. She managed to do it dry-eyed until she took her wedding album out of the sideboard. Tears formed at every page until she was sitting on the floor sobbing when Ellie came in. Horrified, then sympathetic, Ellie squatted on the floor beside her.

'Come on. It's no use doing that.' She eased the album out of her hands.

Andrea gripped it, hugging it close. 'I can't. I just can't.'

'Yes you can. You must.' Ellie took firmer hold of the album. 'Say goodbye and put it away.'

Leaning against Ellie, Andrea let it slip from under her fingers. She covered her face with her hands and sobbed until her throat burned and no more sounds would come.

With one arm round her, Ellie pushed the album out of reach. 'You'll be better if you put it away. Keeping it about will only depress you.'

'It's all right for you.' Andrea's stinging eyes flashed between their puffed lids. 'You didn't like your husband. I loved mine.'

Ellie's head drooped. 'It doesn't mean I don't know how to grieve. I've grieved every day for the past decade.'

'Oh, god. Sorry.' Andrea put a hand to her head. 'Was it ..? Was there ? Did you have someone?'

'I used to. Kenneth. When he was young. There was so much fun. So many dreams.' Ellie wrapped her arms round her legs.

'I remember. You said. What changed him?'

'The restaurant. It was a dream but it turned into an obsession. If it wasn't the latest bit of equipment, it was Michelin stars. It stole my husband from me, not another woman.'

'I'm sorry.'

Ellie shrugged. 'After a while everything that went wrong was my fault. Everything I spent was money the restaurant should have had. Me not letting him put mum's money into it was the final straw.'

Andrea wrapped her own arms round her knees. She leant against Ellie. 'We're a right pair, aren't we?'

'We are that.'

She stood up and pulled Ellie to her feet. 'Right. No album, no booze, no more looking back. Widows United 'R' Us. Agreed?'

Ellie smiled. 'Agreed.'

Despite their good intentions, and fears of the coach-party effect, all five widows crammed into Ellie's blue Golf on Thursday evening. No one wanted to miss out on Harford Manor. Ellie drove through the burgeoning countryside on roads edged with fresh green hedges and clouds of lacy cowparsley.

Mrs Harford Manor - or Lady Harford Manor to be exact - conducted them round her house. By the time they had seen the entrance hall, the drawing room, the sitting room, the dining room, a further reception room, the family room and kitchen, Gwen had to sit down in the hall for quite a few minutes to get her breath back before she felt equal to venturing up to the seven bedrooms and four en-suites. She waved a hand to indicate her wish to pass on inspecting the garages and heated swimming pool, with hot tub, 'Hot what, dear?', and stayed in the drawing room to admire what she could see of the six acres of grounds.

'It's far too big,' Rosie said as Ellie drove round the fountain in the front courtyard and onto the road. 'I could never manage all that garden.'

'Never mind the garden,' Andrea said. 'Who's going to do all the housework?'

'We definitely need something smaller,' Virginia said. 'The bills there must be horrendous.'

On Friday Andrea drove them to Orchard House. It was smaller and only three of its five main bedrooms were en-suite. There were possibilities though, which was why it remained on their shortlist.

'We could take a chunk out of the master bedroom and make an en-suite for the one next door,' Andrea whispered to Rosie when Mrs Orchard House was engaged in inviting the others to look at the master suite's pretty view of the blossoming apple trees.

'We could do the same to that blue one as well,' Rosie answered, sotto voce. 'It's easily big enough.'

Standing on the south terrace looking at the two acres spreading before them, Andrea said, 'What do we think?'

'I like the lounge - I mean the drawing room,' Rosie said. 'And you were right about making two extra bathrooms.'

Mrs Orchard House showed them out.

They gathered round Ellie's Golf while Miffy watered a small patch of drive. 'Doing the bathrooms wouldn't be cheap,' she said.

'We could knock the amount off the price,' Virginia said.

'You're forgetting the roof,' Andrea said.

'What's wrong with the roof, dear,' Gwen asked.

'Haven't you noticed it's thatched? They only last a couple of decades. It got to be longer than that since this one was done'

Four faces turn upwards. Thatched it was, and quite greenly so on the north side. Patches of it there looked beyond mouldy. The curves over the attic's dormer windows were decidedly ragged.

They piled into the car. On the back seat, Virginia said, 'It would see us out.' She eased her left hip away from Gwen's spreading rear.

'It might see you out.' Andrea said, doing a simple calculation. 'But I hope to live past sixty-seven, thank you very much.'

'There was an awful lot of it,' Ellie crunched the car into gear. 'I don't think it's a goer.'

'Don't forget it has an annex with a sitting room and a bedroom,' Rosie said. 'And a kitchen. That would be great if ... I mean, when we have to have someone in to help.'

'OK,' Ellie turned the car onto the main road, sliding Virginia back into Gwen's side. 'We'll keep it as a possible.'

Newcombe Lane was another on their list. It sat behind a severe-looking wall of bricks and stone capping and a pair of chest-high, modernistic metal gates. Standing by the car, on the spread of block pavers, the widows stared at its uncompromising angles. In the flesh - so to speak - it looked more aggressively modern than on the internet. Had it not, it would have been a distinct probable. All four bedrooms on the first floor met with approval, as did their adjacent bathrooms. The ground floor study was big enough to turn into a bedroom. Its side wall could easily be knocked through to the shower room next to it.

'I don't know,' Rosie said. 'It was lovely and had a garden room but it didn't feel ...' She shrugged. 'Comfortable.'

'I think you're right, dear,' Gwen said. 'I'd feel I had to wear my best frock all the time.'

Andrea sighed. 'We've seen all of the ones we thought might do. Now what?'

Silence filled the car. Ellie changed gear and circled the flower-filled roundabout onto the ring road. 'Perhaps some new ones will have come onto the market.'

'New as in new?' Rosie asked. 'Or new as in ones we haven't seen?'

'Ones we haven't seen. I'll stop at Quickmove and ask.'

'It's Sunday,' Virginia said. 'Aren't they closed?'

Ellie shook her head. 'No. Sunday's one of their best days, apparently. Like supermarkets.'

'Good heavens,' Virginia said.

'Let's go home, dear.' Gwen sighed. 'I'm quite tired now.'

Marian was disappointed when Rosie phoned to say they had not really liked any of the houses.

'I'll have another look for you but there's not really anything more you can ... er, see for your budget.'

She tapped disconsolately at her keyboard. No new houses appeared. She crossed her fingers and hoped that someone, somewhere realised they had a five-bedroomed, five-bathroomed house they were desperate to sell.

CHAPTER SEVEN

Not even the several viewers calling on Rosie and Gwen could lift the general mood of depression at the lack of finding a house that they all liked. Gwen kept Miffy hugged to her and ignored Marian's advice to keep the dog out of the way when viewers arrived.

'Oh no, dear. I couldn't do that. We really wouldn't like it, would we, darling?' Gwen rubbed Miffy's ears and smiled at Marian.

Marian handed over the Fixture and Fittings forms and tried to hide her grave doubts about Gwen's real intention to sell. 'God, not another time-waster,' she groaned, starting her car up after a smiling farewell to Gwen standing at the front door, Miffy hugged to her chest.

Rosie had one offer which she turned down as derisory. Only Virginia was yet to receive much, if any, interest in her house. The Old Vicarage was big, impressive and decorated in a style that had not been fashionable for over a quarter of a century. The dust and grime covering it looked pretty-well established too.

'I'm sure you'll get an offer soon,' Rosie said at their next Widows United meeting.

'But I'm not getting anyone in to see it,' Virginia said. 'I don't know why.'

Andrea and Ellie swapped a glance.

Andrea took up the challenge. 'Perhaps if it looked a little more … well, modern it would help.'

'Modern?' Virginia's long nose lifted. 'Why should it have to look modern?'

Ellie leapt into the breech. 'It's a lovely family house. So much space ... at least it looks it from the outside. It's just perhaps anyone with young children thinks they might be too busy to ...' Her voice faded.

'Put their own mark on it,' Andrea finished. 'What about painting the walls cream? That's what they do on those TV make-over programs. I'd help.' She turned to Ellie. 'You would. We all would, wouldn't we?'

'I'm not sure I know how to paint,' Gwen said. 'I've never done it.'

'I don't think -,' Virginia started.

'We really need to get an offer as soon as possible,' Andrea said. 'Once winter, or even autumn gets here, people stop buying.'

The word winter raised hideous visions of broken boilers and freezing houses that would never sell in Virginia's mind.

'If you wouldn't object, then perhaps it might help.' She gripped her hands together. 'Thank you.'

Sunday morning when they were both free, Andrea and Ellie attacked Virginia's second-largest bedroom. Heavily-patterned mauve swirls covered its walls and the matching curtains and bedspread. A Persian Garden style carpet in maroons, purples and forest green rounded it off. A large bedstead in a dark wood stood four-square against the wall opposite the window. From the size of it, the tall carved wardrobe could have housed all the costumes for a major production at Chevelling Market's modest theatre. Three small tables and a couple of straight-backed chairs filled what odd spaces remained.

Ellie elbowed her way through the door, holding an elderly cylinder vacuum and hose. She dumped it on the floor and plugged in the frayed cord. The engine groaned into life. She pushed the brushhead across the carpet. Behind her, Andrea crept round the walls on her knees, tackling the skirting boards.

After five minutes of intense effort a haze rose from the carpet. Ellie sneezed. She rubbed her nose with the flat of her hand and pressed the vacuum switch with her foot. The motor whirred then faded into silence. 'Damn. I supposed the dustbag's full.' She yanked the handle on the lid. It declined to cooperate. After a third vicious tug, it yielded. A cloud of grey dust blossomed into the air. Ellie sneezed again. 'Just look at this.' She pulled out the grey bag. 'It hasn't been emptied for ages.'

'Perhaps it has and it's just the dust in here.' Andrea eased her back from wiping more off the skirting boards and stood up. 'I wouldn't be surprised to find she doesn't come in here any more.' She shivered. 'It's so cold it feels damp. And that wallpaper doesn't help.'

'This is actually a pretty room if you could see it through all this stuff.' Ellie waved her hand around at multiple ornaments on the tables and mantle over the empty, Adam-style fireplace. 'Do you think she'd let us take it all out and start again?'

'She might. She might not. I can't ever tell with her. One minute she's quite friendly then the next she's looking down her nose at me again.'

'Let's just do it.'

'What with? I don't think she'll spend anything.'

'There's all my bedding and stuff in store. Some of that might do.' Ellie rubbed her nose again and looked at the windows. 'Your lounge curtains would fit. And I've a duvet cover that might do.'

Andrea knelt down beside the fireplace. The corner of the carpet pulled back to reveal solid floorboards. 'We could take this up and sand the floor. Or paint it.'

'Would that be best?'

'Anything would be better than this. And I'm not even going to look under the bed.' She levered herself up. 'Let's go and see the other rooms.'

'Virginia.' Andrea perched on the edge of the well-stuffed but slightly sagging green damask sofa. 'Ellie and I think we could make a few changes upstairs that would make the property details more ... appealing.'

'What sort of changes?'

'Well, wallpaper's not so popular now. Perhaps we could paint over it ... just to lighten things up a little. In the other bedrooms, of course. Not yours.'

'I'm not sure about spending money when I'm going to move.'

'Oh, it wouldn't cost you anything,' Andrea said. 'I've got some white paint in the garage.

Ellie shot her a quick look and wondered why she hadn't mentioned the paint before. Assuming she wasn't making it up, of course.

'And I don't know that I could help,' Virginia said.

'You wouldn't have to. Ellie and I can do it, can't we?'

'Oh yes.' Ellie tried not to think how long it would take to slap white paint over dark mauve wallpaper in a room that had to be at least fourteen feet square. Excluding the bay window.

'And perhaps the hall could benefit form a little brightening too.' Virginia said.

Ellie glared at Andrea. The hall was almost as big as her own lounge had been.

Night had fallen by the time Ellie and Andrea walked out of the front door that had lost most of its gloss. Ellie eased her aching arms. 'Have you gone mad?,' she said. 'She'll have us doing the whole house at this rate.'

'I know. It's just that until her house is sold, we can't move.'

'But why the rush?'

Andrea stuck her hands into her jacket pockets. 'It's just ... well, now I've decided to move I can't wait to get out.' A flush of blood spread up her face and turned hers eyes bright and watery.

She bent her head down. 'I don't want to get back to where I was. I'm only amazed I didn't lose all my private pupils. Not to mention my job.'

'Why should you do that?'

'After Anthony died I rather took to an occasional glass of wine.'

'So?'

'The occasions got too close together. On most days they took up the whole evening.'

'Oh, I see.' Ellie pulled Andrea to a halt at the crossroad. 'Well you haven't been drinking much when I've been there.' She examined Andrea's face. 'Unless of course it's after I've gone to bed.'

'No, not at all.' A violent shake of the head. 'It's been better since you moved in.' Her eyes cleared. 'I'm glad you did or goodness knows how I'd be by now.'

Ellie snorted. 'Unless I'm mistaken, after Virginia's finished with us we'll need more than the occasional glass.'

'More likely it'll be DIY therapy and Rosie's remedial massage.'

She was right about that but wrong about Virginia not helping. Rosie was made of stern stuff. Virginia found herself bullied into helping to change curtains, stuff cushions and pack away a lifetime's collection of antique Meissen porcelain figurines. She was allowed to have two left out in her newly-painted cream bedroom but only because the shepherdesses' posies matched the ribbon trimming on Rosie's best duvet cover. Even Marian was impressed by the changes when she was summoned to take a fresh set of photographs.

'These should have people beating a path to your door,' she told Virginia.

'Oh, it was nothing,' Virginia said.

Rosie, listening with interest, choked on her tea and resolved not to mention the comment to Andrea and Ellie when they got back from work.

Gwen's double-fronted house was the next to have an offer, despite her refusal to hide Miffy in her car. Nor would she have a For Sale board in the garden which had stopped at least two would-be purchasers from finding it on a drive-by. Accepting the offer sent Gwen into a turmoil of apprehension.

'Where will I live?' she asked Rosie during a reviving stroll round Laburnum Cottage's pretty garden. 'I don't want to go to a hotel and I'm not going to Caroline's.'

'I should think not. You'll come here, of course.'

Reassured, Gwen let Andrea and Ellie, who were beginning to feel like a firm of removal men as well as painters and decorators, help Rosie clear her house the week before it was due to complete. Gwen fluttered around trying to help but generally just getting in everyone's way. Every cupboard was emptied. All the contents were packed into labelled boxes with Gwen anguishing about each item's safety. By the time the boxes were stacked in the hall and sitting room everyone was in a state of nervous exhaustion.

In the kitchen Ellie tackled the fridge. She put an opened packet of cheese into her cool-box. A half-full bottle of milk stood in the fridge door.

'I'll tip this away,' she said to Gwen.

'Oh no. Don't do that, dear. I can carry it round to Rosie's.'

Ellie put the milk on the worktop. 'All right. If you want to.' She snapped the lid onto the box and raised the handle over it. 'I'll put this in my car then we'll be finished in here.'

She lugged the box out of the front door and past the burgeoning petunias to her blue Golf. It wobbled precariously on the back seat. 'Bugger,' She said. She reached in and struggled to strap the seat belt round it. A car pulled into the drive behind her. It stopped inches from her front bumper. Ellie let go of the belt. It whipped back, smacking the clip smartly under her chin in the process. 'Bugger,' she repeated. She backed out, banging her head on the roof.

A smart-looking woman of about Rosie's age was climbing out of a silver Citroen Picasso. Ellie surveyed her. Tartan pleated skirt, lightweight olive waxed jacket with a vivid scarf tucked inside the collar and a finely knitted jumper underneath. Sixty, if she's a day Ellie decided, admiring the cropped ash-grey hair.

'Hello,' the woman said. 'Who are you?'

'Ellie Duncan. A friend of Gwen's.'

'Is she all right?' Concern tinged her voice and pleated her forehead. 'Not had a fall or anything?'

Ellie smiled. 'No, she's fine. We're just helping her to pack up.'

'Pack up? Why?'

'She's moving. The house completes next week.'

The woman blinked. 'Completes? Next week?' A frown. 'She hasn't said a word.' A sigh. 'But thank goodness for that. We've been telling her for ages to sell up and move.'

'Ah,' Ellie said. 'You're Caroline.'

'Yes.' She shut her car door briskly. The fob bleeped and the doors locked. 'This really is excellent news.' She marched into the house, skirt hem flicking around her knees.

'Oh, God.' Ellie abandoned the wobbling cool-box, locked her own car and hurried after Gwen's daughter.

Caroline burst into the sitting room Andrea and Rosie were denuding of its ornaments, pictures and cushions. 'This is great news, mother. You've seen sense at last but you should have told us, you know. We'd have made all the arrangements for you.'

Gwen sank onto the sofa, clutching Miffy to her blouse. Ellie appeared behind Caroline, making frantic *I'm sorry* signs at Andrea and Rosie.

Caroline dumped her handbag on the sofa. 'Now, have you packed your clothes? And what are you going to do with the furniture.' She glanced round the room. 'We'll take the best pieces for you, of course. You won't want them in Barton Court.' She scanned the room again. 'I don't suppose the rest is worth keeping. The Salvation Army's always after things. They might take it.'

'I'm not selling it.' Gwen's voice barely achieved audible levels. 'And I'm not going to Barton Court.' Miffy squeaked under her clenching fingers.

'What?'

'I'm not selling my furniture. I'm taking it with me.'

'Taking it with you where?' Caroline scowled down at her. 'What are you talking about, mother?'

'She's coming to live with us,' Rosie said. 'All of us. And Virginia.'

All traces of eager anticipation vanished from Caroline's face. She straightened up. 'What do you mean, live with all of you?' She scowled. 'Who are you?'

'Friends of your mother.'

Caroline bristled with tension. She towered over Gwen. 'Mother, what is this nonsense?'

Gwen's hands gripped tighter. Miffy yelped louder. 'We're all going to buy a house and live together in a ... in a commune.'

'Have you gone mad, mother? A commune? At your age?' Her acid scowl swept over the three other women. 'We'll see about this.'

She snatched up her bag and stalked out of the door. Seconds later the Citroen's door slammed, its engine revved and its tyres spat backwards out of the drive.

'Oh dear,' Gwen said. 'I don't think she liked that.'

Rosie patted her shoulder. 'Never mind. You've decided what you want to do and we'll help you do it.' She looked round at Andrea and Ellie. 'Won't we?'

'Oh yes,' they chorused.

Gwen and Miffy sought welcome refuge in Rosie's house, now somewhat tidier than it had been, but not much. Rosie made a point of never leaving Gwen alone with her daughter on the frequent visits she made to stress again and again the stupidity of her actions, for which Gwen was ever after grateful. She had only been installed in Rosie's spare room for a week when Andrea accepted an offer on her own house.

'Where will you two live now then, dear?' Gwen asked at the Monday night Widows United meeting in Laburnum Cottage.

'I've only got one more bedroom,' Rosie said. She stared pointedly at Virginia over her cup of camomile tea.

'Oh. Well … I mean you're welcome to stay of course but I wouldn't think-'

'Good,' Rosie said. 'That's settled.'

Three of the faces in the room looked several shades less than ecstatic.

Virginia eventually accepted an offer on her newly-decorated house. A rather lower one than she considered was its right and proper due but which relieved some of the tightness that had become a permanent feature round her mouth. By then Gwen and Miffy were installed in her second bedroom and Rosie in the third. Ellie and Andrea had moved up to the two smaller attic rooms. The only bathroom was on the first floor. At night, they had to traipse down a dimly-lit flight of stairs to use it.

'I'm not going anywhere that doesn't have en-suites,' Ellie announced when she passed Andrea descending. 'I'm as sympathetic as the next person but there's a limit to the number of old lady's accessories I want to see in any bathroom I'm using on a long-term basis.'

Andrea laughed. 'That's a pleasure still to come, I fear.'

'Not if I can help it. If there's any greater prompt for a tight pelvic floor I've yet to discover it.'

'I can think of one. Not that I've had much practice lately.'

'Slut,' Ellie said with a smile.

'Tart,' Andrea answered.

'I hope we get some viewings organised soon.'

CHAPTER EIGHT

Anxiety printed itself on David Trisk's face when the widows appeared *en masse* on Sunday afternoon in his smart office with its pale wood desks and fetching photographs of attractive properties, all bearing the strap line SOLD, decorating the walls. He levered himself out of his impressive chair. Leather for authority, grey not black for approachability. 'Sit down, ladies,' he smiled. 'I'm sure we can find you something.' He dragged all the spare, non-leather, green chairs into a circle. 'How about some coffee for you while Marian does a quick scan - er, search?'

There were no takers. Marian excused herself to a vendor's solicitor at the other end of her phone and swung her computer screen towards her. Trisk hovered at her shoulder, watching closely.

'I know,' he said. 'There's Langston Rectory Very nice. Langston's an excellent location. Rural but not remote. Only eight miles from the city. Six bedrooms, five en-suite.'

'It's nearly a hundred thousand over their budget,' Marian whispered.

Trisk put his hand on her shoulder and squeezed. 'I'm sure the Rectory'd be open to an offer. It's been on the market for … how long?'

'Since Christmas,' she said, carefully flexing the joint out of his grip.

'Nearly six months then. Let me book you a viewing. Six months is long enough to make them think seriously about a lower offer. There's no harm in looking.'

The widows conferred.

'It's a lot of money. More than we wanted to spend,' Andrea said, conscious of Ellie's white face. She stood up. 'We'll think about it.'

Trisk's face turned ever so slightly grey.

Standing on the pavement of the little parade of shops, Rosie said, 'I hope it's what we're looking for. We've all been lucky to sell so quickly.' See looked at the 8-til-Late, the only other shop that was open. 'I'll pop in and get myself some chocolate. Does anyone else wh=ant some?'

The next morning Ellie's mobile beeped a happy rendition of *The Age of Aquarius* at her. She groaned over her bowl of Special K. 'Who's phoning this early on my day off?' She picked it up. 'Hello?'

'Mrs Duncan?' the estate agent's disembodied voice asked.

'Hello, Marian. What can I do for you? We're not seeing the Rectory 'til later.'

'It's not that, I'm afraid. There's a slight problem with your sale.'

Ellie dropped her spoon. It clattered into the bowl. 'What do you mean a slight problem?'

Virginia lowered her copy of the parish magazine. The corner drooped over Rosie's plate of toast and honey.

'We can't get the deeds to your house. They're tied up in probate.'

'Why are they tied up? They don't need to be. The house was in Kenneth's name and mine. Now he's dead, it comes straight to me.'

'It appears your solicitor - the one who's dealing with Mr Duncan's will - has an issue about the restaurant.'

Andrea walked into the kitchen. 'I've just -'

Ellie held up her hand. 'I'll phone him now. See what he's on about.' She clicked off the phone.

'Problem?' Andrea said.

'Something about the restaurant and Kenneth's will and the house deeds.'

'I thought you said the house and the restaurant were quite separate.'

Ellie chewed a thumbnail. 'So I thought too. Perhaps not.' The thumbnail split. 'Oh, God I hope ...' She swallowed.

'In my experience,' Virginia said. 'Husbands aren't always as honest as they might be.'

The others stared at her. 'In your experience?' Rosie said.

'Er ...' Virginia made a great show of closing the magazine. She picked up her coffee cup and carried it to the sink. 'I mean from what one reads in the press. Occasionally. Injunctions. That sort thing.' She put the cup on the draining board and walked out.

'Oo er,' Rosie said. 'Do you suppose the sainted George was less than perfect after all?'

'Never mind the sainted George, what about my bloody Kenneth? If he's done something with the house, I'll kill him.'

Neither Rosie not Andrea felt like pointing out the obvious.

Ellie's solicitor was less than perfectly helpful. Not something he was prepared to discuss over the telephone, madam. A matter of finances. And tax. If madam would be kind enough to make an appointment?

Ellie made one for that afternoon. Meanwhile she chewed her nails for a couple of hours until Rosie drove them all to Langston Rectory in an ancient Astra that cost more in MOTs than it was worth. Its state did not impress Mrs Langston Rectory when she opened the door to them later.

Langston Rectory, however, impressed them.

'Oh, my,' Rosie said as she bumped the car into the drive.

'Wow,' Andrea twisted round to peer out of the window for a better look.

'Good gracious, dear,' Gwen said.

'I can't see.' Virginia pushed Gwen to one side.

Ellie bit her lip and thought of the solicitor's appointment.

Rosie drove slowly up one side of an oval drive round a lawn that was a good forty feet long and as wide as the house's Georgian front. Five cherry trees had been planted at intervals along each edge. Ahead, the afternoon sun shone on the house's cream walls and reflected off three floors of tall windows topped by four small dormers jutting from the roof. She stopped abruptly in front of the impressive portico over the front door. 'Oh, my,' she said. 'I hope we can afford this.'

Mrs Langston Rectory ignored the car and the grooves in her gravel drive where Rosie had braked to a halt and showed them into her hall, pointing out its spaciousness, its authentic floor tiles and the elegance of the curved stairs rising from them.

All five of them cricked their necks to gaze upwards.

'Oh, my,' Rosie repeated.

They progressed to the drawing room on one side of the hall. Rosie stood stock still on the polished parquet floor, head back again, gasping at the ceiling rose and the white wedding-cake cornice that topped the cream walls. Light streamed in directly through two tall windows at the front and obliquely through wide French doors at the back. The vast garden room beyond them gave glimpses of stunning river views. A carved marble fireplace dominated one wall.

A door on the farthest side led to an annexe containing an office with a separate entrance and a cloakroom. 'That would be perfect for me,' Andrea whispered to Ellie as they followed Mrs Langston Rectory back across the hall. 'My pupils could come and go without disturbing anyone.'

The dining room was equally elegant. Virginia looked at the high ceiling decorated with filigree plasterwork and was apt to think she agreed with Rosie's reaction to the drawing room. Beyond that, the kitchen was as up-to-date as anything Kenneth might have wanted. Ellie doubted he'd have gone for cream units and bronze granite worktops but the double-width range would have earned an approving nod. On a good day.

They ascended the curved stairs behind the gracious Mrs Langston Rectory without having to wait for Gwen to catch her breath. According to the particulars, each of the two bedrooms on the first floor was over sixteen feet square. Smaller than the drawing and dining rooms but just as elegant. A similar pair of tall Georgian windows three panes wide and four high let in the light. A massive walk-in wardrobe in one bedroom occupied the front of the landing. More importantly they both had stunning bathrooms. The second floor was similar, except the wardrobe space and one of the en-suites were occupied by small boxrooms. At the back a single bathroom opened onto the landing.

'Hmm,' Andrea said. 'I thought it was five en-suite.'

The two rooms on the third floor – staff quarters according to the lady of the house - were narrower with dormer windows but had no large landing between them. That space was taken up by a shower room and a miniscule kitchen. A fire escape led down from one room into the garden.

'The stairs are rather steep,' Virginia said to Andrea. 'I couldn't really manage them.'

'I could.' Rosie's eyes shone. 'I wouldn't mind being up here. I could make my remedies in this kitchen instead of the one down-stairs.' She caught her lower lip between her teeth. 'I hope we can afford it,' she whispered.

She was still gnawing her lip until Mrs Langston Rectory led them out to the terrace overlooking the river that wound round the grounds. Rosie plumped herself down onto one of the rattan chairs, face lifted to the sun. 'This is beautiful.' She leant forward. 'Oh look. There's ducks in the stream.' A drake and duck, bobbing for food fluttered sparkles of water into the sunshine.

Mrs Langston Rectory suggested they might like to stop look-ing at the ducks and look at the cottage instead.

A high wall round a kitchen garden several yards away screened the cottage from the house. An open-plan living room and kitchen occupied one end of the ground floor and a decent-sized bedroom the other. A studio filled most of the upstairs with an office at the far end and a small shower room squashed in between. The studio had a skylight in its sloping roof to supplement light from a floor-to-ceiling pointed window at the gable end.

'This would be even better for your pupils,' Rosie whispered to Andrea.

'Better for your aromatherapy clients,' she whispered back, not quietly enough.

Mrs Langston Rectory pointed out that they could let the cottage if they ... er, needed an income. An additional income, of course.

No-one spoke on the journey back to Virginia's house. Everyone, and Ellie in particular, wondered if they would be able to afford it, or anywhere like it, now her contribution was in doubt.

They were pretty silent during the salad Niçoise that Andrea made for supper. Even Virginia forbore to comment when she saw the mix of baby salad leaves, seared tuna, hard boiled eggs, cold potatoes and tinned French beans with black olives and anchovies artistically arranged on top. She had finished every bite before Ellie put her head in her hands.

'Oh, God. I hope Kenneth hasn't messed everything up for us. That place was just perfect.'

'Try not to worry,' Rosie said. 'It might be a lot of fuss about nothing.' Ellie did not raise her head. 'Would you like me to come with you to the solicitor?'

This time Ellie's head did rise. Mild panic filled her eyes.

'I've already said I'll go with her,' Andrea lied. 'I had a lot to do with our solicitor when Anthony died.'

'Are we going to buy the house, dear?' Gwen said.

'I think we'll wait and see what Ellie's solicitor says first,' Rosie told her. 'It'll be better that way.'

'Oh, I hope so.' Gwen popped a last olive into her mouth. 'There was plenty of room for chickens.'

The other four stared at her.

Ellie sat in the faintly gloomy office of the senior partner at Sowerton, Kerton and Gant, Solicitors, Commissioners for Oaths and Notary Public. The senior partner - not a Mr Sowerton, Kerton or Gant, but a Mr Daynes - leant forward in his chair, hands clasped on his desk. 'I asked the building society to forward the deeds to your house as a matter of urgency once you told me you were selling.'

Ellie clasped her hands in her lap more tightly than Mr Daynes was clasping his. 'And?'

'It seems that you were beneficial joint tenants so the house automatically passes to you.'

'And that means what?'

He smiled. 'It means you can go ahead with the sale whenever you choose.'

Ellie unclasped her hands and put one to her forehead. 'Thank goodness for that.'

'There remains, of course, the matter of inheritance tax.'

Ellie's hand dropped. 'What inheritance tax?'

'The value of your late husband's share in the house must be added to his estate for tax purposes.'

'How much will that be?' Ellie asked.

'It depends on what you sell it for. Might I ask ...?'

'Two hundred thousand pounds.'

Daynes opened a new-looking folder. He unscrewed the top of his fountain pen, fitted it onto the rear of pen and noted the price in neat italics on a clean sheet of paper. 'Of course there will be selling costs to come off that. Let's say eight to ten thousand pounds. That would make your tax payable on one hundred and ninety thousand at worst.' He scribbled a few more figures. 'The nil rate threshold is presently three hundred and twenty-five thousand so you are clear of that.' He smiled. 'Good. Now how much is the restaurant worth?'

Ellie stared at him blankly. 'I've no idea. Kenneth never said.'

'Ah.' Daynes leaned back. 'In that case I think we should err on the side of caution, don't you?'

'We're all for caution,' Andrea said.

Daynes smiled at her too. 'The current inheritance tax rate is three percent. Let's say on the entire price just in case ... it's ...' He scribbled some more. 'Five thousand seven hundred pounds.'

'Oh!' Ellie slumped back in her chair. 'How much will that leave me?'

Mr Daynes scribbled. Andrea whipped through some mental arithmetic.

'A hundred and eighty four thousand three hundred pounds,' they said together.

Ellie looked at Andrea. 'I'm not going to have enough.'

CHAPTER NINE

'Are you certain it's as much as that?' Andrea fished her phone out of her bag and clicked to the calculator. One hundred and ninety thousand times nought point nought three flashed up its answer. Her hands dropped to her lap. 'Yes it is.'

Mr Daynes laid his pen down parallel to his folder, nib towards him. 'Quite. I suggest you keep that amount aside, Mrs Duncan. Just in case. A building society perhaps? A little interest might accrue.'

Ellie struggled for the words. 'Thank you. I'll do that.'

'Good.' His smile reappeared. 'You'll still be able to continue with your plans, I hope.'

'I think … I'll have to see.'

'Excellent.' He rose and stretched out a hand. 'I'll keep you informed of any developments, Mrs Duncan.' He shook Ellie's limp hand then nodded to Andrea. 'Mrs Capstowe.' He ushered them out of his office.

Standing on the pavement outside Sowerton, Kerton and Gant in the bright June sunshine, Ellie drew a deep breath. 'Bugger.' She set off at a smart pace down the narrow street and turned into the wider pedestrianised road.

Andrea rushed to keep up with her, trying to zip the top of her shoulder bag shut and failing.

'I need a drink.' Ellie glanced at Andrea. 'Sorry, I keep forgetting.'

'It's OK. Don't apologise. I wasn't a proper alcoholic. Just depressed.' The zip finally buzzed shut.

'Sorry,' Ellie repeated. 'I didn't mean to imply -'

Andrea stopped in the middle of the pavement. The man walking behind her swerved and muttered something about stupid women who shouldn't be allowed on the pavements and definitely not on the roads.

'It wasn't that I liked the drink. It was just that I couldn't get used to Anthony not being here. That, and being glad he wasn't suffering any more. It was a bit ... confusing.'

'I can't imagine how it felt. Watching ...' She sighed. 'At least Kenneth's was quick. That's something to be grateful for, I suppose.'

Andrea heaved the bag's strap onto her shoulder and dug her hands into her jacket pockets. 'The house was so empty all the time.' A woman in jeans and a bright orange jumper angled a baby buggy round them. The infant gurgled an absent smile at her. 'Charlie – our son - lives in Basingstoke so I only see him at Christmas. And Louise and the baby, of course.' She scanned Ellie's face. 'How do you manage to be ... well, so positive?'

Ellie moved towards a building society window out of the stream of pedestrians. She propped her bottom on the deep sill. 'I'm not sure I am positive. I keep waiting for the floods of tears to come back and they don't.' She rubbed two fingers over the fine wrinkles above the bridge of her nose. 'I'm just so angry with him all the time. Between us ...' She twisted round and stared at the large orange and white offers of excellent savings rates behind her. She sighed and turned back. 'Like I said, Kenneth wasn't easy to live with. Came from ordering people around in his kitchen, I suppose.' Her eyes closed briefly. 'And the bloody, bloody Michelin stars.' She sighed again. 'To be honest, it's more peaceful now.'

Andrea stared at her. 'That's one way of looking at it.'

Ellie blushed. 'Sorry. I don't really mean that. It's just ... well, some days are up and some are down. And I'm an angry cow in most of them.'

'Well then, if this works out OK, you'll have enough to rent another salon when the restaurant's sold. Or get a mortgage. You'll be too busy then to be an angry cow.'

'I hope so.' Ellie grinned. 'There's a new one opened up in Market Lane. Let's go and stare through the window. Suss out the competition.'

Andrea linked her arm through Ellie's. 'OK. But how about a cappuccino first? And no more pussyfooting around each other. We're going to be great friends. Not the sort to make catty comments. We'll leave that to Virginia.'

Ellie grinned. 'I think you're right there.'

'We are going to buy the house, dear, aren't we?' Gwen lowered her knitting into her lap on top of Miffy who was curled up there. They were all in Virginia's crowded sitting room. An old-fashion boxy television flickered in the corner with images of Monday's local evening news.

'We're going to make an offer,' Rosie said. 'And we'll see what they say.'

'So that's the nine thousand pounds you were talking about?'

'Nine *hundred* thousand pounds,' Rosie said with heavy emphasis. 'Is that still all right?'

'Oh, yes.' Gwen sat back with a satisfied smile on her face. 'It's fine. I can stop fretting now about Caroline's shoebox. She's a darling girl, but I really didn't want to live there.'

She picked up the knitting. A triangle of peach wool dangled from her needles onto Miffy's nose. The dog opened an eye but decided investigating was too much effort. She closed it and went back to sleep.

Andrea watched Gwen knit three stitches and pondered the notion of sixty-plus Caroline as a darling girl. A certain amount of sympathy for the daughter entered her head. 'You do know we haven't bought it yet, don't you?'

'Yes, dear. Of course.' She knitted two together through the back of the loop and inspected the result.

'And they might not accept what we offer?'

Gwen poked her needle into two more stitches and paused. 'I'm sure they won't refuse our offer, dear. Don't fret.'

Andrea had a shivery memory of a horse's head in a Hollywood bed. She put down a copy of Langston Rectory's particulars. 'So we're all agreed we'll put a hundred and eighty thousand pounds towards it. A hundred and eighty five maximum so there'll be enough left to pay the solicitor's fees.' Murmurs of agreement drifted around the room. 'And have enough for some of us to buy curtains or whatever else we fancy.'

'What sort of other things, dear?'

'There's the three acres of grass to cut so we agreed to get a ride-on mower.' Andrea took a deep breath. 'Don't you remember?'

'Oh, yes, dear.' Gwen nodded. 'Good idea. And there's the chickens too. Don't forget Rosie's chickens.'

Andrea put her hand over her mouth. 'Trust her to remember the chickens and forget the money,' she whispered to Ellie. Rosie glared at her.

'When will we know about it? The offer, I mean,' Gwen said.

'Miss Bowler telephoned them this afternoon.' Virginia glanced at her watch. 'You'd think they'd have had the courtesy to respond by now.'

'Perhaps they're trying to make us sweat so we'll offer them more,' Andrea said.

Virginia, regally enthroned in the armchair with the most decent seat, sniffed. 'I don't like those sort of games.'

'Nor do I, but that's how it goes,' Rosie said. Don't you remember it took three goes to get my buyers up to my price?'

The telephone jangled in the hall. The women stared at the door then at each other.

'You'd better answer it, Virginia,' Rosie said.

'Oh, not me. You do it.'

Rosie marched into the hall. The others strained to hear what she said.

'I see. Right. Thank you.' The handset crashed down.

Ellie and Andrea stood up.

Rosie appeared in dramatic pose on the threshold, chest heaving under her embroidered peasant blouse. 'They said no. Nowhere near enough. They might, just might, consider nine hundred and eighty.'

'That's ridiculous,' Virginia said. 'It was a reasonable offer.'

'It was ten percent less than they wanted. You didn't take ten percent less on this house. Nor did Andrea on hers.'

'What'll we do?' Rosie said. 'Do we offer what they want?'

'No we don't.' Virginia bounced out of her chair as fast as a lady of seventy-two could bounce. 'I suggest we offer them nine hundred and twenty and tell them that is our ... what's the phrase? Better ...?'

'Best and Final,' Andrea supplied.

Ellie did a rapid calculation in her head. 'I can't go that high.' Her head drooped. 'Sorry.'

Virginia swung round to her. 'Why ever not? The price you got on your house is high enough.'

'It's the inheritance tax. The solicitor said I should put some money aside in case there's any to pay.'

Virginia all but snorted. 'The inheritance tax level is way above your house.' She persisted. 'What about your salon? There must be some profit from it.'

'There is but I need it to live on'

'I'm sure you could manage if you tried.'

'It's a village hairdresser's.' Ellie's eyes glittered. 'Not Vidal Sassoon's.'

'But you won't need as much as before. We've agreed the bills are going to be smaller.'

'Virginia. I'm not going to commit myself to paying out money I haven't got.'

'Well, what about the restaurant? You won't want that any more.'

Andrea came to the rescue. 'Ellie doesn't know how much it's worth. And that's what might push her over the zero tax limit.'

'Did it have a mortgage?' Virginia stared at Ellie.

'Yes, it did.' Ellie's hands clenched. 'I just don't know how much. Kenneth never talked about it.'

'Well you should have asked,' Virginia said.

Ellie's voice cracked. 'Asked? Asked? Did you ever try asking Kenneth anything?'

Rosie hurried across and put her arm round her. 'Sit down.' She eased her towards an armchair. 'I'll get you some nice camomile tea.'

Ellie shrugged her off. 'I don't want any bloody camomile tea. I don't … oh, I don't know. Excuse me.' She ran out of the room.

'Well.' Virginia sat down. 'I must say -'

'Don't,' Andrea said. 'Don't say anything. She really can't go any higher than one eighty. It's her absolute limit. If they won't take our offer, that's it. We'll just have to find somewhere else.'

'There'll have to have room for the chickens,' Gwen said.

'Oh, bloody chickens,' Andrea whispered to herself through clenched teeth.

'What, dear?' Gwen looked up.

Rosie sighed. 'I'll telephone Miss Bowler now. Tell her the upped price and see what happens.'

'But what if they accept?' Andrea said. 'Ellie won't have enough.'

Gwen counted finger and thumb along the stitches on her needle. 'Let's not rush our bridges, dear.'

Andrea sighed. 'I think it's rush fences and cross bridges.'

The counting stopped. Two bright eyes looked up at Andrea. 'Is it, dear? I'm sure you're right. I'm just not counting chickens.'

Andrea had a sudden, surprising urge to find the cooking sherry. She settled for a strong coffee instead.

No-one expected an answer that evening and they were not disappointed. Virginia retired to bed early. She lay there, staring at the newly-painted ceiling, turning numbers over in a mind still quick despite its advanced years. In her schooldays, mental arithmetic had been an essential and tests on it frequent. It stood her in good stead now. Ellie could manage no more than a hundred and eighty thousand. If Langston Rectory wouldn't take their latest offer and stuck to their new price, then it meant one hundred and ninety-six thousand from each of them. Rosie would be pushed to her limit, not that she seemed to fret about things like that. Virginia threw back the duvet. She got up again and pulled Andrea's curtains more tightly closed, unnecessarily. Her mind still calculated. If she paid Ellie's extra they would get the house. If she didn't, they wouldn't. It was that simple. The question was, did she want the house? No, the question really was did she want to live with these people in the house they all liked? She climbed back into bed not knowing the answer. Her mind continued chasing the problem through the highways and byways of her psyche until she fell asleep.

At breakfast next morning she faced the others. 'I've been thinking. If they refuse our offer and we can't go any higher -' Her glance flicked over Ellie. 'The best thing will be if we all stay here. There's plenty of room and I haven't completed yet.'

A flinty silence greeted her words. Eventually Andrea said, 'That's very kind of you, Virginia, but it wouldn't work. There's no room for my pupils to practice even if we could agree about the bathrooms.'

'And I'd feel like your lodger,' Rosie said. 'I wouldn't like that.'

'Your garden's not big enough for chickens either, dear' Gwen said. She lifted a spoonful of Rice Krispies to her mouth. 'I quite like the idea of chickens.'

Andrea found something very interesting to look at outside the kitchen window. Her shoulders quivered.

'Well,' Virginia said. 'I only thought it might help.'

'It was very kind of you,' Rosie said. 'Thank you.'

Virginia stomped out.

'Would you pass me the sugar, please, dear?' Gwen said to Andrea.

Their offer was refused at ten o'clock that morning.

'I'm so sorry,' Marian Bowler said. 'Would you like to increase it at all? Or perhaps have a second viewing?'

'I don't think so, Marian.' Rosie clasped a hand over her ear to shut out the sounds of Andrea's pupil slaughtering Clair de la Lune on the baby grand now in Virginia's dining room. 'I'll ask the others. Not Ellie, of course. She's gone to work.'

She put the phone down and trailed into the sitting room. 'They've turned us down.'

Virginia scowled. She twitched the cushions beside her into place. 'Well, really,' she said at last. A car sounded in the drive, followed by a knock on the front door. 'Excuse me.'

She opened the door. Gwen's daughter, Caroline stood outside, barricaded inside a well-cut navy jacket with her fists clenched at her sides. A slightly younger-looking man with thinning grey hair and a somewhat thickened middle hovered beside her. He grasped a briefcase to the front of his dark suit.

'This is Christopher,' Caroline said. 'We've come for our mother.'

CHAPTER TEN

Virginia conducted Caroline and Christopher into the sitting room. The pair stopped by the door. Christopher smiled at his mother.

'Oh. I wasn't expecting you, dear.'

'I don't suppose you were.' Caroline surveyed Virginia and Rosie. 'We'd like a word with our mother. In private.'

Gwen clutched Rosie's hand. 'Oh no, dear. I want them to stay.'

'I think not,' Caroline said. She held the door wider. 'Ladies.'

Virginia's long nose had its moment. She looked down it. 'And I think not, too. Gwen has asked us to stay and I will not be ordered around in my own home.' She took station behind Gwen's armchair.

Caroline flashed a look at Christopher that betrayed previous, lengthy conversations.

Spurred on, Christopher slowly took up the challenge. 'Mum, we want you to be sensible and come with us. To Caroline's.'

'No, dear. I want to stay here.'

He hesitated.

'Get on with it,' Caroline said.

'In that case, Mum, we've some forms for you to sign.' He balanced his briefcase on an upraised knee and flicked it open. The lid fell forwards, jerking some of the contents onto it.

Caroline caught it. She pulled out a green manila folder and pushed the half-closed case at her brother. 'Here, let me talk you through it, mother.'

She perched on the arm of Gwen's chair, inhibiting Virginia's view. Christopher positioned himself with a faint smile on the other side, still fiddling with the clasps on his briefcase.

Gwen looked at the top paper in the folder. 'What is it?'

'It's a form for you to say that if you're ever ill, or not able to look after your ... yourself, mother, we can do it for you.'

'It means we'll be able to take care of you, mum' Christopher said. 'It'll stop you worrying about things.'

Virginia peered over Gwen's head. 'It's a Lasting Power of Attorney. If you sign it, Gwen, it will give your children control over all of your money. To put it bluntly, they can stop you buying another house.'

'Or buying anything, come to that,' Rosie added. 'If they don't want you to come and live with us, you won't be able to because they will control your money.'

Caroline's face flushed puce. 'Will you mind your own business?' she hissed. 'What our mother wants to do is nothing to do with you.'

'Yes it is.' Virginia's voice stayed calm but frost chilled its edges. 'Gwen has made it quite clear she wants to share with us, not live with you. Or in some shoebox of a flat.'

Gwen's hands trembled. Virginia gave her a second to speak.

Gwen gritted her teeth like a determined hamster. 'That's perfectly true. Dear.'

Virginia sighed. 'Good. That's settled.' She folded her hands across her waist. 'Now I'll thank you to leave my house.' Her eyes raked Christopher. 'I assume, Mr Fellowes, you have work that you should be attending to, it being a Tuesday.'

Christopher snatched the folder. He stuffed it into his briefcase and snapped it shut, trapping a corner of green manila in the process. He followed Virginia out of the room in silence. Caroline favoured Rosie with an acidic stare before walking after her brother.

'Isn't she marvellous?' Gwen said.

'Caroline?'

'No. Virginia. I've never dared say anything like that to Caroline.'

'Now's the time to start.' Rosie patted her head. 'Better late than never.'

'I think perhaps you're right, dear.'

Caroline complained to Christopher all the way to his car that their mother had been latched onto by a harridan and a New Age charlatan who were going to take their entire inheritance.

In Virginia's green-draped dining room, Andrea led her final pupil of the morning laboriously through an introduction to five-finger exercises. After forty minutes, she hustled child and parent out of the front door and hurried into the sitting room. 'Ah, good. You're all here. I wanted a word before Ellie goes back after lunch.'

Rosie looked up from a game of gin rummy with Gwen. 'Something important?'

'Yes.' She flung herself onto the empty end of the sofa. 'Look, we all liked Langston Rectory. It suited us perfectly. Losing it's not on.'

'Absolutely.' Rosie slid her fan of cards shut.

'Good,' Andrea continued, sitting on the sofa. She leant forward, forearms propped on her knees, hands clasped. 'I think we should increase our offer by twenty-five thousand. An extra nine grand each.'

'But -' Ellie said.

'I know.' Andrea held up a hand. 'You've to put almost that much aside in case of tax, so you can't increase your contribution. As yet.' She scanned three faces.

Gwen's cards drooped onto her lap. The six and seven of hearts, nine and Jack of clubs, two threes and the Jack of diamonds showed their faces.

Andrea ploughed on. 'So I suggest we four make up the difference.'

'Oh no, you can't,' Ellie said.

'Ellie's right,' Virginia said. 'She can borrow the extra. From the bank. Or one of those people who advertise on the television.'

'The interest rates would be horrendous,' Andrea said. 'Given that Kenneth's affairs are still in probate.'

Rosie counted on her fingers. 'I think I could manage it.'

'Manage what, dear?' Gwen put down her cup of tea.

'To lend Ellie two thousand five hundred pounds until her husband's will is sorted so we can buy Langston Rectory.'

'Oh, that's an excellent idea. I like the Rectory.'

'No.' Ellie put her mug down with a thud. 'I can't agree to it.'

'Nor I,' Virginia said. 'I think we should wait until probate is granted.'

Andrea banged her fist on her knee. 'It's no use saying wait until probate's granted. That could take a year or more. You have to decide now if you want to live in the Rectory or not. If you do, it means lending Ellie the difference.'

'Is anyone listening to me?' Ellie said. 'I'm still in the room, in case you hadn't noticed. I don't want you to lend me any money. I can do what Virginia says and borrow it.'

Virginia folded her arms across a well-washed twinset at least three years old. 'As I said, that's the best idea.'

'Good grief.' Andrea ran a hand through her hair. 'Don't you understand? She won't have enough collateral for any bank until she gets probate. That means taking dreadful rates from people who don't ask for it. That means loan sharks and you might not mind seeing her in their clutches but I do.'

Ellie looked at her watch. 'I've got to go. I've a cut and blow dry in fifteen minutes.' She glared at everyone. 'This is my problem. I'll sort it out. I don't want your charity.'

She rushed out of the room.

'Now she's gone we should decide,' Andrea said. 'Let's have a vote. Who's in favour?'

Rosie put up her hand. 'Gwen, dear. Put your hand up if you want to lend Ellie two and a half thousand pounds so we can buy the Rectory.'

Gwen's hand shot up. The cards spilled onto the floor. 'Would you like a cheque now?'

Andrea looked at Virginia. 'It's up to you.'

'I don't see why I should have to pay to sort out Ellie's money problems.'

'In that case,' Andrea said. 'We won't increase our offer. We'll have to look for somewhere else.' She left the room.

'That's a pity,' Rosie said. 'I liked it.'

Gwen patted her arm. 'Don't worry. I'm sure Virginia will reconsider.' She smiled at Virginia. 'Won't you, dear?'

'That is blackmail and I'm not going to tolerate it.' She picked up her pen and Wordsearch book and left the room.

Virginia sat in the cane backed armchair by her bedroom window, listening to the creaks and closing doors of the house settling down for the night. Outside the window the sky drained from rose, to lilac, to navy blue. Inside, Ellie's huge cream rug that hid most of the Persian garden carpet between the chair and the bed glowed in the half light. Its pair occupied the space between the bed and the door. Rosie's duvet in her best white cover mindlessly embroidered with lavender sprigs by whatever machine the manufactures used lay on the bed. Two cushions carefully embroidered by Rosie leant on their points against the pillows. The white candlestick lamp with a pale green shade on the bedside table was Gwen's and the apple green curtains had hung in Andrea's lounge until a few weeks ago.

Virginia let her eyes sweep slowly over them all. She had never had friends like that before. Friends who did things for you. All her so-called friends had been the wives of George's colleagues. Ladies who knew how to behave, how to attend coffee mornings, how to hold dinner parties and charity events. If she were honest, none had been more than acquaintances really. None came to see her now George was dead. There were none like Ellie, who had turned up after a day on her feet cutting, colouring and perming hair to paint Lilac White over the bedroom walls.

Stop being so maudlin and sentimental, she told herself. She tugged the collar of her brushed cotton nightdress up round her ears. The large alarm clock on her bedside table ticked loudly. Virginia wrapped her arms tighter. The front gate swung shut with a decent clunk. Pushing herself upright she tweaked a crack in the curtains. Andrea was walking up the front path. Back from some concert or other, Virginia thought. Bossy, blackmailing woman. She let the curtains fall back into place. Andrea's curtains. She wrapped her thin arms around her. George's photograph stood on the tall chest of drawers. Its dark walnut frame matched the newly-polished wood. He'd left her finances in a mess too. Was Ellie's position any different from hers? She climbed into bed, shoving the hot water bottle down the sheet until her cold feet could rest on it. She closed her eyes but did not sleep.

At five past one by the bedside alarm the floorboards outside her room creaked. Virginia sat up. Footsteps tiptoed down the stairs. She lay down for a few minutes, listening. No returning footsteps came up again. She pulled on her dressing gown.

Ellie sat in one of the curved wooden kitchen chairs, elbows propped on the ends of the sweeping arc that formed its back and arms. Her head drooped in her hands.

'Am I disturbing you?' Virginia said.

Ellie's arms swung down onto the table. She turned her face away but not quickly enough for Virginia to miss the damp, red eyes and the pink nose. She pulled out the high-backed Windsor chair next to Ellie. 'Is it the money?'

Ellie nodded, returning one hand to her forehead.

Virginia sat down. She leaned forward, her hands inches away from Ellie's single one still lying on the table. 'I've been thinking about Andrea's idea. If you agree it would mean we could still buy the house.'

'Oh no.' Ellie jerked upright. 'I couldn't do that. No, really. Thank you, but no. I couldn't take your money.'

Virginia captured the free hand. 'There wasn't a mortgage on my house so ... you know, I do have some to spare these days. And it would only be a temporary loan. Until this tax business is sorted.'

'It wouldn't be temporary if I have to pay it.'

'We can cross that bridge when we come to it.'

'No, really. I'd feel too bad about it.'

'But listen. We've agreed we all want that house. Won't you feel just as bad if we can't buy it because of you?'

The spirit went out of Ellie's body.

'So you'll feel bad either way. Better to choose the way that gets us what we want, don't you think?'

Ellie slid her hand from forehead to her eyes. Tears escaped from under her little finger.

'You could always give me free hair-dos until it's repaid. I haven't had a proper trim for - oh - eighteen months at least.'

A watery chuckle emerged. 'You're a very persuasive woman.'

'So you'll agree?'

Ellie lowered her hand. Tear tracks shimmered on her cheeks. 'As long as we tell the others. It isn't fair otherwise. I don't want to start this on a lie.'

'Agreed.' Virginia patted Ellie's hand. 'Now, I'll make us some warm milk and pop a little brandy in it. I've a miniature bottle I was saving for a Christmas pudding.'

'Thanks, Virginia.'

Virginia looked down and up and down again. 'When I was a girl my friends used to call me Ginnie.'

Ellie gently squeezed the fragile hand with its paper-thin skin. 'Thanks, Ginnie.'

Virginia made her announcement to the assembled company at eight-thirty the next morning.

'I've persuaded Ellie to let me put in all of her extra nine thousand until the probate's granted.' She smiled at Ellie who was steadily turning pink round the ears. 'I'm going to have free hair-dos until it is.'

'Oh, good.' Gwen clasped her hands together. 'I'm so glad, dear. Can we do it quickly before Caroline and Christopher come back?'

'We'll do it this morning,' Virginia said. 'If you two agree.'

'Marvellous,' Rosie said. 'Brilliant idea.'

'OK with me.' Andrea grinned. 'As long as Ellie's fine with it.'

'Oh I am,' Ellie said. 'Ginnie's been ...' She smiled at Rosie. 'Brilliant.'

'Ginnie?' Andrea said.

Virginia cleared her throat. 'It's my ... it's what they called me at school. You can too. But only if you'd like to.'

Rosie marched forward and wrapped the thin body in an enthusiastic hug. 'Thanks Ginnie, we will.'

Virginia walked out of the kitchen to the telephone sitting on its table in the hall. Its dial clicked round. The ringing tone burped in her ear.

'Miss Bowler,' she said. 'Please tell the vendors we will increase our offer by forty-five thousand. That represents our Best and Final. Take it or leave it.'

At three twenty-nine Marian phoned back. The Rectory was theirs.

CHAPTER ELEVEN

Ellie flipped open her appointments book and telephoned Mrs Richards to put her colour off for half an hour then hurried home. Andrea arrived back from school in a rush, clutching a bottle of champagne.

They stood in the kitchen holding Royal Albert Old Roses tea-cups filled with pale straw liquid. Sparkling bubbles rose through it.

'Sláinte, everyone' Andrea said. 'And thanks to Ginnie for changing her mind.'

A wave of cheers bounced round the room.

'Thank you all,' Ellie said. 'I need to give you an IOU, Ginnie, or something in writing anyway.'

Andrea drained her teacup. 'You can do that later. Right now we need to get organised. We need Lists. Follow me.'

She marched into the dining room and swept the centre runner and silver rose bowl off dining table onto the sideboard. 'Paper,' Andrea said.

'There's my wallpaper,' Rosie said. 'I'll get it.'

'Why on earth did you bring that with you?' Virginia asked.

Rosie coloured up a fraction. 'I was trying out some plans for a herb garden.'

'But we didn't know what shaped a garden we'd have. Or even if we'd have one.'

'I know.' Rosie shrugged at her. 'I was just ... hoping.'

'Just as well you did,' Andrea said. 'Go and get it – there's lots to plan.'

'You'll have to manage without me. I've got to get back for Mrs Richards. Just put me down for whatever you need to.' Ellie dashed out, still grinning.

By tea time Virginia's dining table was covered with a schedule of form filling, cupboard emptying, rubbish dumping, contract exchanging, meter reading, sale completing, money transferring, Big Yellow Box room emptying, furniture removing and delivery, and essential items unpacking. Everybody had tasks allocated to them. It was not entirely coincidental that Gwen had very few.

'Done.' Andrea flung her self back in the dining chair. She tossed the ballpoint onto the table. 'I think we deserve a take-away tonight. Fish and chips, Chinese or Indian?'

'I've never had an Indian,' Virginia said.

'You want to be careful where you make remarks like that, Ginnie,' Andrea said. 'You might be misunderstood.'

It took Virginia several seconds to recognise the joke.

A sense of humour turned out to be a necessity the next four weeks but at last, at ten-fifteen on August the thirty-first when every last penny had flashed across the ether, Marian Bowler handed the five widows five sets of keys to Langston Rectory.

Virginia Lesage stood at the bottom of The Old Vicarage drive. Quickmove's For Sale sign had a white label screwed diagonally across it with the word SOLD on it in five inch high red letters. She stared at the house for several seconds then said, 'Goodbye, George.' She turned her back and climbed into the rear seat of Andrea's Peugeot, directly behind Gwen who was clutching her handbag and Miffy rather tightly in the front. Andrea revved the engine and pulled away, leading Rosie's Astra and Knight's Move removal van to Langston Rectory.

They arrived as a pantechnicon loudly labelled VanMan Transfers turned into the drive, closely followed by Ellie's Golf. It pulled up level with the front door.

'At this rate,' Virginia said, peering past Gwen's fluffy hairstyle. 'The place is going to look like a used vehicle shop.'

Andrea slowed to a halt. 'Just be grateful the drive's long enough for five removal vans and all our cars to get in it.' She scanned the drive. 'I'm going to cut across the grass. That way I can park near the garage and be out of the way of the vans.' She bumped over the stone edging between two of the cherry trees and drove onto the long stretch of lawn.

Rosie's horn blared behind her. 'Be quiet, Rosie dear,' Gwen said to the window. 'It's only grass. It will grow again if we squash it.'

Ahead, Ellie's Golf stalled. The engine coughed back into life. Ellie heaved on the wheel, following Andrea across the grass to the triple garage.

Rosie pulled up three feet behind the removal van. She had her door open before the car had stopped moving. The engine stalled with a lurch.

'Oh gosh, where's my list?' She rummaged in her skirt pockets. An untidily folded square of wallpaper emerged. She ran to the van.

A dark-haired man in his forties looked down at her. A miniature version of VanMan Transfers was embroidered in two rows on his blue overall pocket. 'Nice place you've got here, missus.'

'Oh, it's not all mine. We're sharing.' She unfolded her list. 'This is where everything has to go. Some of it in my bedroom - I've got a label for the door but it's on the third floor ...' She faced the house, flapping her hands from side to side. 'On the right.' The hands stopped flapping. 'And -there's some for the kitchen. That's beyond the dining room. Or you could go round the side there.' She pointed. 'And in the back door. Be careful of the river though.'

The driver stopped admiring the rectory. 'Thanks, missus. We'll be sure not to fall in.'

The true nature of his comment failed to stop Rosie mid-flow. 'And one or two things for the drawing room.' The hands flapped again. 'Through the front door on the left.' She took two steps forwards. 'Oh, and the garden things can go in the garage.' She pointed. 'It's over there.'

'Really? Wow.' He pointed to the Astra. 'You'll have to back off a bit before we can start. We can't get the tailgate down with you that close.'

'I'll do it in a minute.' Rosie bounced through the door, pushing ahead of Ellie who had opened it. Dark, masculine mutters about grannies, experts and sucking eggs failed to reach her.

Three paces inside, she stopped abruptly.

Ellie cannoned into her. She disentangled herself from Rosie's crocheted shawl. 'What's the matter?'

Rosie's nose turned pink. Her eyes became distinctly watery. She sighed. 'I'd forgotten how lovely it is.'

Ellie linked an arm through hers. 'I know. We're so lucky. I feel like nothing will ever upset us again.'

The VanMan driver stood in the doorway, muttering. Eventually he stopped and called, 'You ready yet, missus?'

Rosie spun round. 'Oh, yes. I'm coming.'

She backed her car away, watched the tailgate descend then hurried inside the house.

One minute later the man stood on the threshold clasping a medium-sized cardboard box. 'Where d'you want this, missus?'

Rosie tilted her head sideways. The black magic-marker words on the side said KITCHEN. She pointed to the door. 'In there, please. It's the tea things.' She pointed again. The man muttered again.

'Come on.' Ellie urged Rosie forwards. 'Let's go and brew our first cuppa.'

'Oh yes. I just fancy a rose hip tea.'

The removal man looked at her sideways. He plodded off towards the kitchen, still muttering, this time about tea and its readiness, or otherwise, to appear.

'Where do you want us?' Another man, this one in smart green overall, shouted from the front door.

Ellie stopped. 'Who are you? I mean which firm?'

Virginia walked out of the drawing room, scowling. 'Why aren't you unloading my furniture?'

'Are you Knight's Move?' the green man asked her.

'Knight's Move is whom I've employed.'

The VanMan emerged from the kitchen. He stopped beside Virginia. 'Knight's Move, eh? 'You need to tell 'em to get on with it, love.' he whispered. 'That lot's notorious for taking their time.'

Virginia scowled. She stomped out of the front door, green-clad man trailing in her wake. A slight frown pleated his forehead.

Ellie grinned at the blue man. 'You can expect them in here, fully laden, any second now.'

The noise of another heavy vehicle drifted in through the open door. A bright pink removal van with *Girl Shifters* in green letters scrolling along its side pulled up behind the Knight's Move van.

Virginia's mouth dropped open seconds after it had clamped shut from telling the Knight's Move gentlemen what they were going to do and how quickly they were going to do it. 'What on earth is that?'

Andrea hurried across the gravel. 'It's my stuff. They were the only people available.'

'But they're women.'

The driver, a particularly well-endowed young woman in a tight pink T-shirt, jumped down from the cab. 'Well spotted, madam. We provide a guaranteed service to those ladies who prefer the security of female movers.'

The sight inspired the Knight's Move men to move themselves far more quickly than anything Virginia's comments had achieved.

By the time **Richford's Removals** and *budgetmoving.com* had started to unload, the men and women staggering in through the front door with furniture and assorted boxes were colliding with those exiting for the next load and cursing every ten seconds. Miffy had barked herself hoarse.

Ellie, standing in the hall directing traffic like an old-time policeman, received a fourth apology for language in as many minutes. 'This is chaos.' She ran a hand through her hair. 'Look. Bring stuff *in* through the front door and go *out* through the office.'

'OK, missus,' a green-clad man said. 'But keep that mutt out of the way before someone trips over it.' He growled at Miffy yapping round his boots. 'Or drops something heavy on it.'

'Of course.' Ellie scooped up the furry bundle. She beckoned the dog-lover and his competitors to follow her through the drawing room door. 'This way.' She went into the office. Clutching Miffy in the crook of one arm, she picked the key to the outside door off the windowsill. The door creaked open.

The romance of the wide outdoors beckoned Miffy. She wriggled out of Ellie's grasp, landing on the threshold with a squeak. Hurdling over the doorstep, her short legs sank into the gravel as she made good her escape.

'Miffy,' Ellie yelled. 'Oh, good grief.' She bit back her opinion of the dog and headed after her at speed. 'Tell your mates to come out this way,' she called over her shoulder.

Ellie cornered Miffy before she could squeeze under the arched door in the wall connecting the house to the garden. Unconcerned, the men continued their way to their respective vans. She carried a protesting Miffy back to captivity. The older Girl Shifter winked as their paths crossed and cast her eyes skywards.

In the kitchen Rosie and Andrea stood every mug they had so far unpacked on the vast, bronze granite worktop.

'Can you remember how many teas had sugar?' Andrea paused, a bag of golden granulated in her hand...

'I think it was five with and four without.'

'But that only makes nine and there's fourteen of them.'

'Oh.' Rosie scratched her head. 'I'd better go and ask again.'

'Take something to write it down with,' Andrea yelled after her.

Gwen wandered into the kitchen. 'Are you making tea, dear?'

'Trying to,' Andrea said.

'Lovely. I'd like one too, please.' She slumped down on one of Virginia's wooden kitchen chairs that had been pulled up to the worktop. 'Those men in the blue romper suits keep asking me where to put things. I've told them where my bedroom is so they're putting everything in there. I think I'll have to carry the birdbath downstairs again.'

'Oh dear God,' Andrea muttered under her breath. 'Put the milk in the teas, please, Gwen. I'll be back in a minute.'

Virginia stood at the bottom of the stairs, arms outflung barring the way to two men sofa-carrying men like Horatio at the Tiber bridge.

'What's the matter, Ginnie?'

'They're taking my sofa upstairs and I want it in the drawing room.'

'But we agreed that it would be Ellie's sofa and my two in there. Rosie's is in the office and yours and Gwen's are in your bedrooms.'

'Well, I've changed my mind.'

'Look, if we all keep changing our minds we'll still be unloading at midnight.

'It's not you unloading, missus. It's us and this thing's bl-, very heavy.' The Knight's Move man shifted his grip on Virginia's sofa.

'Upstairs, on the left,' Andrea said. 'Ginnie, we'll sort it out later.' A Richford's Removals man walked in carrying a triple dressing-table mirror. 'While you're up there,' Andrea said. 'Please will you bring down the bird bath and put it on the terrace?'

Richford's Removals and Knight's Move exchanged looks.

CHAPTER TWELVE

Lunchtime found the staff of five removal firms sitting round their vans eyeing each other like gladiators. The oldest Girl Shifter gulped the last of her tea.

'Come on. Let's show this lot we can outdo them.'

The second of the three young women took her empty mug. 'The piano?'

The slim girl twisted round. She groaned. The piano stood on its cradle lashed to the side of the van. 'It's not exactly small, is it?'

'It's a baby grand. They're never small. Or light.' The oldest held out her hand. 'Give me your mugs, I'll stick them in the cab.'

The piano, minus its legs, was wrapped in blankets. Foam protected every edge, corner and polished plane. The slim girl edged the brakes off the wheeled cradle supporting a lengthy board underneath the piano's flat back edge.

'Hang on, Trish,' the eldest said. 'Wait while I flip the spare straps round it. Hold it steady.'

'Steady? Are you joking, Megs.' Trish edged her weight awkwardly against the curving rear. 'Hurry up then.'

Satisfied, Megs untied the piano from the wall. It balanced perfectly. They started to ease it out of the van. The two at the keyboard end backed down the ramp, straining to look over their shoulders. 'I can't reach the brakes now,' Trish said.

'I know, I know,' the oldest girl gasped. 'Just keep it steady.'

Round their vans, the men put down their mugs, folded their arms and prepared to enjoy the spectacle.

One of the blankets covering the polished wood slid gently down the side. Trish tried to catch it.

'Leave it.' Megs said. 'It doesn't matter. I'll watch out for it.'

Ellie emerged from the house. 'Good grief,' she said. 'Rather you than me.'

'Indeed.' Megs wiped at the perspiration trickling into her left eye.

'Well, I'll leave you to it. I'm off back to work.'

She dashed across the gravel, started her car and drove it down the middle of the grass between the cherry trees leaving two flattened ruts behind her.

Eleven pairs of interested masculine eyes followed her progress, then turned back to enjoy Meg's expression. A quick smirk and they directed their gazes to the pink T-shirted figures bending and heaving at the piano. Trish, a newcomer to the job, wore gratifyingly tight jeans.

The girls inched the cradle across the gravel. Its wheels dug in at every second step. Progress to the office door was slow. And it was closed.

'Damn,' Megs grunted. 'Too much to hope any of them,' she flicked her head at their audience, 'will come and open it.'

Andrea appeared at the front door. 'Oh, my. Can you manage? Shall I ask the men?'

Megs grunted again but not with effort. 'Just open the door, please.'

'Oh, yes. Of course.' Andrea hurried across the gravel.

Feet were shuffled, knees were bent, shoulders were tensed until the piano cradle bumped over the threshold. Inside was no easier. Bitten lips, wrinkled brows and held breath continued until the cradle was balanced on the office carpet.

Megs relaxed. 'There. Safely in. It just needs its legs. You two keep it steady, I'll go and get them.'

Fifteen minutes later three perspiring women left. Andrea looked at the piano standing in the corner, upright and scratch-free. Only its music support was still in the van. She lifted the lid, exposing the bones of the playing mechanism. It looked like an enormous coffin. A coffin for Anthony's wonderful music. The image blurred. Tears overflowed her bottom lids. One salty teardrop slid down her cheek into her mouth. She wiped it away with the back of her hand. On the threshold Megs paused, music lyre in hand. She stepped back, pulling the door closed.

'Don't let anyone in for a minute,' she said to the other two. 'I'll just go and find someone.' She pushed the fragile support at the slim girl and went in through the front door.

A few moments later Gwen toddled into the office. 'Feeling a bit sad, dear?'

Andrea sniffed. She rubbed her forehead. 'It's just seeing it again where Anthony's never played it. He loved it so.' She ran her hand across the polished flank. 'I remember the day we bought it. He was so pleased. So happy.' Her voice waivered into silence. She sniffed and dug in her jeans pocket.

Gwen pulled out a small, inadequate hanky from its place tucked round her belt. 'Here, dear. Use this.'

Andrea dabbed it at her eyes. 'I'm sorry. I'm being stupid.'

'No you're not. It's hard to be on your own with just happy memories.' She put her arm round Andrea's waist. 'Come for a walk round the garden with me and have a little cry. The sun will make you feel better.'

Andrea looked down at the grey head that barely reached her shoulder. 'I don't think so.'

'I never thought so either but it will, dear. Even if it doesn't feel like it now. It does get better. That never feels true either.'

Andrea scanned the room. 'An office is so cold for it.'

'Well, dear, we'll call it The Snug instead. And it will be with Rosie's sofa in it.'

They walked away from the piano, into the garden room and onto the terrace.

'Where are you going?' Virginia called after them from the drawing room.

'Andrea's feeling sad so she's going to have a little cry in the garden.'

'Whatever for?'

'Her husband's piano, dear. It's making her miss him.'

Virginia stared at them. 'The piano? Good heavens. I can't say I feel the same about George's bureau.'

'No, dear,' Gwen said. 'I dare say you can't.'

budgetmoving.com finished first. Their less than pristine van was empty save for a bulbous hairdryer on a tall stand. The youngest of the three youthful budgetmovers carried it into the hall.

'Where d'you want this space helmet thing?'

Virginia looked at it from top to bottom, and then did the same to him. 'It's a hairdryer.'

'In the bathroom then?'

'No. In the right-hand bedroom on the second floor.'

The youth hoisted it up. The wire unwrapped. The yellowed plug crashed to the floor and shattered.

'You'll pay for that, young man. Make a note of it.'

The young man made several mental notes, grabbed the wire and started up the stairs.

'I'll get you a brush and dustpan so you can clear that mess up.'

The youth deposited the hairdryer in the first floor, left-hand bedroom and returned to sweeping duties in the hall.

'Empty the bits in the dustbin then wait there.' Virginia walked up the stairs. A few minutes later she descended, beckoned to the lad to follow her to budgetmoving's van.

'This person,' she indicated the youth to the driver. 'Has deliberately put an object in the wrong room. Come with me.' She stood back from the door and waited.

The driver cast a glowering look at the lad. 'Sorry, madam.' He climbed down and followed Virginia inside. In her bedroom, she pointed at the hairdryer. 'I distinctly told him to put it in the right-hand bedroom on the second floor. This, you will have noticed is the left-hand bedroom on the first floor.'

'Sorry, madam,' the driver repeated. 'He's only been with us a week. Work experience, you know.'

Virginia folded her hands across her waist. 'In my day, we didn't have work experience. We had doing as we were told.'

'Yeah, well, they're all full of themselves nowadays. Never heard of discipline. Only their human rights.'

The driver picked up the hairdryer and carried it up to Ellie's room. 'Right, ma'am,' he said on the first floor landing. 'I'll say cheerio.'

Virginia nodded. 'I hope you'll take that young man to task.'

The driver walked out of the door. 'You can be sure of that. Madam.'

At half past seven the final van disappeared down the drive. It met Ellie's Golf at the gate. She braked, the van swerved, the iron gate shuddered. Car and van lurched past a bare inch apart.

Virginia, watching from the front door with the others, put her hands to her face.

Ellie scrunched to a halt on the massacred gravel. 'Did you see that? He almost hit me.' She slung the long strap of her shoulder-bag over her wrist. The metal clasp on the bag banged against her ankle. 'Damn.' She reached for a large carrier bag laying on its side on the passenger seat, hoisted it out and slammed the door shut with her bottom. 'Is everything unloaded? All my stuff?'

'It's either in your room or the lounge or the kitchen,' Andrea said.

'Good. At least something's gone right. Mrs Wilkinson-Brent was in today and she's a pain. Doesn't seem to realise nothing I can do is going to turn a fifty-year-old, overweight woman into Princess Di re-incarnated.'

Virginia folded her hands. 'Mrs Wilkinson-Brent is a friend of mine.'

'Is she, Ginnie?' Ellie said. 'Sorry. I didn't know. You haven't mentioned her at all.'

'Truth to tell, I haven't actually seen her since George's funeral.'

'Not much of a friend then.' Ellie dumped her handbag on what had been Gwen's round mahogany dining table but now stood in the centre of the entrance hall.

'Do be careful, dear,' Gwen said. 'Caroline quite likes that table.'

'Well she won't be getting it any time soon,' Andrea told her. 'Not now we're all here to look after each other.'

'Come on,' Ellie said, heading for the kitchen with the large bag. 'I'm starving.'

'Me too. Thank God it's Ginnie's turn to cook tonight. I'm whacked.' A slight element of glee entered Andrea's voice.

'Me? No-one said anything to me about turns. Much less mine. You can't expect anyone to cook anything in all this muddle.'

'Why am I not surprised?' Andrea said.

'What?' Virginia's drooping eyelids flicked open.

Ellie put the bag down flat on the worktop. 'Just as well I stopped off for some pizzas, then, isn't it?' Four Heavy Guys pizza boxes slid out. 'There's two ham and pineapple, a four-cheese special and an extra spicy pepperoni.'

Rosie meandered in from the garden. 'Oo, dinner. Good. I'm hungry. I've been checking the greenhouse. It needs a good clean and there's not much in there worth saving. Never mind, we'll soon have our own veggies.' She peered in the nearest pizza box. 'Is that sausage?'

'Pepperoni,' Ellie said. 'But I asked them to put mushrooms on half the cheese one. There no meat in it.'

'Excellent. Are we eating here or in the dining room?'

'In here, of course,' Virginia said. 'Pizzas aren't suitable for the dining room.'

Andrea's teeth clenched briefly. 'Oh, no. It's the dining room for me. I think we should eat in style.'

Ellie lifted five non-matching table mats from a pile on the kitchen table. 'Start as you mean to go on,' she whispered to Andrea as she passed.

Twenty minutes later, Rosie picked up the last piece of cheese and mushroom pizza and followed the others out to the kitchen. 'I'm going to open a bottle of my elderflower champagne. Who wants some?'

'I'm not sure I've ever had it before,' Ellie said.

'Oo, I have.' Gwen carried her plate to the sink and ran some water over it. 'It's lovely.'

'Don't bother with that.' Andrea dumped the empty boxes into the recycling basket. 'We've a dishwasher.'

Gwen stood back from the sink and looked around. 'I can't see one. I use a sponge.'

Andrea walked to the sink and clicked down a cupboard front beside Gwen's knees. 'Here.'

'Oh. That's strange.'

'Give me your plate.' Andrea slotted it into the stainless dishwasher. 'Any more takers?' She loaded everyone else's plate and cutlery and flipped the door up. The buttons were lined in a row along the top. She pressed the 'rinse' one. 'Right. Where's this champagne?'

Rosie opened one of the cardboard boxes on the long worktop. 'Here. Any glasses handy?'

'Here, dear.' Gwen lifted a large, light box with a big green cross on it. She opened the lid and pulled out a substantial-looking blue box. Eight champagne flutes glittered inside it in dips in the dark blue satin. Gwen stood five of them up. 'These were a wedding present. I've never used them before.' The cut glass sparkled in the twelve downlighters lined along the ceiling.

Rosie unscrewed the bottle top. Pale citron liquid foamed out. She caught it in one of the flutes. 'Let's have a toast.' She handed the glasses round. 'Here's to Langston Rectory.' She raised her glass.

'Here's to us and Langston Rectory,' Ellie said.

'Langston Rectory,' they repeated. 'And us.'

CHAPTER THIRTEEN

By tea time on Friday all the rooms had curtains, most of which fitted, and agreement had been reached – more or less – about the locations of five dining tables and twenty-four associated chairs, Ellie having disposed of her teak ones on eBay for an interesting amount that had her seriously considering several other pieces that were not actually hers. In the conservatory strips of Rosie's wallpaper covered three kitchen tables lined up along the side wall. Trays of her transplanted seedlings stretched across them from end to end.

The drawing room had only three sofas: Andrea's two blue linen ones and Ellie's green and blue striped one. A multitude of Rosie's embroidered cushions lined the backs of all three in soldierly ranks. Virginia's pair of piecrust tables stood at either end of Ellie's sofa and Gwen's chinoiserie table and lamp occupied the angle between Andrea's two. Six unmatched lamps stood on the floor along the window wall in front of the radiator.

Gwen sat in her Comfort Easyriser by the fireplace, Miffy on her lap and her feet on her large, washed silk rug that covered a sizeable amount of parquet floor. A rolled up Turkish kelim was propped against the far wall. 'This is nice, dear, isn't it?' She pulled the lever and the chair swung on its pivots, hoisting her nearly vertical and almost shooting Miffy onto the rug. 'And I like your mirror there.'

Andrea lifted a tissue out of her pinafore pocket, bent forward and huffed on the Viennese mirror hanging over the marble fireplace.

She rubbed at numerous fingerprints until the sun reflected diamonds of light across the room from the mirror's bevelled edges.

'It was a wedding present from Anthony's parents. I've always loved it. They told us to choose something special when we were on honeymoon in Vienna.' She gave the mirror a gentle caress. 'Lovely,' she sighed.

The sun did not reach the left hand wall. Gwen's watercolour of the Grand Canal occupied the centre rectangle of three plaster-edged panels.

'I think it's really nice,' Gwen repeated. 'I think I'm going to like it here.'

Andrea laughed. 'That's just as well. We'd be in a real mess if you decided to leave.'

One Widows United meeting that no-one really remembered had agreed everyone was to clean their own bathroom and tidy the kitchen after they had finished in it. Boxes containing enough bottles, tubs, aerosols, dusters, sponges and brushes to stock a small village shop stood on the floor at the far end of the kitchen.

Early next morning, Ellie walked towards them. 'We'll have to take our own stuff into our bathrooms.' She half-lifted several boxes. 'Ah! This one's mine.' She picked up an Amazon box with a large black B drawn on one side, accidentally nudging the neighbouring box. Something white and fluffy flopped over its edge. Miffy charged across the room, yapping loudly. She clamped her teeth onto the offending object.

'No, Miffy. No.' Gwen got up from her half-eaten breakfast and rescued her crocheted poodle toilet roll cover. She put it on the table where it surveyed her cup and plate.

Ellie dumped her box on the worktop. 'I'll take that upstairs before I leave.' She rubbed her hands together. 'Right. What have I got for lunch?' She held open the door of the built-in, full-height fridge and rummaged inside. She gave up trying to find her last pot of Muller rice for her lunchbox. 'This idea of separate shelves in the fridge isn't working. We'll have to do something else.'

Gwen sat down by her cup of tea and quarter slice of toast and strawberry jam. 'I'm sure I had some Flora left too and now it's gone.'

'Here's some.' Ellie yanked a two hundred and fifty gram packet out of the egg container in the door. 'Look, I've got to dash - Saturday's always an early start. When the others come down, tell them we need to do something about the food situation. Say we'll sort it out this evening.' She picked up her Star Wars lunch box and rushed out of the door.

Gwen poured herself another cup of tea, her fifth since she had come downstairs at a quarter past five. Since then she had sat at the table staring out of the window at the garden brightening in the morning light. Another forty minutes passed before Andrea appeared.

'Morning, Gwen. Been up long?'

'Not long, dear. I sleep very well.'

'Ellie's up and gone, I suppose.'

'Yes. She wants us to do something about the ...' She frowned. 'About the food situation.'

Andrea paused, a box of crunchy cereal half out of the cupboard. 'For tonight?'

'For always. She said these shelf things aren't working. Something about a pot of hers. And there's my Flora.'

'Who?'

'My margarine, dear. It's better for you than butter.'

Andrea put the cereal box down carefully. 'Do you think she meant we had to stop trying to keep our food separate?'

'I think so. If we all ate Flora and Muller rice it would be easy. But we don't.' She bit into the remaining quarter of cold toast.

'Let's wait until the others are up, then we can think what to do.'

Gwen smiled 'That's what Ellie said.'

'What did Ellie say?' Rosie walked in, swathed in Black Watch quilted cotton.

'She told me to say she wants us to do something about the food situation, dear.'

'For dinner?'

Andrea shook her head. 'I think she means we should have some sort of communal agreement. Perhaps a kitty then we wouldn't have any bother about who's eaten what.'

'We could take turns in cooking.' Rosie beamed. 'I wouldn't mind. I like cooking.'

'Oh, dear. I'm not sure I could cook for all of us.' Gwen's face puckered round the eyes and mouth and turned as pink as her fleece dressing gown.

'You used to cook for – what was his name? Arthur? And your children.'

'That was a long time ago, dear. I don't know I could do it now. I mostly have sandwiches.'

'Well, you could make sandwich lunches for us. That's what I have when I'm gardening.'

Andrea looked at the enormous kitchen clock. 'Er, I've got to go into town. The shop phoned to say my music is in and if I go now I'll miss the worst of the crowds. I won't be long. If you come up with a roster for shopping and cooking we can cost it out when I'm back.'

'Won't Ellie mind, dear?' Gwen said.

'No. She never complains,' Andrea said. 'Unlike some.'

Rosie swung open a cupboard door beside the ovens. 'I put my cook books in here. Gwen and I can make up menus.'

'OK.' Andrea put her mug in the dishwasher. 'But not too many with dandelion leaves and rutabaga.'

That evening, ten pages of sample menus that everyone liked, or at any rate did not hate, spread over Virginia's table in the dining room.

'I'll cost it out if you want,' she said.

'Don't go too mad, I'm still on a tight rein until this probate is sorted.'

'I won't. I'm good at finding bargains.'

'Are you, dear?' Gwen said. 'That is a surprise. I didn't think you needed bargains. Not with George being a doctor.'

Virginia inhaled deeply through her nose. 'Consultant. He was a consultant.'

'Really, dear? I dare say he was. I suppose that house cost a lot to run. I was always very cold when we were there.'

Virginia's mouth folded into a narrow line.

Ellie and Andrea exchanged glances.

'If you're willing, Ginnie,' Ellie said. 'Then thanks very much.'

'Right, that's settled.' Andrea stood up. 'I'm going for some fish and chips. Anyone else fancy some?' Four hands waved. 'Cod OK?'

Virginia shook her head. 'I'd prefer haddock.'

'Of course you would,' Andrea said.

Rosie scrunched up the remains of the fish and chips papers. She trod on the nearest of three pedal bins and shoved them inside. She sat down. 'Right, cooking roster.'

'What?' Virginia all but spluttered into her tea. 'What cooking roster?'

'It'll be much easier if we have one meal for all of us,' Rosie said.

'I'm making the sandwiches.' Gwen smiled at the faces round the table. 'For lunch.'

'I prefer my cooked meal at lunchtime,' Virginia said.

'We can't do that or Ellie won't have one,' Rosie said.

'She could heat it up,' Virginia scowled.

'Thank you very much,' Ellie said. 'If it's all the same to you I don't want to spend my life on reheated meals. You could always heat up your dinner for lunch the next day.'

'I don't think that's a good idea at all. Not if I'm paying for it.'

'So it's all right for me to pay for reheated meals but not you.'

'But I'm –'

Rosie tapped her knife handle on the table. 'We won't get anywhere if we squabble. Let's say we have cooked dinners during the week and cooked lunches at weekends. It'll be better for Andrea too, when she's at school all day. Won't it?'

Andrea nodded.

Virginia and Ellie stared at each other across the table. 'I'm ok with that,' Ellie said.

Virginia took a deep breath. 'And I - I suppose.' She sniffed. 'Will I still be making the sandwiches at weekends?'

Andrea closed her eyes briefly. 'Yes, Gwen, you will. But for tea, not lunch. Let's get back to the cooking roster.' She held up a hand as Gwen's mouth opened. 'Apart from Gwen.'

'If we're having a cooking roster, are we having a gardening one too?' Rosie asked.

'I thought you wanted to do all the gardening,' Virginia said.

'Well I do, but it will make a big break in the day if I have to come in to cook lunch. Especially in the winter.'

Andrea propped her elbows on the table and sank her head into her hands. She took a deep breath. 'Right. Gwen does sandwiches for lunch – or tea - every day. Rosie does the gardening. Ellie, Virginia and I will do the cooking. Agreed?'

Gwen and Rosie nodded.

'I'll cook at weekends,' Ellie said. 'Or rather, on Sundays and Mondays. Hairem's open on Saturdays. It's my best day with girls who're going out for the evening.'

'Right. Ginnie and I will do Tuesdays to Saturdays. OK?' She looked directly at Virginia. 'Do you want to do alternate days, or swap three days and two every other week?'

All eyes turned to the head of the table.

'I suppose alternate days would be better. Though I'll still be cooking more often than Ellie.'

'Ellie goes out to work, dear,' Gwen said. 'Don't forget that. And she said she'd do the shopping on the way home on Tuesdays.'

Virginia's nose lifted. 'Very well.'

'Good.' Rosie scraped her chair back and stood up. 'That's all agreed.'

She escaped from the kitchen into the garden holding a clean bucket. At the edge of the terrace, she stood arms flung wide. The lawn spread from her feet to the river the best part of two hundred yards away. Across the shining water, fields of rye blushed pale gold.

'Beautiful. So beautiful.'

She crossed the terrace into the walled garden. Two long paths bisected it at right angles, cutting it into quarters. At the junction, the paths expanded into a circle round a raised stone pool filled with brackish water. Low, unkempt box hedges outlined the weed-filled beds where occasional remains of run-to-seed vegetables and herbs struggled to survive. Ragged fruit espaliers covered the west wall. A greenhouse spread along the wall nearest the house. After several hours of effort with an old brush and gallons of soapy water, Rosie had its glass sparkling in the sun. Inside, the seedling trays, transferred from their temporary home in the conservatory, sat on disinfected slatted benches.

Rosie bent over a tray of late-sown broad beans. 'How are you now, my babies?' The fat dicotyledonous leaves waved in her breath. 'You'll have some wonderful pods for us by November.' She nodded at three trays of Blue Lake French beans, twitched two of beetroot into line, tutted at the limp feathery tops of autumn carrots and smiled at two more trays of Kohl Rabi. She hurried past neatly-labelled aquilegias, aubrietia, foxgloves, delphiniums and lupins until she reached some trays of herbs. A wide smile puffed her cheeks up towards her eyes. 'Beautiful.'

A green and beige striped apron with a large half-oval pocket hung on a peg by the door. She slipped the top band over her head and tied the two ribbons round what could almost still pass as her waist. Sturdy fabric gloves bulged out the pocket like young kangaroos. She pulled them on. 'Urtica dioica, prepare to meet your doom.' She grasped a pair of shears and the bucket and went outside. 'If I'm going to keep bees I'll need you to salve any stings. Or …' She let herself out of the walled garden. 'Some soup. That will help poor Gwen's joints.'

The patch of nettles behind the garages trembled in the breeze.

CHAPTER FOURTEEN

Sunday morning Andrea rearranged her sheet music on the bookshelf in the snug for the third time. Ellie walked in. 'Are you OK?'

'Why wouldn't I be?'

'Because a certain person was getting your goat yesterday.'

Andrea straightened the pages of Chopin Nocturne No 4 in F. 'She was rather. Is. I really shouldn't let her wind me up. It's just that she does.'

'She's old and, I think, not very happy.'

'I know.' Andrea sat on the piano stool. 'I'm beginning to wonder if this has been a wise move.'

'Sharing, you mean?'

Andrea nodded.

Ellie knelt on Rosie's floral sofa beside the fireplace and curled herself into a corner. 'I don't think you should worry just yet. Selling and moving's a trying time. It's bad enough for us but Ginnie's older and she'd been in her house much longer. Probably all of her married life.'

'I was in mine all of my married life too.'

Ellie tried to decide which way to go. 'Me too. But that's gone.'

'You said you didn't like yours. Mine ...' Andrea's voice faded.

'We've all got our troubles.'

A stricken expression filled Andrea's eyes. 'Oh, I'm sorry. I'd forgotten about the probate. Is there any news?'

Ellie shook her head. 'No. Nothing. Snails move faster.' She swung her knees round and hugged them. 'There was a mortgage on the restaurant. Quite a big one apparently, so there won't be much money from that to mess things up.'

'Is it still open? I never thought to ask.'

'No. I closed it. Had to let everyone go.'

'That's a pity. Not a good time to be looking for a job.'

'I gave them all a good reference. The pastry chef's gone to Madringham Hall.'

'Wow, that's a good move.'

'Yes. Still no news though. Apparently a couple of people have asked to see the books. See what the turnover was and so on.'

'Was it good? It always looked a good place.'

'Not bad ... I think. Problem is, until it's sold I'm liable for the rates and stuff. Buying this –,' She waved her hand around. 'Has taken all my money.'

'That's not good.' Andrea frowned. 'But the rent from the flat must help.'

'Yeah, but being occupied makes it harder to sell apparently.'

'Can't you give them notice?'

'Kenneth renewed their year's tenancy just before ... well ...' She cleared a sudden constriction in her throat. 'There's six month break clause that I don't quite understand. I *think* it means I can give them two month's notice, I'm not sure.' She folded her lips tight. 'I'll be in a real mess if I have to sell up here.'

'Why didn't you two live there?'

'What?' Ellie gasped. 'So I could listen to them clattering around clearing up at one in the morning?' She shuddered. 'No thanks.'

'What about Kenneth? Didn't he want to?'

'Yes he did.' She flung herself round on the sofa. 'He shouted a lot when I refused.'

'But I thought ...'

Ellie snorted. 'That I always gave in to him?'

'Something like that.'

'We'd agreed before we married to live away from any restaurant he got. He just didn't like being held to it.'

'If you don't mind me saying, he sounds a right bastard.'

'You're not far wrong.' Her face crumpled. 'He never used to be.' She bit her lip. 'It still feels strange without him. It's odd.'

'People are odd. Come on, let's go and have a coffee and see if there's any of Rosie's cheesecake left.'

Ellie unfolded herself from the sofa. 'Cheesecake to banish the blues?' She stood up. 'You do realise we'll all end up Rosie's shape with all the cakes she keeps baking?'

The morning sun smiled on the garden. Rosie rocked back on her heels and surveyed the row of transplanted broad bean seedlings. She pulled off her floppy sunhat to wipe the back of her hand across her forehead. Freshly dug and raked soil lined with rows of seedlings covered one entire quarter of the walled garden. Low box hedges now edged it with clipped military neatness. Rosie tossed her trowel into the wheelbarrow. She levered herself up with a hand on its side. Dust and small pieces of gravel from the path clung to her crinkled floral skirt. One worn leather gardening glove followed the trowel before she brushed at the dirt.

'Haven't you done well?'

Rosie turned. Gwen, minus her stick, hobbled along the path towards her. Miffy waddled around her feet. 'You're not doing too badly either,' Rosie said.

'It must be the soup you made. Look –.' She waved both hands away from her sides. 'I can manage without my stick now.'

'Just you take care Miffy doesn't trip you up.' Rosie bent down to pat the overweight dog. It plopped its bottom onto the path. Its tail swept a semicircle in the gravel.

'What are you going to do next?'

'I was thinking of beehives.' Rosie pointed to the farthest corner. 'Over there.'

'Bees? Won't they be dangerous this close?'

'Well – they might be. I suppose I could put them down by the river.'

'Where will we put the chickens?'

'Oh, they'll have to be in here. To keep them safe.'

'Won't they eat your seeds?'

Rosie shook her head. 'We'll have a run for them.'

'A run? Like sports people have?'

A gentle look spread over Rosie's round face. 'It's the name we give the pen they're kept in. It keeps them under control.'

'And safe. Little Miffy won't be able to reach them.'

Rosie looked down at Miffy, now stretched out on the path like a small furry scarf, nose on paws, tail out straight. A small snore drifted upwards. She rather thought the odds would be on the chickens. 'Were you just having a little stroll?'

'Oh no, dear. I came to tell you I'd made you a cup of tea.'

Rosie pulled off the remaining glove and tossed it onto its fellow in the wheelbarrow. 'Come along. Let's go inside.'

Arm in arm, she and Gwen ambled up the path towards tepid cups of tea.

Just before twelve, Ellie tied one of Rosie's many aprons round her waist and stuck two spurred forks into the lump of gammon bubbling in the pan. She lifted it out. Cloudy liquid dripped onto the worktop between pan and spiked, stainless steel carving dish. The gammon settled into place. One fork caught on the string tying the poached skin round the meat. Hot liquid sprayed onto the apron.

'Damn.' She picked at the string. 'Ouch. Ouch. Ouch.' She sucked her scalded fingertips and rummaged in the drawer for scissors. The strings parted but stuck to the indentations they had made in the skin. Ellie slipped a knife under its leading edge and gently wriggle it from side to side. It peeled back revealing a glistening shroud of fat. She dropped the gruesome lump of boiled skin into the sink. 'Ouch, ouch,' she repeated.

'What's the matter, dear?' Gwen opened the kitchen door. Rosie followed her in.

'Nothing really. I'm only ruining my fingers on this.' She waved the knife at the ham.

Rosie peered at it. 'Meat,' she said.

'Don't worry. I've made you a cheese and tomato flan.'

'That'll take eggs, won't it?'

Ellie stared at Gwen. 'Well, yes. Four of them.'

'Good.' Gwen smiled. 'We'll be able to have lots of flans when the chickens arrive.'

Ellie's stare transferred to Rosie. 'Chickens? Live ones? Where are you going to buy chickens?'

'From battery hen places. You can rescue them.'

Ellie slumped one hip sideways and propped her hand on it. She waved the knife at Rosie. 'Why would anyone want to rescue a battery hen?'

'Because the poor things can still lay eggs, just not quick enough for the horrible battery people. They don't cost much, just a four pound donation or so.'

'Don't they need stuff? Houses and such?'

'Yes but once you've got them, you're away.'

'How many of the dear little things are we having?' Gwen asked.

'Three to start with, perhaps more later.'

'Just a minute, Rosie we haven't agreed to have any at all yet.'

'Where do you get them, dear?' Gwen sat down and lifted Miffy onto her lap. 'I haven't seen any hen shops in town.'

'On the internet. There's a site for them. They sell food and Eglus too.'

'Egg loo's?' Ellie put down the knife. 'Why in God's name do chickens need a loo?'

'It's not a loo. It's a plastic house with a pen attached so they've a space to run around in. You can move it from place to place.'

'But –', Ellie started.

'Can I watch you order them?' Gwen looked hopeful. 'Is this net thing the same as the one with houses on?'

'I didn't know you had a computer. Andrea has but …'

'Had one for ages,' Rosie said. 'It's where I where I do all my accounts.'

'Accounts?' Ellie's face went blank. 'But you don't look … I mean …' She waved a hand at Rosie's floating cotton skirt and gold-threaded scarf over another of her peasant blouses. 'Sorry.'

Rosie chuckled. 'Don't worry about it. I used to be a wages clerk, you know.'

'No, I didn't. Sorry. I say, are you any good at business accounts? My chap costs a fortune to do mine.'

'Of course I am. I'll do them if you like.'

'You bet.' Ellie ignored the cooling ham. 'How much would it be?'

'Nothing, of course. Not for you.'

'That's not right. You'll have to take something.'

Rosie shrugged. 'Buy me some seeds. Or a few roses. I don't want anything more.'

'That's great.' Ellie smiled. 'I'll be able to give the money I save to Ginnie.' She returned to the ham and sliced quick diamonds into the fat before dribbling honey over it.

'How clever, dear,' Gwen said.

Rosie wasn't sure if she meant the ham or the accounts. 'What is?'

'Doing your accounts yourself.'

'I enjoy it. I've been doing the ones for here too. Meter readings, council tax, insurance bills, food. I've got them all worked out.'

'Good gracious. I've never done anything like that. Arthur did it all.'

Ellie licked honey off her fingers. 'Well it's about time you learnt.' She screwed the honey lid back on, twisting it in the curve of her little finger and palm. 'You can show us all tonight, Rosie. We need to sort this kitty out properly rather than just forking out the odd forty quid for food every now and then.'

Virginia's nose was in fine form. She looked down it at the four seated around her dining table. 'Who said Rosie was in charge of bills?'

'Rosie's a financial whiz,' Ellie said. 'And she has all the costs listed already I think she should ... er, carry the burden.'

Rosie picked up the sheaf of printer paper beside the plate with the remains of a salad and cheese and tomato flan on it. 'If you all take one of these I'll run through them. Then you'll be able to have a think before we decide what to do.'

They stared at the spreadsheet of figures.

'Oh, my,' Gwen said.

'Good grief.' Andrea pulled her paper towards her. 'You've done a lot of work on it. I'd never have thought it of you.' She flushed. 'Sorry – that didn't quite come out as I meant.'

'Don't worry about it. Not many people think I've anything but flower pollen in my head.'

Virginia scowled.

'Have I left anything out, Ginnie?'

She ran a finger along the columns. 'No. Not at all. As far as I can see.' The finger stopped at a column headed Proposed Expenditure. 'What's an Eglu?'

'I know that,' Gwen said. 'Rosie showed me one this afternoon on the net thing. It's a dear little house for three chickens. We're going to buy one.' She sat back, triumphant. 'And three chickens.'

'Well I must say I think it's very high-handed of you to expect us to pay for your hobby, Rosie.'

Andrea glanced at her sheet again. 'Will you be eating any of the eggs, Ginnie?'

Virginia glared at her. 'It looks as if I'll have no choice.'

'Good. That's settled then. Rosie, buy your Eglu and hens.'

Eglu arrived by special delivery two days later. Rosie installed it on the last remaining unweeded patch in the walled garden. She collected the hens in three small crates the next afternoon and carried them gently into the garden. All four women watched her unlatch the lid of the first crate. A bird poked its head out. It blinked at them all then cowered back inside. Rosie wrapped her hands round its body and lifted it out. It squawked weakly.

'Oh dear,' Gwen said. 'How sad. The poor little thing's lost half its feathers.'

Virginia peered forward. 'I can't see that thing laying any eggs for us. It looks like it won't last another day.'

'You wouldn't be looking too good if you'd spent all your life caged in a wire box in a shed.' Rosie popped it into the Eglu's run. It squatted on the ground, staring at her. 'She'll be fine in a week or so, you wait and see.'

The second hen looked worse. Most of the feathers up its neck had gone, its comb hung limp and pale over its head and it could not stand at all.

'God,' Ellie said. 'I didn't know they looked as bad as that. Makes me want to rush out and save them all.'

'Three will be more than adequate, thank you,' Virginia said. 'I'm going indoors.' She marched off up the path.

Rosie put the last two hens into the run. The first did not exactly greet them as long lost sisters. 'I'll keep an eye on them for a while,' she said. 'Just to make sure they don't hurt themselves. Or each other.'

'Why would they do that, dear?'

'Where do you think "pecking order" comes from?' Andrea said. 'One of them has to be boss.'

'A bit like us then, dear,' Gwen replied.

CHAPTER FIFTEEN

It was another four days before Virginia consented to discuss Rosie's accounts. They gathered round Virginia's pedestal table in the dining room. Rosie handed out teacups, plates and more Excel printouts. The three-tier stand of cupcakes, each one topped with swirls of pastel butter icing and a tiny sugar flower, stood on a doily in the centre.

'Oo, lovely.' Gwen helped herself to a lemon one. Miffy jumped onto Gwen's skirt. 'None for you, sweetie. Get down.' She pulled off the paper case spraying crumbs around her plate. The dog subsided onto the floor, one eye watching for descending crumbs.

Virginia scowled. 'If we could get on.' She grasped her copy of the spreadsheet with both hands.

Three pairs of eyes scanned the spreadsheets; Gwen ate her cake. Rosie waited.

Virginia's scowl deepened. 'This allowance for heating seems rather high. I can't believe we've spent that much in two weeks. Not in this weather.'

'We haven't,' Rosie said. 'Marian got me copies of last year's heating bills. This is what it will cost us for a whole year. Divided by twelve.'

'Oh.' Virginia's face fell. 'I didn't think it would be that much.'

'It's a big house,' Andrea said. 'It takes a lot of heating.'

Virginia persisted. 'The idea was that the bills would be lower. This,' she waved the paper at her, 'isn't lower.'

'How much did it cost to heat your house?' Ellie asked her.

'Was it heated, dear?' Gwen said. 'I didn't know that. I was always so cold I had to wear an extra vest.'

Andrea strangled a cough. She thumped her chest. 'Sorry. Crumb went down the wrong way.' She looked at Virginia. 'This is less per person than it cost me to heat my house and it was smaller than yours. I think it's very good.'

'Very well then, if you say so. But I still think it's too high.'

'Look on it as a form of saving. If it's not that expensive, we'll all have a rebate to share.'

Virginia's grip on the paper lessened slightly.

Gwen finished the last mouthful of cupcake. She frowned at her sheet. 'Is boiler insurance really that expensive?'

Virginia snorted. 'It's not as expensive as having a boiler break down on you.'

The others stared at her.

'Your boiler was tested before we left, wasn't it?' Ellie said.

'It was working the day we moved out.' She avoided everyone's eyes. 'If you remember, the bathroom was warm.'

'Warm-er,' Rosie said. 'But not exactly spa temperature, was it? Not what I'm going to have in my aromatherapy room.'

'What aromatherapy room?' Paper crinkled under Virginia's fingers.

'The one I'm going to open in the cottage.'

Virginia flushed. 'Really? That's another plan you've made without the courtesy of asking us first.' Her face turned redder. 'I think you're taking far too much upon yourself, Mrs Reynolds. This is a shared house in case you'd forgotten.'

'I only said I had a plan, not that I was doing it.'

'I had the distinct impression there was mention of the cottage being let to holiday makers. To bring in some money.'

'Just a minute.' Andrea patted her fingertips on the table. 'We always said Rosie might use it.' The pats became a smack. 'Don't you ever think about anything other than money, Virginia? Every single time anyone says anything, it's money, money, money with you.'

Virginia gasped. 'How dare you speak to me like that just because I was brought up to be thrifty?'

'Brought up to be miserly more like it.'

'I think it would be nice to have an aromatherapy place,' Gwen said. 'I had one once when Arthur took me to that lovely hotel in the Peak District.'

Ellie took a quick glance at Gwen. The faded blue eyes looked straight back at her. 'I wanted one in the back room of my salon,' Ellie said, dreamily. 'To bring in more custom.' She looked from Andrea to Virginia to Rosie. 'Anyway, it's too late to get it ready for this year so why don't we let Rosie have it for now and let it next year?'

'I don't see why we can't let it straight away.' Virginia stared at Andrea. 'Those people left some furniture in it. Too cheap to bother taking, I expect.'

'They also left a year's worth of dust,' Andrea said. 'But that wouldn't bother you, would it? Not judging by the state of my room at your house.'

'Andrea, dear,' Gwen said.

Andrea pulled in a breath and held it. No-one spoke. After ten seconds the tension left her face. Her shoulders drooped, squashing the breath out back of her lungs. 'I'm sorry, Virginia. That was unforgivable.'

Virginia clenched her hands. Her mouth opened. A small cough emanated from Gwen's direction. Virginia looked down and up. 'My sight isn't as good as it was. I don't see things as well now.'

'Have you had it checked, dear?' Gwen helped herself to another, pink-topped cupcake. 'It's important to have it checked.'

'You should do,' Rosie said. 'At our age the backs of your eyes can go all blotchy. If you do something straight away, you can stop it getting worse.'

'Perhaps I should. I haven't been to an optician's for years.'

'Let's phone now and I'll run you in when you get an appointment.'

'Oh, I don't know about that.'

'It's quite free, dear,' Gwen said.

'Well in that case ... thank you, Rosie.'

'And the cottage?' Andrea said.

Virginia paused. She looked at the waiting faces. 'I think I've seen enough dust for this year. We'd better let Rosie have her room.'

'Good,' Gwen said. 'Can I have first go, please, Rosie?'

'It's a date. Now.' She picked up two pages of printer paper Sellotaped together. 'About paying for things, I checked up online and we can have a joint account – all of us. We can each pay our share into it by standing order.'

'All five of us?' Andrea said. 'On one account? I thought that was only for couples.'

'There's no limit apparently. Not according to the Citizen's Advice Bureau.'

'My bank's very good,' Ellie said. 'I have my account for the salon with them.'

'Ah.' Rosie lifted a finger. 'There's a problem if a joint account's at the same bank where you have a current one. If the joint one gets into debt, the bank can help itself to money in the other without asking.'

'Damn cheek,' Ellie said.

'They're banks,' Rosie shrugged. 'What do you expect?'

Andrea looked at Rosie. 'I'm with a building society. Do you think they're the same?'

'Probably.' Rosie said. 'I don't think we should take any chances. I'm with the Co-op. Is anyone with Lloyds?'

'Oo, I think I am,' Gwen said.

'Barclays?'

'Me,' Virginia raised her hand. 'It was the Woolwich but they were taken over.'

They eliminated all of the better known banks. 'Right,' Rosie said when they had found a one none of them used. 'We'll go with them. I'll set an account up online now.' She picked up her papers and disappeared upstairs.

Five minutes later she was back.

'No go, I'm afraid. They'll only let me enter details for two people. I phoned them up and they said we'd only be allowed to have one for two.'

'What?' Andrea said. 'One for two?'

'They'll only let two people share a joint account.'

'But you said there was no limit,' Andrea said.

'I know, but just because they're allowed, doesn't mean they will. I rang every bank I could think of and it's the same for all of them. Computer systems again, I suppose.'

'So we've got to chose two of us, have we?' Andrea looked round the table. 'I think it should be Rosie and Ginnie.'

Virginia's eyebrows shot up. 'Me?'

Andrea shrugged. 'Yes. No-one could say you're very not careful about money. I'd trust you with mine.'

'Here, here,' Ellie said. 'Is that alright with you Gwen?'

'Oh yes, dear, of course. I don't like things with money.'

'Well it's about time you learned,' Rosie said. 'You can come and help Ginnie and me set up our account.'

'Oh,' Gwen almost wailed. 'Does it mean your computer again?'

'It does. And it's easy. We'll turn you into a silver surfer yet.'

Virginia looked as enthusiastic as Gwen.

She saw it through but escaped into the garden room as soon as she decently could. It was not as sunny as usual. The sun had disappeared behind a cloud and an occasional raindrop dropped onto the roof. Virginia looked around, pondering whether to fetch an extra cardigan. Not cold enough, she decided, to struggle up the stairs to her bedroom. She wandered towards five neat piles of old books sat on the middle of the three kitchen tables still lined up along the house wall. Most of them were hardbacks with faded covers and wilting spines. She snatched the top one from the tallest pile and sat down.

Gwen tip-tapped in quite some time later, smiling. She and Miffy toddled across the room. 'I've bought a book on Amazon.'

'On the river?' Rosie's copy of *Vinegar - 1001 Practical Uses* drooped onto Virginia knees.

'It's a large shop – sort of – that you can go to on the internet.'

'Why would you want to do that?'

'Because they deliver. It saves you going into town.' She lowered herself, with care, into one of Rosie's armchairs. Her stick, propped against the outside corner of the arm and chair-back, slid gracefully onto the floor. Miffy eyed it with suspicion then curled up on the quilted knitting bag beside it. 'You can do your groceries on-line too. Sainsbury's. And Waitrose. Everybody does it.' Her face glowed. 'Isn't it marvellous?' She looked up at the roof, now closely patterned with raindrops. 'It'll be so handy when it's wet. Or when we're too ancient to drive there.'

Virginia refrained from mentioning Mr Alex James and Abbey Cars. 'We'd still have to go out to get to the library.'

'Ah, no you don't.' She peered over the arm at the knitting bag. 'Ellie has a kind doll. Amazon will send books to it for you. Not that it looks anything like a doll. More like ... like one of those slates Victorian children used.' She lifted the bag's two wooden handles. Miffy slid off, complaining. Gwen pulled out a small heap of lavender wool with needles sticking out of it like antennae. One needle clanked onto the tiled floor. She stretched down and rescued it, puffing.

Virginia watched her. 'What are you talking about? What kind of doll thing?'

'I'm not too sure, dear, but Rosie said they're marvellous. And you can make the font bigger.'

'What font? Why would you want a bigger font? The one in the church is ample.' She snapped the book shut. 'You're wandering, Gwen. And you're far too susceptible. Anyone can persuade you to do anything.' She levered herself out of her armchair and marched over to the tables. *Vinegar - 1001 Practical Uses* joined the middle pile. 'Rosie could start a library all by herself. Whatever does she need all these books for?'

Gwen stopped counting stitches along one needle. Her index finger and thumb marked her place. 'She's copying out the useful bits. She's going to make them into a book.'

'Why?'

'I don't know. Perhaps she thinks it might be useful.'

Virginia picked up and put down *Classic Household Hints: Over 1000 Tips for a Happy Home. Hedgerow Medicine: Harvest and Make Your Own Herbal Remedies* met the same fate. She flipped open the somewhat battered cover of *1001 Natural Remedies*, tilted her head and said, 'Was that the doorbell?'

'Was it? I didn't hear anything, dear. Perhaps it's the rain. Or one of Andrea's pupils.'

Virginia looked unimpressed. 'Today is one of Andrea's school getting ready days. And Rosie's moving the chickens down the garden. I suppose I'll have to go and see.' She sniffed. 'Just when we were having a little peace to ourselves. I hope it's no-one who wants to stay.'

She walked into the hall. The doorbell rang again, long and angrily. 'Well, really,' she said.

She opened the door. Caroline and Christopher stood on the step sheltering under a large golf umbrella.

CHAPTER SIXTEEN

'We want to speak to Mother,' Caroline said. 'Be good enough to let us in.' She took a pace over the threshold, forcing Virginia backwards.

Virginia pointed at the floor immediately in front of Caroline's polished brogues. 'Wait here. I'll tell her you've arrived.' At the drawing room door she stopped. Christopher received a Medusa look. 'Close the door, Mr Fellowes.'

He did not instantly petrify but closed the door quietly.

Cosy and calm in the sunny garden room, Gwen paused her clicking needles halfway along a knit one, pearl one rib row. 'Who was it, dear?'

'Your children.'

The knitting collapsed. Three stitches fell off the left-hand needle. 'Oh, dear.'

'Don't worry. I won't let them bully you. I'll -'

'Mother.' Caroline stood at the French window from the drawing room.

Virginia spun round. 'I told you to wait. This is not your house to do as you please.'

'This is our mother. And we want to speak to her.' Her heels scrunched across the cream tiles. Christopher trailed behind her, clutching his car keys. Half-way to his mother he stopped and cast a look at the plaster around the French doors. His discomforted expression cleared. 'Is that a crack?' He took two steps towards the doors.

Caroline glared. 'For heavens sake, Christopher. Can't you stop the surveyor business just for once? You're retiring next month.'

Miffy disappeared out of sight behind Gwen's chair.

'What is it, dear?' Gwen's hands clenched on the unravelling knitting. The glossy pattern for a Ladies Classic Raglan Cardigan and Matching Jumper, larger sizes, drifted to the floor. The smaller-sized model on the front gazed sightlessly at the ceiling.

Her daughter stared at Virginia. 'Alone, mother.'

'Certainly not.' Virginia put her hands on the back of the rattan armchair nearest to Gwen's and pulled it closer. Its legs scraped across the floor. 'We've made that clear before.' She sat down, back straight, skirt twitched neatly into place, and put one hand on Gwen's arm. Gwen dropped the knitting and clutched at Virginia's thin fingers.

'Chair, Christopher.' Caroline waved at the dining chairs lined up in front of the kitchen tables.

The nearest was a high-backed pine with a heart-shaped cut-out in the top rail. A small, red gingham heart padded within a whisker of bursting its seams was tied through it with ribbon. He lugged the chair forwards, his eyes glancing sideways to the crack. Caroline grabbed the rail and dragged it, screechily, the last few inches to Gwen's toes. The gingham heart swung frantically. She sat down facing her mother, handbag on her lap. Christopher stood at her right shoulder. The floor appeared to grasp his interest more than the crack.

'We've some questions for you, Mother.' Caroline pulled pages of folded paper and a pen out of her handbag. She opened them out. 'First of all, try to remember horse, pencil and rose.'

'Why, dear?'

'Just do it, please, Mother.' She balanced the sheets, blank one uppermost, on her handbag and held it and the pen out to Gwen. 'Draw a clock for me, please mother, saying ten to two.'

'Well, if you say so, dear.' Gwen took the pen. She drew a circle on the paper. 'Ten to two, ten to -'.

'Mother!' Caroline's eyes closed briefly. 'Make the time on the clock ten to two.'

Gwen drew two strokes. She leant back, tilting her head. 'It looks like an angry face.' She drew a semicircle under the joined strokes. 'Now it's happy. Look.'

Caroline did not. 'What were the words I asked you to remember, mother?'

'Ten to two, dear?'

Caroline pressed three fingers to her forehead. 'Before that, Mother. Before you drew the clock.'

'Have you forgotten them? That's rather worrying, dear. It was horse, pencil and rose.'

Caroline's fingers curled into a fist.

'What are you doing?' Virginia asked.

'Mind your own business, please.'

'It is my business. You are harassing a friend of mine in our house.'

Caroline ignored her. 'Mother when did the Second World War start?'

'You really should know that, dear. You did history at school, didn't you?'

'Yes, but I want you to tell me.'

'Well, father always said it was the twelfth of November, nineteen eighteen.'

'What?'

'Your father always said it was -'

'I heard that. What I want to know is when you think it started.'

'I think I agree with father but if you mean when did we start fighting, it was September, nineteen thirty-nine. The third. Two days before granddad Patterson's birthday.'

Caroline sighed. 'Alright -.'

'I know it was right. I'd never forget granddad's birthday.

'Never mind granddad's birthday, Mother. Tell me this. If I give you a pound coin, a penny and two twenty pence pieces, how much will you have?'

Gwen frowned. 'I don't know, dear.'

Caroline twisted to cast a triumphant look up at her brother.

'I haven't got my purse, dear.'

The triumphant look wilted.

'It's in my handbag in the drawing room. Christopher, dear, would you fetch it please?'

'This is ridiculous, Caroline,' he said.

'I quite agree.' Virginia stood up. 'Whatever it is you're after, it's not working so I'll thank you to leave now.'

The French doors opened. Rosie walked in carrying a fraying wicker basket full of herbs. 'Hello.' Perspiration stuck the white muslin blouse to her bosom. Her crinkled cotton skirt billowed dust onto her bare legs. Scents of rosemary and sage blossomed round her. Christopher blinked.

'Rosie, dear, this is Caroline and Christopher.'

'I know it is, Gwen. We met at your house. Remember?' She smiled at Christopher who smiled back until Caroline sniffed loudly. Rosie pulled off her floppy hat and dropped it onto the nearest table. A strand of salt-and-pepper hair slid out of its grips.

'Oh, yes, so you did, dear. Well they're here again. Asking me questions.'

Rosie put the basket beside her hat. 'What sort of questions?' She cast a very un-Rosie-like look over the siblings.

'Oh – can I remember horse, pencil and rose? And draw a clock.'

'I see.' Rosie folded her plump arms. 'You're testing her for Alzheimer's, aren't you?' She looked from Caroline to Christopher. No smiles for him this time. 'Trying to prove she's going gaga?'

'What?' Virginia stared at the two visitors.

'My dear Malcolm had Alzheimer's, Ginnie. Had it quite young. The doctor used questions like that to identify the first signs.'

'Really?' Virginia faced Gwen's children. Her stare turned into one sufficient to eliminate several years' concern about melting ice caps. 'So it's another attempt to make your mother do what you want, is it? Not what she wants.' She rose. 'You should be ashamed of yourselves, bullying her like that. I'll show you out.'

She marshalled the pair back through the drawing room and out of the house.

'Oh dear,' Gwen said. 'Oh, dear.'

Rosie perched most of her bottom on the arm of Gwen's chair. The arm creaked. 'Don't fret yourself.' She patted Gwen's hand. 'You've bought part of this house. If you want to stay here –'

'Oh, I do. I do.'

'Well, we'll make sure you do.'

'We certainly will.' Virginia reappeared. 'Horrid little people.'

'Oh, no, dear. They're not horrid. They're just … just …'

'Just not very nice to try to stop you living where you want to.'

Gwen's face crumpled. 'Why would they do that?'

Rosie cast a warning glance at Virginia. 'I expect they're worried we're trying to make you stay when you don't want to.'

'Oh.' Gwen fiddled with her knitting with her free hand.

'It's easily settled,' Virginia said. 'All you have to do is keep saying no if they ask you.'

'I'm not sure that's easy, dear.'

Rosie took Gwen's other hand. 'Now. Listen to me.' Gwen looked up. 'It is easy. You're quite capable of doing it. You can do anything you want to if you set your mind to it. You've learnt how to surf, for goodness sake. Ginnie can't do that, can you, Ginnie?'

Appealed to, Virginia shook her head.

'And you've even set up a standing order for the bills.'

'I suppose it have, haven't I?' A small smile crept onto Gwen's mouth. 'Arthur hadn't done that and he was the bank's area manager.'

Rosie let go of her hands. 'There. See? You can do things.'

'Will you show me that doll again, please? The kind one.'

'What doll?'

'That square thing you put books on.'

Rosie quickly rubbed the bridge of her nose. Her lips folded together briefly. 'It's called a kindle, dear. Kin-dull. Not doll.'

Memories of household hints and vinegar afflicted Virginia. 'Are they expensive? I might have a look if they're not.'

'Oh dear.' The knitting unravelled further. 'You won't get all … short with me if I get it wrong, will you?'

'Short?' Virginia blinked.

'I think Ginnie will be really patient. Won't you?'

Virginia's features struggled a little. At last she said, 'Of course I will,' and followed the toddling Gwen and the wide, bouncy Rosie out of the leaking garden room. Left alone, Miffy settled onto the knitting bag again.

Ellie flicked off the spotlights in the salon. The cream and pale green room faded into peaceful twilight.

Andrea slid her jacket up over her shoulders. 'Thanks for that.' She hunched down to stare in the mirror. 'Looks good. I'm glad you persuaded me about the colour.' Her head twisted left and right. 'Stops it looking so … drab.'

'You'd be surprised what I can do.'

'Are you OK for Sainsbury's?'

'I'm fine. The sooner we get it done the sooner we can get home.'

Ellie locked the door. They walked round the back of the short parade of shops. Marian Bowler was flipping her key-fob at a shiny Honda Accord. The car bleeped and flashed its yellow lights.

'Wow. That's new,' Ellie said.

Marian grinned at her. 'It's what comes of selling five houses and one very large rectory.' She opened the rear door and flung a shopping bag inside. 'How are you all getting on together?'

'OK – more or less.'

Marian hesitated. 'Even with Mrs Lesage?'

'Ah,' Andrea said. 'She's softened up a lot.'

'I'm glad to hear it. I have to admit I did wonder.'

'Everything considered, it's going fine. In fact the only problem is that I have to share a bathroom with this scissors freak.' Andrea jerked her head sideways at Ellie.

'You think yourself lucky you're not sharing with Ginnie. Or Gwen.'

Marian frowned. 'Ginnie?'

'Mrs Lesage,' Ellie said.

'Good grief.' Marian closed the rear door. It shut with an elegant, expensive-sounding click. 'I'd never have thought of her as a Ginnie.' She climbed into the driver's seat. 'Wonders will never cease.' That door clicked elegantly shut too. 'Cheers. Have a good evening.'

Ellie and Andrea watched her swing the Honda out of the small car park.

'Nice to know we got her a new car,' Andrea said.

'Huh,' Ellie said. 'Perhaps I'll get one one day. Come on. Sainsbury's beckons.'

The nearest Sainsbury trolley refused to cooperate. Ellie rammed it back into line and pulled out the one beside it. She rolled it back and forth. 'Good. At least this one's wheels all seem to be going the same direction.' She looped the cool bag beneath the handle and reached into her pocket. 'Damn. I've lost the list somewhere.'

'I'm sure we'll remember.'

The high, double glass doors breathed open in front of them. They proceeded up and down the fruit and vegetable aisles, avoiding a pensioner who was steering her trolley, or rather not, with just her forearms propped on the handle.

'Why do they do that?' Andrea whispered.

'No idea. Annoys me every time. Absolutely no control at all.' Ellie dropped seven apples into one of the flimsy plastic bags. One shot straight through onto the floor. 'Bugger.' She clasped the bag to her stomach. Three more apples fell out. 'For God's sake. Is nothing going right today?'

Andrea snapped another bag off the roll. 'What is it?'

Ellie's mouth drooped. 'The restaurant. It's such a worry. I sometimes think I'll never be rid of it.'

'Can't you do anything to hurry it along? What about the tenants?

'I've terminated that.'

'Given them notice?'

'Yeah. I wasn't too happy. They're only a young couple, but what else could I do?'

'Nothing. You need to get as much as you can for it. And quickly.' Andrea picked up another apple. 'What'll you do if you can't sell?'

Moisture brightened Ellie's eyes. 'It'll be the salon. It'll have to go.'

They finished the shopping and drove home. A girl in head-to-toe black holding an old-fashioned, boneshaker bicycle was staring at the house's carved name on the tall left hand gate pillar.

Ellie twisted round for a better look. 'Who's that?'

'No idea.'

'I'm sure I've seen her here before.'

'Don't worry about it. She's probably just lost and looking for somewhere.'

At the gate, the girl stepped back behind the pillar and watched the car drive up to the door.

CHAPTER SEVENTEEN

Next morning, Rosie lugged her purple cylinder Dyson downstairs from the second floor boxroom. In the hall the coiling hose slithered out of her grasp onto the tiles. She put the vacuum down beside it and leant against the newel post, panting.

Gwen tip-tapped out of the kitchen with Miffy pattering behind her. 'Would you like elevenses, dear? I'm going to make a coffee with Andrea's machine thing.'

'I'd better get on thanks. Anyway, it's only nine o'clock.'

'Get on with what?'

'Cleaning the cottage. The sooner I get it done, the sooner I can start my aromatherapy.'

'Oh, what a good idea. I'll help.'

Rosie eyed her. 'I can manage, thanks. You just take it easy.'

'I've been taking it easy, dear, ever since Arthur went. It's time I took it busy.'

Rosie eyed the short, plump, slightly bent figure. 'I'll tell you what – you can do the dusting when I've done the vacuuming.'

They walked through the walled garden, Rosie with the vacuum and floor mop, Gwen with three dusters in one hand. In the other she held her stick, the supply of inflammation-easing nettle soup having run out. Miffy raced ahead, charging towards the Eglu between neat box hedges she could barely see over.

'Miffy, come here.' Gwen quickened her pace to little effect. 'Oh, you naughty dog.'

Miffy ran up and down outside the wire run, yapping at the squawking chickens. In the confined space, the three birds raced around flapping their wings and colliding with each other. Cream and russet feathers flew into the air.

Gwen dropped stick and dusters and wobbled towards the chaos. She scooped up the dog. 'Naughty, naughty girl,' she scolded. Straightening up again, she swayed on her heels. 'Oo, dear,' she gasped. Recovering her balance she toddled back to the centre path at a slower pace, face flushed. 'They will be alright, won't they?'

The vacuum slid in Rosie's arms. She clutched it tighter. The mop escaped. Its sponge head scraped on the gravel path. Rosie muttered and hoisted it up again. 'They'll get over it. Might miss a day or two's eggs.'

She bent again to retrieve Gwen's stick then led the way to the second door out of the garden. Single handed, she dragged a large black key out of her skirt pocket with difficulty.

'Why lock the doors at night, dear? There's only us here.'

'Keeps the foxes out.' Rosie eased the key round in the uncooperative lock. Metal screeched on metal until it clicked. She opened the door and ushered Gwen through.

The cottage could have graced any up-market chocolate box, with or without a ribbon bow. The pointed porch over the weathered door turned the entrance into a sentry-box. The roof almost reached down to the tops of the green-painted windows at either side.

The main room rang hollow when they entered. A musty smell hung in the air mixed with the delicate fragrance of Domestos. All of the furniture left by the previous owners had gone. In their place, some of the contents of Rosie's house were grouped at the far end of the ground floor. Beside them stood a padded massage table. Three snowy white bath towels wrapped in cellophane were piled on its pink surface. At the kitchen end, all the pine cupboard doors stood open.

Gwen looked at the pink and green checked linen curtains. 'Aren't those Ginnie's? I'm sure I saw them at hers.'

'Andrea's. She said I could have them.' Rosie deposited the vacuum on the floor. The mop clattered onto the tiles. 'They're far too short for any of the windows in the house.'

'They're nice in here.' She looked around the empty room. 'I like this. It will look so comfortable.' Miffy ran across the long-haired pale green rug and jumped onto the more respectable of a pair of painted Lloyd loom armchairs. She settled onto its cream linen cushion. 'Oh dear,' Gwen said.

'Never mind. She'll soon get down when I switch the vacuum on.'

'No, I'll get her.' Gwen walked slowly towards the chair, stick tapping on the tiles. She propped it against its back and bent over. One hand reached out for Miffy, the other, for the chair back. It missed.

She fell sideways, hand grabbing uselessly at the chair. She crashed onto the floor pulling it on top of her. Miffy landed on her hips.

Rosie dropped the vacuum hose with a clatter and ran forwards.

Gwen lay on the floor, moaning. She screamed when Rosie tried to lift her.

'Oh, my God.' Rosie grabbed the cushion, batting Miffy out of the way. She raised Gwen's head gently and slipped the cushion underneath it. 'Stay still. I'll get an ambulance.'

Gwen lifted a limp hand. 'No, dear. Don't bother them.' Her mouth clenched. 'I'll be fine in a minute or two. I just need a little rest.'

'Rubbish.' Rosie pulled her mobile out of her pocket. The nine button clicked three times.

The paramedic lugged his grip along the path. 'This way,' Rosie said.

He crossed the floor and knelt beside Gwen. Rosie squatted on the armchair. She bent forward and took hold of Gwen's hand. Neither found a small, anxious dog licking its mistress's face at all helpful. Virginia walked to Gwen's head and clamped a struggling Miffy to her cardigan. She walked away, and hovered at Gwen's feet.

'Could you put the animal outside, please madam?' The paramedic clipped a pulse oximeter onto Gwen's index finger.

'Oh, don't,' Gwen said. 'She likes to be with me.'

'It'll bark,' Virginia said.

'Outside, please,' he repeated.

Virginia scooted the dog outside and shut the door. Miffy barked. Continuously.

'What's your name, love?' the man asked.

'Gwendolyn.' She looked at his green overalls. 'Are we moving again?'

The paramedic raised an eyebrow at Rosie.

'We've only just moved in,' Rosie said. 'My removal men wore green overalls.'

'Ah. I see. Well, I'm Peter, Gwendolyn.' He laid Gwen's hand on her midriff. 'Now, can you tell me where it hurts?'

'I don't know.' She tried to reach her left knee. 'I think it's here.'

'You lie still. I'll just have a look.' Peter lifted Gwen's pleated skirt out of the way. A hint of long pink bloomer appeared. He gently smoothed his hands over the joint.

Gwen winced.

Rosie leant forward. 'Is it broken?'

'We'll need an X-ray for that.' He smiled at Gwen. 'Let's make you comfortable until the ambulance arrives.'

'Why haven't you got one?' Virginia scowled. 'We dialled 999.'

'I'm rapid response. We have cars. People don't always need an ambulance.'

'She's eighty-two. She's had a fall. Of course she needs ambulances.'

'Ginnie,' Rosie said. 'Let's let him get on.'

Peter flicked her a look before pulling out his radio. He walked out of the door. Miffy rushed in between his legs. She jumped onto Gwen's stomach and licked her chin. Gwen squeaked.

Virginia scooped the dog up again. She leant over Gwen. 'Are you cold? Would you like a blanket?'

'There's these.' Rosie pulled the towels off the massage table with one hand.

'No, don't,' Gwen gasped. 'You'll spoil them.'

The cellophane ripped apart. A white towel unravelled onto the floor. Rosie caught it and dropped it over Gwen's legs. The paramedic came back in. 'Should we lift her onto the rug?' Rosie asked. 'The floor's bound to be cold.'

He looked at his would-be helpers, one not much younger than the patient and the other not much younger than that. 'Best not. We'll wait for the ambulance.'

'A cup of tea, then?' Virginia said.

'Not that either,' he said. 'Just in case she needs an anaesthetic.' He knelt down beside Gwen. 'When did you last have anything to eat or drink?'

'Oh dear.' Gwen put her hand to her mouth.

'She had breakfast at eight-thirty. Rice Krispies, the last peach and a cup of tea,' Virginia said.

The paramedic twisted his wrist. 'An hour ago. Roughly.' He pulled a clipboard out of his pack and wrote on a form. 'What's your full name?'

'Gwendolyn Mary Fellowes.'

'And when were you born?'

'April fifteenth, nineteen thirty-one.'

'And do you live here?'

'I do now.'

He wrote some more. 'That's great.' He stood up, looking from Rosie to Virginia. 'Would one of you wait for the ambulance up at the house?'

'I'll go,' Virginia said.

'Take the dog, please, love.'

Virginia favoured him with one of her less enthusiastic looks. She waited in the hall for seventy-three minutes until the ambulance arrived. In the cottage, Gwen shivered on the flagstones.

Four ambulances were lined up outside the entrance to A&E, their doors open and at least one of their crew loitering at the main door. Rosie sat on the passenger seat beside Gwen, smiling encouragement and patting her hand. 'Don't fret. They'll soon let us in. You'll be warmer then.'

Gwen shivered. 'How long have we been here?'

Rosie looked at her watch. 'Twenty-five minutes.'

'Why are we waiting out here and not inside?'

'I don't know. We must be going in soon.' Behind her the double glass doors hissed open. A young man flat on a board and with his head in a neck brace was wheeled in.

'There,' Rosie said. 'There's only two more before it's our turn.'

'Why can't we go inside now?' Gwen said, her fingers plucked at the pale blue cellular blanket folded in half across her legs.

'There's no cubicles,' the girl paramedic told her.

'But it's huge,' Rosie said. 'And new.'

'Yes, but they're all are full. And there are trolleys all round the nurses' station.'

'Oh, dear,' Gwen whispered. 'Can't we go home instead? I don't like hospitals. I really don't mind going home.'

'Well, I do,' Rosie said. 'Someone needs to get themselves sorted.'

Gwen winced. 'You're squashing my hand, dear.'

Rosie let it go. 'Sorry.' She turned back to the paramedic. 'Why are they full? Aren't there enough doctors and nurses?'

'It's beds, not staff. There's none available for A&E admissions.'

'That's ridiculous.'

The paramedic sighed. 'Tell me about it. Sometimes I think I spend more time hanging around here than I do on the road.'

'Well –'

The second paramedic arrived. 'Right. Here we go.'

The pair slid Gwen's trolley out of the ambulance. It's legs snapped down and they wheeled her into the hospital.

Rosie scanned the large room. Only one of the cubicles lining its perimeter had its curtain open. Four trolleys stood around the centre desks, each with a paramedic beside it. 'I don't think this is going to be quick.'

It was not.

Andrea walked into Gwen's cubicle at twenty past one. 'What do they say? Is it broken?'

'We don't know,' Rosie said. 'We've only seen a nurse so far. Not a doctor.'

'This is ridiculous. I'll go and see why not.'

'Oh, don't fuss, dear. I'm sure they're all very busy.' Gwen lifted a hand. It shook.

Andrea marched to the centre spread of desks, charts, computer screens, light boxes, a whiteboard and a water cooler. Three nurses were talking in a group near the board. One of them wiped a name off it.

'Can you tell me when my friend will be able to go home? She's getting anxious.'

A short nurse with dark hair scraped back and wearing a plastic pinafore looked round. 'What name?'

'Gwen Fellowes.'

The nurse scanned the whiteboard. Gwen's name appeared three quarters of the way down. 'She needs an X-ray.'

'Why hasn't she had one? She's been here since just after breakfast.'

'The doctor has to authorise it.'

'So? What's the delay?'

The taller of the two other nurses took a plastic-pinafore-covered deep breath. 'We are rather busy.'

Andrea looked round the room. All of the medical staff were gathered at the desks. 'That's a matter of opinion.'

She walked back to Gwen's cubicle. 'This is ridiculous.'

Two and a half hours later Gwen was back home, in bed with a hefty dose of analgesics inside her. Ellie arrived in a rush. She dumped her handbag on the kitchen table.

'Has anyone told the dreaded Caroline?'

Rosie shook her head. 'Gwen said not to. Said she'd only make more fuss and say we weren't to be trusted.'

'That's true enough.' She pulled a chair out and sat down. Miffy stood on her hind legs, pawing at Ellie's skirt. 'Has anyone fed her?' she said.

'Oh God, no.' Rosie put her hand to her mouth. 'I never thought of it.'

'I'll do it.'

'No, don't you get up. You've been at work all day.'

'Better than all day hanging around A&E.'

Ellie took a foil dish of Mini Fillets in Jelly with Lamb & Chicken out of the cupboard. The white dog on its lid looked exactly like Miffy. She ripped the foil off and put the dish on the floor. Miffy pounced on it. The dish scraped inch by inch round the floor with each bite.

Virginia came in, stared at the dog and sniffed. 'Caroline's on the phone. She wants to speak to her mother.'

Rosie and Ellie stared at each other.

'Oh, dear,' Rosie said.

'Ah,' Ellie added.

'I'll tell her Gwen's in the bath shall I?'

'Take a message,' Rosie said.

'Do be sensible.' Virginia crossed her arms. 'She won't tell us anything.' She walked out.

'I wonder what bloody scheme they've come up with now,' Ellie said.

CHAPTER EIGHTEEN

Gwen sat on the Golden Lily sofa in her bedroom, propped round with cushions, feet level on the matching square padded stool and Andrea's spare spring-weight duvet over her legs. She tapped inexpertly at Rosie's laptop balanced on a tray across her lap. The padded underside of the tray kept it level. Miffy raised her head briefly from the edge of the nearest cushion before lowering it again. Furry eyelids descended; small canine snores whiffled across the cushion's pink satin pleats.

Gwen tapped some more. Saga's website flashed up, turquoise, blue and white. She read, mouse-clicked, read some more then tapped the keyboard again. Fed Olsen's site bloomed onto the screen, also turquoise, blue and white. Five minutes later, Gwen discovered P&O kept to the same colour scheme. The gentle clatter of keys continued for several more minutes.

The door opened. Virginia walked in carrying a miniscule tray with a single cup and saucer on it. Two digestive biscuits were propped on the saucer.

'Are you using that thing again? I don't know why you bother.'

'It's amazing, dear.' Gwen closed the lid and twisted round to put the laptop down beside her, away from Miffy. 'I've just ordered three cruise brochures.'

'Why ever do you want cruise brochures?'

'To go on a cruise of course. I've always wanted to.'

Virginia looked up and down Gwen's legs. 'You're not in any condition to go on a cruise.'

'I will be though. There are some cruises round the Mediterranean at the end of next month that I think I'd like.'

'The Mediterranean?'

'Yes. One stops at Barcelona and Rome and then goes all the way round to Venice.'

Virginia put the tray down on the laptop. One biscuit fell off the saucer. 'I may not know about *technology* but I do know Rome isn't on the coast.'

'Don't be so negative, dear. The boat stops at Civitavecchia. You take a little train in from there.' Gwen picked up the cup and saucer. Her hand shook. The cup rattled and the second biscuit fell onto the laptop. 'Wouldn't you like to see Rome? And Venice? Or the Canaries? Quite a few go there.'

'I'm far too old to go gallivanting about like that.'

'I'm not and I'm older than you. I'm going to book one. If I don't do it now, I'll never do it.'

'You're mad.' Virginia turned to go then stopped, hand on the door handle. 'Can you find anything you want on that?' She waved her free hand at the laptop.

'Of course. Rosie showed me. You goggle things.'

'Goggle? What's goggle?'

The cup and saucer wobbled from Gwen's hand to the side table. 'Come and look, I'll show you.'

Virginia eyed the laptop. She slid two of the cushions away from Gwen's other side. Miffy's head bumped onto the linen upholstery. She yelped. 'Shoo,' Virginia said. The dog jumped down.

'Quiet, darling. Mummy's busy.' Gwen settled the laptop onto the padded tray and opened the lid again. The multicoloured Google logo blossomed.

Virginia sat. She peered at the screen, eyes scrunching. 'That's not goggle. It's Google.'

'That's what I said, dear. Now, what do you want to know?'

'Well -' Virginia gripped her hands together. 'Some builders, please.'

'Builders? Why do you want them?'

'Well -' The hands gripped tighter. 'I rather thought I might – possibly - see about changing the boxroom next to Ellie's room into a bathroom.'

Gwen stared.

'I thought it would be fairer if we all had a bathroom of our own.'

'That's a kind thought, dear.' Gwen tapped on the keyboard. Google told them it had found *About 3,490,000 results (0.29 seconds)*.

'Oh, my,' Virginia said. 'That's far too many. How about stair lift people?'

'Do you want a stair lift too?'

'I might. And it would mean you could get downstairs again.'

Google told them there were over two million hits.

'Oh dear,' Virginia said. 'I thought there might be fewer of them.'

'You don't have to look at them all. Let's just look at the first ones.'

Two grey heads leant together.

'None of them tell you the price,' Virginia said.

'I suppose it's like dress shops. The ones that don't put prices in their windows. They're scared it will put you off.' Gwen tapped some more. 'This one says we can get someone to come and give us a quote.'

Virginia peered at the screen. 'I don't sales like people coming to the house. They push and push until you buy something.'

'Ginnie, dear, when has anyone pushed you into spending money you didn't want to?' Gwen tapped their address into the on-screen form. 'I'm sure you could see anyone off.'

'You make me sound like a Rottweiler.'

'Not quite, dear. More of an Afghan hound. Very slim, elegant and down-putting.'

Virginia was so taken with the Afghan hound idea she agreed to email six different firms to come and quote. Three to builders, three to stairlifts.

When Ellie arrived home from work two days later and opened the front door a smartly-suited man, middle-aged with a round face and an extending metal tapemeasure wavering from his hand heaved himself off his knees beside the bottom stair. He flicked a knob on the case and the long metal rule zipped back inside.

'What's going on?'

'Good evening, madam.' He held out his hand and walked towards her. 'Laurence Goodward, Homelift UK. Mesdames Lesage and Fellowes have asked for a quote.' He looked around the hall. 'Such an elegant place. Just the sort of location our lifts are designed for.' He picked a brochure off the round table in the centre of the hall. One corner brushed the darkest of the delphiniums Rosie had stuck in a tall glass vase. A blue petal fell unnoticed. 'As you see, there's nothing of the utilitarian about them.'

Ellie took the brochure. 'I didn't know we were having a stairlift.'

'Ah –'

'I called them.' Virginia appeared from the drawing room. 'Or rather, Gwen and I did.'

Ellie looked from her to Mr Goodward and back again. 'Ginnie – could you come into the kitchen for a moment, please?'

Mr Goodward busied himself ostentatiously with his tapemeasure as they walked away.

Ellie snapped the kitchen door shut. 'Ginnie, I can't afford any more money. I haven't paid you back for the loan yet.' She twisted her hands.

'I – we, weren't expecting you to. Or the others. You and Andrea are barely forty and Rosie's only sixtyish. None of you will need a stair lift for years. It's only Gwen and I who are getting ... creaky.'

'Well, if you think so.' Ellie picked up the kettle and held it under the hot tap. 'What do the others think?'

'Are you really intending to fill it with hot water?' Virginia said.

Ellie's head whipped round. She swung the tap lever off and emptied the kettle. Cold water rushed in.

'Rosie is fine with it. Andrea's not home yet.' Virginia frowned. 'She didn't say she'd be late, did she?'

'Not as far as I know.'

'Well, I'm sure she won't disagree.'

'Probably not, but she might point out that you complained when Rosie didn't mention her aromatherapy room.'

Virginia waved a hand. 'Oh, I'm sure that's long forgotten.'

A tap sounded on the door. Mr Goodward's head appeared round the edge. 'I've finished measuring, Mrs Lesage, if you'd like to discuss a quote.'

'Thank you. I'll show you into the drawing room.'

'Won't Gwen want to be in on this?'

'Ah, yes.' Virginia folded her hands and bestowed an Afghan hound nod in Goodward's direction. 'If you'd wait here, I'll just see if Mrs Fellowes is awake and receiving.'

From the expression on Goodward's face, Ellie doubted that he had ever been 'received' before. 'Let's go into the drawing room,' she said.

Goodward slipped another brochure off the hall table, en route.

Ellie stood in the middle of the silk rug in front of the marble fireplace. Mr Goodwood admired the room's proportions and aspect.

'You'll see we have four different levels of chair, madam.' Goodward flipped through the brochure. 'Depending on style. And budget, of course.' He pressed it open and held it out.

Madam took the brochure. A large photo showed a chair, nicely padded and upholstered in beige, fastened to a metal rail in a hall much like theirs. Three smaller photos of narrower, less well padded and, presumably, cheaper ones were printed underneath it.

'And of course there's a wide choice of upholstery, madam.' Mr Goodward stressed the word 'wide'. He leant forward pointing as if his finger would cause the pages to turn. 'They're at the back.'

Madam flipped over two more pages. Several small coloured squares spread across the left hand page, none of them very adventurous, all of them with pretentious names. Blenheim taupe, French claret, Sherwood Forest leaf, Burmese sapphire, and, quite simply, Russet.

'All with a Scotchguard finish of course, madam. Or there's the plasticized version.'

'Of course.' Madam really didn't want to think why that might be a necessity.

Virginia sharp footsteps sounded in the hall. 'Mrs Fellowes is available now.'

'Er ... you go on,' Ellie said. 'I'll catch up later.' She left Mr Goodward ascending the stairs in Virginia's wake and went to finish making her coffee. The yellow leather tote on the worktop beside the kettle burst into a jangling version of *The Age of Aquarius*. Ellie dropped the teaspoon and rummaged inside. Andrea's number flashed the mobile's screen.

'Hello?'

'Ellie. Thank god.'

'What's up?'

'Look, sorry about this but can you do dinner tonight?'

'Yeah. Why? Are you alright?'

'I'm fine. It's just... well, I've had an invitation to dinner.'

'Wow. Anyone I know?'

'Just the new deputy head. He wants to discuss an idea for a concert.'

'Oh, ho.' Ellie grinned. 'Right, well … enjoy. See you later.'

'Thanks. It's just school stuff though, nothing special. Bye - oh, it's veggie lasagne and chicken breasts. It's all ready, in the fridge. Yours, not the built-in one.'

Ellie disconnected. The American fridge and freezer were taller than she. Inside were a square Pyrex dish of pasta and a bowl of marinating chicken. She lifted the pasta from fridge to oven and clicked the dial up to one ninety. The dish looked very sad sitting alone in the range's four ovens. Ellie checked the fridge door. Two full and one half empty two-pint plastic bottles of milk stood in the bottom rack. She took the open milk bottle out.

'Fruit and custard, I think.'

The freezer hissed open. She lifted out a clear bag of sliced apples and a brightly-coloured one of forest berries. They clouded while she snipped the corner of the berries bag. The door bell rang.

'Damn.' She laid the scissors and bag down. Two frozen black-currants rolled out. She popped them into her mouth and grimaced. Wiping her hands on a tea-towel, she crossed the hall. Virginia reached the bottom of the stairs with Mr Goodward behind.

'Who is it?' Virginia said.

'How do I know?' Ellie opened the door.

Caroline stood there, holding firmly onto a small child either side of her. Their heads swivelled from person to person. 'I've come to see my mother since you won't let me speak to her on the phone.' She pushed her way in. The children's feet tattooed across the tiles. The boy stared blatantly round the hall and tried to peer into the drawing room. 'Where is she?' Caroline demanded.

Ellie, flattened against the front door by the trio's passage, said. 'In her room.'

Caroline swung round. 'Why? What's the matter with her?'

'She's hurt her knee,' Virginia said. 'Slightly.' She looked down at the children. 'And who are you?'

The girl on the left edged closer to Caroline's skirt.

'These are my mother's great-grandchildren. They want to see her.'

'Do they have names?' Virginia said. 'Or are they merely accessories?'

The boy, about seven years old, said, 'I'm Michael Bradley Arthur Thackary. Michael for me. Bradley for daddy and Arthur for Great-granddad. He's dead now.'

Ellie choked.

'So I gather,' Virginia said.

'And she's Felicity Gwendolyn May. Felicity –'

Caroline tugged his hand. 'Be quiet, Michael. We're going to see Gran-gran. Now.' She frogmarched the children across the hall. Mr Goodward stood hastily aside. 'Are you the doctor?'

'Laurence Goodward, madam, Homelift UK. Delighted to be able to improve your mother's access to her house.'

Caroline glared at him. 'It's not her house.' Her glare transferred itself to Virginia without losing a fraction of its frost. 'And she won't be staying here much longer for people to make free with her money.'

'Yes, well.' Mr Goodward dug a smile out of his repertoire. Half a dozen strides took him to Ellie. 'I'll put the quote in the post, madam.' He escaped.

'Right,' Caroline said. 'Mother.'

CHAPTER NINETEEN

Andrea stared into the mirror in the female staff's loo, lipstick suspended in one hand. Her bottom lip caught between her teeth briefly before she spread the colour evenly. She dropped the slim case into her handbag and left.

Mark Western looked across the empty staffroom when the door opened. 'Ready?'

'Yes, thanks. Sorry to keep you waiting.'

'No trouble.' He walked to the door and held it open. Andrea lifted her hand a little too quickly off the edge. 'I thought the Old Swan,' he said. 'If that's OK with you?'

'It's fine, thanks.'

They walked down the corridor.

'Good. I wasn't sure. It looked OK on-line but I've never been there. Never been much of anywhere round here as yet.'

'You'll soon get used to it.' Andrea pulled the outside door open. Mark held it back for her. His hand brushed hers. 'I hope so.'

'There's not much doing unless you go into the city.'

'I haven't seen much of that either, apart from estate agents and the solicitor. Pleasures yet to come.' He dug his keys out of his pocket. A silver Touran, the newest addition to the carpark, bleeped its lights. He opened the passenger door.

Goodness, Andrea thought. I haven't had this many doors opened for me for years.

Mark opened The Old Swan's dark oak door too. He settled her at a table and came back with a peach J2O, a half pint of larger and menu folder labelled All Day Bites. The jolly strains of Mozart's thirty-second danced from several speakers fixed into the angles between walls and ceiling.

Andrea held her glass in both hands. 'What did you have in mind for this concert?'

'Time enough for that. Tell me about you. I don't know anything about anyone yet.'

'Not much to tell. I'm part time. I teach music. At school and for a few private students.'

'Your house or theirs?'

'Mine. Well, part of it's mine. The others own the rest.'

'What others?'

'Ellie, Rosie, Gwen and Virginia.'

'That's quite a few. Family?'

'No. We're all widows. We decided it would suit us to share.'

Mark looked away from her face. 'Ah, yes. I'd heard you, er ... I mean ...' His voice trailed away. 'Sorry.'

'Thanks. It was all a bit bloody but I'm OK now.'

He smiled. 'So tell me about your housemates.'

'Ha. We're a strange bunch. Ellie has Hairem - that's a hair-dresser's. Rosie is our homoeopathic, earth mother. Very into aromatherapy and meditation.'

'An off-the-planet type?'

'You'd think so but actually she's a whizz at finances.'

'Surprising. Who else? A Gwen and a Virginia, I think you said.'

'Gwen's sweet. I used to think she was an off-the-planet type too but there's more in her head than you'd ever suspect. Hideous daughter, though. Bossy.'

'That leaves Virginia.'

Andrea laughed. 'Nobody leaves Virginia, not if they know what's good for them.'

'She's bossy too?'

'Not really. I don't suppose you know many headmistresses from girls' public schools but magnify that about twenty times and you've got Ginnie. Never puts a foot wrong. Probably starches her petticoats.'

Mark laughed. 'I must remember that if I ever meet her.'

'You'd better. Best behaviour all the time. I'll bet she kept her husband up to scratch.'

'Poor chap. Now –,' He handed Andrea the menu. 'Let's order then we can discuss Christmas.'

The music changed. Andrea's hand paused on the red plastic folder. She stared at the nearest speaker.

'Something wrong?' Mark asked.

Andrea blinked and folded her lips tightly. After three breaths she said. 'That music. It's the march from Sibelius. The Karelia Suite. It was Anthony's favourite. We had it at our wedding.' Her eyes moistened.

Mark laid his menu down. 'I'm sorry.' He looked at the reddening face. 'Would you prefer to go?'

Andrea sniffed. She shook her head. 'No. It's alright. It's just the music … I'm susceptible to it.'

'Isn't everyone? Isn't that why we have military marches, national anthems and plainsong?' Mark watched her face.

The pain left her eyes. 'I'm sorry. Let's eat.'

Caroline marched across the bedroom floor. 'Now Mother, what's this all about?' Miffy galloped past her on her short little legs and hid behind Virginia's feet. Its plume of a tail drooped. 'Why are you letting them spend your money on this place?'

'Darlings.' Gwen flung open her arms. The children rushed towards her.

Michael swung over the sofa arm. 'Gran-gran, I like your house. It's ever so big. Can I stay?'

Felicity climbed onto the seat and wrapped her arms around Gwen's neck.

'Get down at once, Felicity. Gran-gran's not well. She doesn't want pestering. Now mother, tell me about this lift.'

'I'm buying it, dear. It will come in very handy.' She settled Felicity beside her. 'What have you been doing, darling?'

'Mother –'

Gwen looked over her great-granddaughter's head. 'And I'm going on a cruise.'

'What?'

'I'm going on a cruise. To the Canaries.'

Caroline strode forward and laid a hand on her mother's forehead. 'I think you've a temperature. What did the doctor say?'

'That I should rest my knee for a week or so until the swelling went down, then I could get up as usual.'

'Mother, you're eighty-two, not some jet-setting teenager. I want you to stop this nonsense and come home with me.'

'Gran-gran, can I stay here too?' Felicity pushed her feet under the duvet. 'It's nicer than Grannie's.'

'Of course, darling. Any time.'

Michael climbed onto the padded window seat and stared out at the drive. 'You've loads of grass. If Grannie leaves us here when she's picked us up from school, I could play football until mummy finishes.'

'Be quite, Michael,' Caroline ordered. 'And get off the sofa Felicity. I've told you once. You'll squash Gran-gran's legs.'

Virginia advanced towards Gwen. 'I think your mother can make up her own mind about the lift.'

'If I want your opinion, I'll ask for it.'

Miffy chased after Virginia who bent down and picked her up. The dog's bright little eyes buried in its fluffy white head stared at Caroline. It growled deep in its throat.

'And you can forget this silly notion of a cruise.'

'No I can't, dear. It's booked. A bridge deck stateroom. Single occupancy. Very comfortable. I'm leaving at the beginning of half term.'

Caroline's voice shot up an octave. 'Daddy would be horrified if he knew. He hated things like that.'

'I know, dear. That's why I'm doing it now. And you're not to worry. Rosie's helped me set up an email so I can keep in touch. If you have one too, of course. And I'm getting Sky. Lots of lovely programs.'

Caroline's mouth opened and shut a few times. Her face coloured. 'I'm going to tell Christopher.'

'What an excellent idea,' Virginia said. 'Let me show you out.'

'You stay out of this.' Caroline's words spat out. 'It's between me and mothAuguster.'

'Now, dear let's not argue. I've decided to go, and I'm going.'

More colour flooded Caroline's face. 'If that's how you want it, mother, among these people instead of with your family, so be it. Just don't expect to see these two when you're back.' Her finger stabbed at the children.

Felicity wriggled off the sofa and ran to hold Michael's hand at the window seat. Her face puckered.

So did Gwen's. 'You can't mean that, Caroline.'

'I most certainly do. If you prefer these people ... well, it's your choice.' She marched to the window and grabbed hold of the children. 'We're leaving.' She dragged them out of the room.

Virginia stared after her.

'Bitch,' hissed Virginia Henrietta Lesage. 'Selfish, malevolent bitch.'

The following Wednesday morning held the promise of the sort of early autumn day that lifts the heart. Rosie clattered around the kitchen with a mop, collecting a lemon, a bottle of vinegar and a box of baking soda into her garden trug. She balanced four large sponges in vivid colours on top.

Gwen yawned. 'What are you doing?'

'More of the cottage.'

'Really? Can I help?'

Rosie looked at Gwen's dumpy figure and the stick propped against the table. 'You've only been up a couple of days. You're still supposed to be resting your knee.'

'But I could do things that don't need bending down, dear. Dusting.'

'Like before? When you hurt yourself?' She sighed. 'Alright. Come down when you're ready.'

'I'll come now. It's too early to make sandwiches.'

Rosie was glad for that. Gwen normally made the sandwiches straight after her breakfast which could be from six o'clock onwards-. Any that had tomatoes or anything moist in them turned the bread soggy well before lunchtime. She handed a pile of dusters to Gwen who followed her outside onto the sunny terrace.

At the cottage door, Rosie slid the trug's handle up her arm and fished a key out of her pinafore pocket. Inside the lock, the key declined to turn. She struggled, the trug swung. The pile of sponges wobbled and fell to the ground. Dropping the key, she slapped a hand over the vinegar bottle and soda that were within a hair's breadth of following them. The lemon bounced into the foaming lime-green alchemilla mollis beside the doorstep. Rosie put the trug on the ground and piled the sponges and lemon back into it. A spray of green flowers caught in the handle. She picked it and waved it at Gwen.

'Lady's mantle. Good for healing wounds and inflammations. That's what I gave you. And arnica. Good for shock and bruising. That's why you're doing so well.' She heaved on the door latch, pulling the warped door straight. The key crunched in the lock. Its metal innards squealed and clunked. 'Done it.' The door sprang open.

The inside of the cottage struck cold despite the warm day. Rosie turned right into the kitchen. She dumped her collection of cleaning things onto a small, scrubbed table. She sniffed at the white china sink. 'Yuk. It's still not clear.' She stuck her finger into the side of the soda box and pulled open the triangular tab. A heavy spray of crystals tipped down the plughole followed by a large slurp of vinegar. The plughole fizzed and foamed. 'I'll put a kettle down it too, that'll sort it.' A minute later the kettle, so battered it looked as if it had been part of the original furnishings, was hissing on the gas cooker.

'Right,' she said to Gwen, pushing open the window over the sink. 'I'll open the upstairs ones too. Let it air.' She unlatched a cupboard door that stretched from floor to ceiling in one corner of the kitchen.

'What's in there, dear?'

Rosie's voice echoed from inside the cupboard, accompanied by heavy footsteps. 'It's the stairs.'

'What a strange thing to keep in a cupboard,' Gwen said.

Between them, but almost entirely by Rosie's efforts, the cottage was aired, the windows cleaned and a start made on washing the living room flagstones.

Pink-faced and puffing, Rosie straightened up. 'It must be past lunch-time,' she said. 'We'd better stop. I'm taking Ginnie to the opticians this afternoon.'

'Oh, dear. I haven't done the sandwiches.'

Virginia was in the kitchen eating a round of tuna sandwich. 'I wondered when you were coming in,' she said. 'I thought I might have to come and find you.' She waved a half sandwich at them. 'I had to make these myself.

'I'm so sorry, dear. We were cleaning the cottage.' Gwen sat down rather heavily on the nearest chair.

Rosie washed her hands under the running tap. 'We've plenty of time, Ginnie. Your appointment's not 'til half past three.'

'I thought you wanted to go to that healthy shop as well.'

'I do but it won't take long. It's only round the corner from the optician's. I'll pop in while they're testing you.'

Virginia fidgeted until Rosie finished her lunch, washed up and said, 'Right. Time to go.'

Gwen hobbled after them to the front door. 'Bye, dears. Take care.' She waved until Rosie's Astra had reached the end of the long drive and turned onto the road. The door swung shut. Her stick tapped across tiles, parquet, rugs and more tiles to her favourite chair in the garden room. She lowered herself into it and hooked the handle of her stick under a large footstool. Its legs dragged noisily across the tiles. Feet in pink, velcroed slippers settled onto it, she leant back. Her stick slid along the arm of the chair and rattled to the floor. 'Silly thing.' She looked at her knitting bag. 'Later.' She patted her lap. Miffy jumped onto it. Two pairs of eyes drooped. Five minutes later both were asleep.

Andrea called, 'I'm home.'

Gwen woke, lifting her head with a start. The cushion under it fell off the side of the chair.

'I'm in here dear. Have you had a good day?'

Andrea swung her music case onto the nearest kitchen table. 'Trying to teach year sevens to play all the same notes of 'O, Little Town of Bethlehem' at the same time will never make for a good day.' She slumped into an armchair. 'What've you been doing? Knitting? Surfing?'

'Oh, no, Rosie and I have been cleaning the cottage.'

'Have you? Was that wise?' She pointed at Gwen's knee.

'Now don't nag. You're turning into a regular Caroline.'

Andrea shuddered. 'No thank you. Is the cottage ready? I could do with a relaxing massage just now.'

'Not quite. We've left some stain stuff on the rug Rosie's put down. I think it was from Ginnie's. There was a mark. Rosie said if that doesn't move it, she'd like to borrow your blue one instead, please.'

Andrea shrugged. 'That's fine. I'm not using it.' She wriggled her shoulders. 'It's a cuppa for me. Would you like one?'

'Yes, please.'

'OK. I'll see if there are any more takers.'

'Everyone else is out. Ellie said she might be late and Rosie's taken Virginia into the opticians.'

'Oh, yes. I'd forgotten. I hope it goes OK.'

'I'm sure it will. Will you look in the cake box, please, dear? See if there's any left.'

'I don't think there is. I think someone ...' She put a stern head-mistressy expression on her face. 'Ate the last of it.'

She and Gwen sat in peaceful, companionable silence, feet up, drinking tea and looking through the wide conservatory windows at the garden. Three sets of eyelids drooped until someone banged on the front door.

Andrea looked at her watch. 'They can't be back already. I'd better go and see.'

A girl of about twenty, dressed from head to toe in silver-studded black, with aggressive hair like something from a 'before' shampoo advert stood on the top step scowling at the door. An old-fashioned bicycle was propped against the right-hand pillar.

'Virginia Lesage lives here, doesn't she?'

'She does.' Andrea paused. 'Weren't you outside the gate the other day?'

'Never mind that. I want to see her.'

'She's not in I'm afraid. Can I take a message?'

'I'll wait.'

'I think not. Give me your name and I'll tell her you called.'

'Livvie Lesage.'

'Oh.' Andrea blinked. 'A relative?'

'You could say that. I'm George Lesage's daughter.'

'You can't be.' Andrea frowned. 'Virginia hasn't got a daughter.'

'You aren't listening. I didn't say anything about *Virginia* Lesage. I said *George*.'

Andrea blinked again. 'Oh. Well ... I'll tell her you called.' She started to close the door.

The girl pushed it. 'Don't think I'm leaving. I'll sit on the step and wait if I have to.'

'As you wish.'

'Too right. She's not going to keep all dad's money for herself. My mum's going to have her share.'

Andrea shut the door and locked it. 'You're never going to believe this,' she told Gwen.

CHAPTER TWENTY

'Believe what, dear?'

'There's a girl outside. Says she's Ginnie's husband's daughter.'

Gwen struggled round in the chair, tipping Miffy off. 'Says what?'

'That she's George's daughter.'

'Oh, dear.'

Andrea shrugged. 'Illegitimate, presumably.'

'Ginnie's never mentioned a daughter so I suppose she must be.' Gwen settled herself back in the chair and picked up her knitting. 'Ah, well.'

'You don't seem unduly surprised.'

'Well no, I'm not really.'

Andrea sat herself down. 'Do tell.'

'Now, now. It's not nice to gossip.'

'But if she's what she says she is, we might lose the house. She says she wants some of his money.'

'Oh dear. I hadn't thought of that.' Gwen lifted Miffy back onto her lap. The dog settled itself carefully, avoiding the knitting needles. 'Well, there always was gossip about George. Of course, no-one ever said anything to Ginnie. Arthur certainly knew about it. Something to do with setting up an account at a different bank.'

'That makes it sound more permanent than a bit of a fling.'

'I don't know, dear.'

'But Ginnie must have known. Eventually. It would have come out in probate. Perhaps she's been lying.'

'Now that's not a nice thing to say, dear. It might not have come out.' She patted Miffy's head. 'I think ... I'm not sure, but I think it was put down as lifetime membership of another golf club. And some sort of insurance.' She frowned. 'Or was it an investment?' She shook her head. 'I'm not sure.'

Andrea folded her arms and sat back 'Well that's a new name for it.'

'Don't be coarse, dear.'

'Sorry.' She frowned, then grinned. 'It'll be a bit of a shock if she doesn't know. Poor Ginnie.'

Gwen peered over the top of her reading glasses. 'You aren't gloating, are you, dear?'

Andrea stopped smiling. 'Sorry. It will be though.'

'A shock for all of us if you're right and it means we lose the house.' It was her turn to frown. 'Or Ginnie's part of it.' The frown deepened. 'What if the girl wants to live here?'

'It's Ginnie's share, not George's.'

'Yes, but the money ...'

'I'll text Ellie. See if she can get home early. We'll need all our guns lined up for when Ginnie gets back.'

'I'd phone her, dear. She might not have her mobile in her pocket.'

A disbelieving Ellie arrived home twenty minutes later. She came up the path from the river straight into the kitchen.

'This is ... well, amazing. Where is she?'

'Sitting on the front step.' Andrea beckoned. 'Come and see.'

They tiptoed across the hall. Ellie peered through the leaded stained glass beside the door.

'Careful,' Andrea whispered.

A hunched figure sat on the top step, arms round its knees.

'Gosh,' Ellie whispered. 'She doesn't look like anybody George would know.'

'I rather think it was her mother he knew.' They crept back to the kitchen.

'What are we going to do?' Ellie asked. 'About Ginnie coming home? She'll have a fit if she's accosted on her own doorstep.'

'I've texted Rosie to come the river way.'

'Did you say why?'

'No. Ran out of characters. I just said it was an emergency.'

'Have we any brandy?' Gwen asked. 'Brandy's very good for shock. Better than arnica.'

'Good idea,' Ellie said. 'There's some in the sideboard. I'll fetch it if you get the glasses, Andrea.'

'I was thinking more about Ginnie needing it than us,' Gwen said. 'But now you mention it …'

Andrea took three small glasses out of a cupboard. They sat, sipping brandy and watching out of the windows for Rosie and Virginia.

Virginia did not pass out. Nor did she have any brandy. She marched straight to the front door and flung it open. The girl jumped up.

'I don't know who you are, or what you think you're doing but if you don't leave at once I'll call the police.' Four interested faces peered round Virginia's shoulders.

'Do that. I don't mind.' The girl stuck her hands on her hips. Her face coloured, her eyes flashed. 'I can prove I'm his daughter.'

'Rubbish!' Virginia folded her arms. 'I know my husband.' She paused. 'Knew. He'd never do anything like that.'

'Really? So why did he pay my mother every month? And made sure she got a pension.'

'I have no idea – and less interest - in your mother's occupation.'

The girl's eyes moistened. 'Don't you dare speak about my mother like that.' She swung the shabby patchwork tote off her shoulder. 'Here's my birth certificate, if you don't believe me.' The heavy metal zip declined to open until the third attempt. The girl stuck her hand inside and yanked out a long brown envelope. 'Look.' She held it out to Virginia.

'Certainly not.'

Andrea reached round and took it. 'Perhaps we ought …' She lifted the unsealed flap and drew out a folded paper. Holding both envelope and paper, she unfolded the certificate.

'Olivia Margaret Lesage,' she read out loud. 'Date of birth, twenty-four June nineteen ninety-one. Place, Mansfield. Mother, Margaret Helen Swinton. Father –' She looked up at the girl. 'Father, George Robert Lesage.' She turned to Virginia. 'Occupation - surgeon.'

Virginia's voice came faintly. 'Let me see.' She held out a hand which shook slightly. Andrea gave her the certificate.

No-one spoke.

Virginia read the names. The dates. The place of birth. Worse still, the name of the person registering the birth. *George Robert Lesage, father, present with the mother.* Her hand drooped. The certificate fluttered towards the ground. The girl snatched it inches before it reached the step.

'See? I told you I could prove it.'

Virginia swayed. Rosie grasped her arm above the elbow. 'Come and sit down. We'll see to this.' She led the ashen-faced Virginia towards the drawing room.

'I think you should go,' Ellie told the girl. 'Just give me your details first.'

The girl pulled another paper from her bag. A number was scrawled on it. 'Here. That's my mobile. You can get me on that. I'm not telling you lot where we live.' She shoved the paper into Ellie's hand then yanked the zip of her bag closed. 'And don't think you're getting rid of me. I'm – Mum's – going to have her due.' She glared at the three women, grabbed her bike upright and pedalled off down the drive.

'Oh, dear,' Gwen said.

'Quite.' Andrea said. 'We'd better see how Virginia is.'

They went into the drawing room. Virginia was sitting on the sofa nearest the door staring at nothing. Rosie sat beside her, patting her hand.

'I think we need the brandy,' Ellie said. She left and returned moments later with a large glass tumbler containing a considerable slug of brandy. In her other hand she carried the bottle. 'Here, Ginnie. Drink this.'

Virginia drank. And coughed. Colour came back into her cheeks. 'It's lies. All lies. It must be.'

'It was George's name, though,' Ellie said. Did you recognise his signature?'

Virginia turned her head slowly and looked at her from a great distance. 'Signature?'

'Yes. On the certificate.'

'I didn't look.' Her expression lightened. 'Perhaps it was someone pretending to be George.'

'I saw it,' Andrea said. 'If you've something he's signed I might be able to tell if it looks the same.'

'How about his will?' Ellie said. 'Have you got it?'

'Er ... yes.'

'Where?'

'I think it's in my diddy box.'

'What's a diddy box?' Ellie said.

'It's what you call a box you keep all your important papers in, dear. Wood usually. I had one until Caroline sorted all mine into a nice new metal one.' Gwen's face fell. 'Red.'

Rosie patted harder. 'Where's yours, Ginnie?'

Virginia put her free hand to her forehead. 'It's on top of my wardrobe. I think.'

'Shall I ...?' Ellie began.

'We'll get it,' Andrea said. 'Come on.'

She took the stairs two at a time.

'Slow down,' Ellie called. 'Some of us have been on our feet all day.'

Andrea stopped on the landing. 'And some of us have had year sevens practicing Christmas carols.'

Ellie arrived, panting. 'Do you think this is for real?'

'It looked genuine to me.'

'What do you think will happen? Does an illegitimate child have a claim?'

'I don't know.' Andrea stood on tiptoes to peer at the top of the wardrobe. 'There is a box up here.'

Ellie carried the dressing table stool over to the wardrobe and stood on it. She handed a dark polished box inlaid with marquetry to Andrea. They opened it on the bed. It was stuffed full of yellowing envelopes and papers.

Andrea upended the box. 'Look for something official. My lot used thick white envelopes.'

Ellie spread the papers. She grabbed one. 'This?' She squeezed the sides and pulled out the contents with finger and thumb. 'Ah ha! Gates, Merton & Braithwaite.'

Andrea peered at the papers. 'It'll be on the last page. Here –' She took the papers from Ellie. Two three four leaves flipped over her hand. 'Oh.'

'What? Is it his signature?'

'It looks awfully like the one I saw.' She tipped the pages back together. 'God. What's Ginnie going to do?'

'I don't know. Come on, we'd better let her read it.'

'But Ginnie must have read it already so there can't be anything in it about the girl.'

Virginia was on her second glass of brandy and her seventh tissue from a box Rosie had on her lap. 'Have you found it?'

Andrea nodded. ''Fraid so. I'd say it was George's signature on the girl's certificate.'

'Er, I'll just go and check something.' Rosie disappeared, skirts and scarf flying.

'Oh dear,' Gwen said. 'Oh dear.'

Virginia unfolded the will. 'It can't be true. She must be an impostor. Why would George sign her certificate but not mention her in here?'

No-one offered any suggestions.

They sat in silence until Rosie came back.

'Did you find what you were looking for?' Andrea asked.

'Unfortunately.' Rosie sat on the armchair next to the sofa.

'Well?' Ellie said.

'I checked the Law Society website for claims on estates. There was nothing I could see on there and the government one went on about 'issue' and 'intestacy'. I did find one that said an illegitimate child would have a claim on its father's estate but if it was working it probably wouldn't get any money. Not unless it was a carer for the mother … I think that's what it meant.' She frowned. 'And there was something about making a monthly allowance if it was still in full-time education.'

'Do you think she was young enough to be at school?' Ellie asked.

Andrea shrugged. 'She could be. Or she could be at college. Or uni.'

Ellie looked at the others. 'We need to find out more about her. And the mother. If there really is one.'

'Good idea,' Rosie said. 'We need a campaign. You go in the kitchen. I'll get my wallpaper.'

'Come along, dear,' Gwen stood up and pulled at Virginia's arm.

Virginia tried to stand. She swayed. 'I feel a little strange.' She put a hand to her cheek and blinked her eyes.

'Lean on me, dear,' Gwen said.

The pair set off unsteadily towards the door.

'She's drunk,' Ellie hissed to Andrea.

'I'm not surprised. If I'd spent my life in social corsets demonstrating to everyone just how superior I was, I'd be knocking back tumblers of brandy too.'

CHAPTER TWENTY ONE

'Right.' Rosie carried her laptop and wallpaper into the kitchen. 'Let's see about this.'

She sat down, flipped the lid up and started to type.

'Hmm. There's no Olivia Margaret Lesage on facebook. There's three Olivia Lesages, but the names of their friends all look foreign so perhaps they are too. Lesage does sound foreign. I never thought of it before.'

'What's a face book?' Gwen asked.

'Somewhere on the internet that people go to chat,' Ellie told her.

'But you can't hear anything,' Gwen said.

Ellie patted her arm. 'I'll explain later.'

Andrea lent her arms on the kitchen table. 'She could be using a pseudonym.'

'Then we'll never find her.' Rosie tapped the keyboard. 'Nothing useful on twitter.' She looked at the others gathered round the table. Virginia was still staring blankly into space. 'What now?'

'Electoral roll?' Ellie suggested.

'Could be. She looked over eighteen so she ought to be on it somewhere.' Rosie tapped again.

'Somewhere's the point, isn't it? We don't know where to start.' Andrea put her fingertips on Virginia's arm. 'Ginnie. Ginnie. Did George go away anywhere in particular? Often?'

The blank face turned towards her. 'Away?' A slow frown appeared. 'I suppose so. Conferences in London. That sort of thing. Not often though.'

'That means it must be somewhere near here so he could … um …' Ellie shot a quick glance at Virginia. 'Get there.'

'Wasn't the place on her birth certificate?' Gwen said. 'I'm sure Caroline has Chevelling Market on hers.'

'Brilliant,' Rosie said. She looked at Andrea. 'What was it?'

Andrea's face turned as blank as Virginia's. 'I don't know. I can't remember. Did I read it out?'

Ellie bit her lip. 'I can't remember either.'

'Think, dear. Try hard,' Gwen said. 'Let's all think. I'll make some coffee.' She shuffled over to the sink. Water hissed out of the flexitap and rumbled into the kettle.

Andrea bent her elbows on the table, rested her cheekbones on the heels of her hands and tapped her fingertips on her forehead. 'I can't remember.'

Mugs clattered onto the worktop. 'Mansfield.'

Andrea looked up. 'What?'

Gwen paused, a teaspoon of coffee suspended over Rosie's china mug with a robin on it. She turned round. A sprinkle of granules cascaded off the spoon. 'It was Mansfield. There used to be shoe shops called Mansfield. I bought a pair of peep-toes there when I was a girl. Pale blue suede, they were. Very pretty.' She turned back and tipped the coffee into the mug.

'Praise be.' Rosie's fingers pattered on the keyboard. She held her breath. 'Ah, we have to pay.'

'Where's my bag?' Ellie swivelled in her chair. 'There.' She rocked backwards and dragged it off the dresser behind her. 'Here.' She gave her credit card to Rosie.

'Right. Oh … we need her date of birth too.'

'It was June,' Ellie said, stuffing her card back into her purse. 'I can remember that but not the year.'

'She looked about twenty. Let's try nineteen ninety-two.'

Two pairs of eyes watched Rosie type. Virginia stared at the apples in the fruit bowl in the middle of the table and sucked the nail on her forefinger.

'Got it. Fifty-one Estelle Pankhurst Road. God, what an awful address.'

'Found her, dear?' Gwen toddled back to the table and put the robin mug beside Rosie. 'Now what are we going to do?'

The three younger women stared at each other.

'That's a point,' Ellie said. 'What are we going to do?'

'Well ...' Andrea chewed her lip. 'We could go and have a look. See how she lives. If it's a squat or anything.'

'Spy on her, dear?'

'Well, yes.' Ellie said. 'We've got to do something to see if she's genuine. God knows what will happen if she is.'

Andrea shot a quick glance at Virginia and lowered her voice. 'What will we do if ...' She jerked her head towards the silent woman at the end of the table. 'Has to give her some money?'

'I can't afford to buy her out,' Ellie whispered. 'I still don't know what's happening about the restaurant.' Her eyes filled with tears. 'Not to mention I'm still paying its tax and utilities.' She pressed her hands to her mouth. 'In fact if it's not sold pretty quickly you might be buying me out too.'

'Oh, don't say that, dear.' Gwen put her hand over Ellie's. 'It's so lovely with all of us here.'

'If the worst comes to the worst,' Andrea said. 'Could you get a mortgage on the salon?

'I don't want to do that. It's too much of a risk.' A tear slid over an eyelid. 'I've worked so hard for it.'

'Let's not cross that fence before we get to it, dear. Let's just think about this girl.'

'George didn't leave me much of a pension.'

Four heads whipped round to Virginia.

'Sorry?' Andrea said.

Virginia turned her head slowly towards her. 'George. His pension wasn't as big as it should have been. Now I know why.'

'Er … I thought you were pretty comfortable,' Ellie said.

'No. Not really.' A flush of colour rose in her cheeks. 'And to think he's kept me short just to pay off his … his tart.' More colour rushed back. She stood up, turning from side to side at the chairback. 'The … the bastard. Well *his* bastard's not getting any more money. I'll see to that.'

'We've found out where the girl lives,' Andrea said. 'Or at any rate where she was on the last electoral roll.'

'Good.' Virginia sat down again. She picked up her coffee. 'We'll go and see what he bought them.' She winced at the scalding liquid.

At ten o'clock the next morning Rosie walked into the drawing room a navy suit and orange blouse.

'Good heavens, dear,' Gwen said. 'You look smart.'

'Ginnie and I are driving to Estelle Pankhurst Road so she can see what sort of place it is.'

'Dear me. Is that wise? Won't she recognise you?'

'I hope not. She wasn't looking at me much. Only Ginnie. I thought I'd try to look different though, just in case.'

'Oh,' Gwen said. 'Oh,' she repeated when Virginia appeared.

Virginia's usual pleated skirt and twinset were gone. In their place were a pair of dark green trousers and a padded patchwork jacket, both somewhat too wide for her. A long, fringed, silver-threaded scarf was looped twice round her neck.

'Ginnie, dear. I hardly recognised you.'

'That's why Rosie lent me these.' Virginia tugged the scarf looser. She pulled the padded jacket down over a white blouse, flexing her shoulders inside it. She ran a hand over the green, red and navy patterned materials. 'I'm not sure about this. It's a bit – well, Christmassy.'

'You'll be fine,' Rosie said. 'Everyone will look at it, not at you.'

'I never thought of that.' She took a deep breath. 'Let's get going.'

'Take care,' Gwen called after them.

Estelle Pankhurst Road was a long curving avenue lined with mature plane trees and double-fronted, Edwardian terraced houses sheltered by low walls. The angular bay windows stared out at passers by. Rosie drove slowly along the road.

Virginia sniffed. 'Not exactly a slum, is it?'

'No. It looks pretty well established to me.' She frowned. 'If they're as old as they look, why's the road called Estelle Pankhurst? Wasn't she a suffragette?'

'I thought that was Emily.' Virginia shrugged. 'Never mind. Where's ... ah, that's it.' She pointed ahead. Number fifty-one had a blue painted front door inside a narrow porch framed by two stone pillars and topped by an elaborately carve arch. The same carving decorated the lintels of the angular bay windows on either side. Straggly purple and white striped petunias tumbled disconsolately over the edges of terracotta flower boxes on the downstairs sills.

Rosie slowed so they could have a good stare. 'I'll pull in if I can.' She found a space four doors further along the avenue and parallel parked with one sweeping manoeuvre. 'Good. Now we can walk back for a proper look.'

'We don't look like we'd be together.'

'We'll go separately then.' Rosie reached and clicked open the glove compartment. It flopped onto Virginia's knees. She winced. Rosie pulled out a small bundle of flyers. 'I picked these up in the post office. I'll put one through the letter box. That way I might see into the window.'

Virginia took one. 'How to apply for house insulation?'

'Quite appropriate as it happens. I don't suppose they're very efficient with those windows.'

Rosie got out and walked to the nearest house. She stuffed a leaf-let through the letterbox. She did the same for the next two houses then stood at the gate of number fifty-one. Its blue paint was dull but intact. Same for the front door. Rosie opened the gate and walked the three steps along the red and black tiled path to the door. Net curtains covered the bay windows. Their heavily-embossed, scalloped border flopped onto the sills. Through the undecorated weave of the right-hand one she could see a woman sitting on a sofa with her back towards Rosie. She stopped staring and pushed a leaflet through the brass letterbox, tarnished where the lacquer had chipped off. A move-ment in the lounge caught her eye as she stepped away from the door. The woman was struggling to stand. Rosie hurried down the path and back to her Astra. She dragged open the door and jumped in.

'Well?'

'I couldn't see much. There's nets at the window but a woman was sitting on the sofa.'

'What did she look like?'

'No idea. I could only see the back of her head.'

'That's not much use.' Virginia gnawed her bottom lip. 'Can we wait? See if she comes out?'

'I'll have to turn round. We're facing the wrong way.'

'Go on then.'

Rosie lurched the car into the centre of the road. There was no room to turn. She drove to the T-junction with the high street. A quick glance left and right and she shot forward, executed a U-turn that had Virginia clinging to the door handle and dived back into Estelle Pankhurst Road. A white van approaching from the right hooted. The driver shook his fist at them.

'Rosie! Be careful.'

''S alright. I could see him.'

'Quite possibly but I'm on the side he was going to hit.' Virginia uncurled her white-knuckle grip from the door handle and grasped the crunched scarf round her neck, pulling it looser.

Rosie swerved into another space, stopping millimetres from the back bumper of an aging Toyota.

'Have you ever considered taking another driving course?' Virginia asked with a certain amount of asperity.

'Been on one. Advanced driver, me.'

Some of Virginia's composure was returning. 'I'd never have guessed.'

'Did I hit anything?'

'No, but –'

'Well then.' She switched off the engine. 'Look. Someone's going in.'

CHAPTER TWENTY TWO

They peered through the windscreen. A short woman in a checked nylon tabard over a navy summer skirt and white T-shirt that showed her loose upper arms slammed the door of a small car. She turned a key in the lock and hurried into the house without knocking.

'The mother?' Virginia said. 'A cleaner?'

Rosie shrugged. 'Don't know.' She sucked her bottom lip. 'Perhaps there's something in her car that might say.'

'I'll go. I'll drift past and drop my handkerchief.'

'People don't have handkerchiefs to drop any more. Here –' Rosie reached back and pulled a magazine off the rear seat.

'*Health and Revitalisation*? Good heavens.' Virginia took it and heaved herself out of the car. She took a firm grip of her bag and crossed the road.

Rosie watched her thin figure meander down the pavement. Virginia paused to look at the various horticultural interpretations in the narrow walled strips that separated house from street. A green windowbox here, a blue pot there, slate chips, limestone slabs, pea shingle. Net curtains, vertical blinds, burgundy swags. A red door, two black ones. Level with the faded blue door and with her back to the car, she dropped the magazine. She turned round, bent down, wobbled and supported herself with a hand to the bonnet. The car shrieked. Virginia straightened up rapidly. The front door opened and the mystery woman emerged. The tabard flapped as she hurried to Virginia, now leaning against the car, pressing the back of her hand holding the rescued magazine to her forehead. The woman said something and pushed her hand into the kangaroo pocket on her tabard. She waved a small and dark object under Virginia's nose. Virginia's head snapped back. She blinked rapidly several times. The woman smiled, spoke a few words and patted her arm before letting her continue along the pavement.

Rosie waited until the woman was back in the house then started the car and drove along the road.

'Well?' she said as Virginia sank into the passenger seat.

'Not sure. There were lots of leaflets and two plastic folders on the passenger seat.'

'What did she say?'

'She said "Are you all right, dear?" and gave me some smelling salts.'

'Smelling salts?'

'I said I was feeling dizzy.'

'Oh.' Rosie negotiated the junction at the end of Estelle Pankhurst Road. 'That's not much of clue. What were the leaflets about?'

'The print was too small for me to read. And they were upside down.'

'We're not really any the wiser then, are we?'

Virginia shook her head. 'Let's go home. I need a cup of tea.'

Rosie glanced at her. 'Don't get down-hearted. We'll tell Andrea and Ellie what we've seen. Perhaps they can think of something.'

'So what sort of person has smelling salts in her apron pocket?' Andrea said as she bundled her duvet cover into the washing machine. 'Has to be a nurse or a carer of some sort, surely?'

'Perhaps.' Ellie rummaged in the tea caddy for a fruit tea bag. One emerged trailing a shower of fine dust. 'But it doesn't mean she was there for anyone in the house. She could be a friend who's a carer.' She turned to Rosie and a drooping Virginia. 'How long was she in there?'

At the table the would-be spies looked at each other across Gwen. 'We didn't stay,' Rosie said.

'Perhaps we should have,' Virginia said.

Rosie stiffened. 'But you said you were feeling dizzy.'

Virginia huffed. 'I was acting, of course.'

'Oh.'

'Why don't you go back, dear, and watch how long she stays?'

'We can't. She might recognise us.'

'I could go, dear.'

All movement in the kitchen stopped.

'Um,' Rosie said.

'Er – I think that mightn't be so good, Gwen,' Ellie said. 'Perhaps Andrea and I should go.'

'Be safer,' Andrea muttered into the washing machine.

'But you two are at work during the day, dear. I could manage.'

'It's quite a difficult drive. You might get tired. Or hurt your knee again.' Rosie received grateful looks from the others. 'We don't want that happening, do we?'

'But if I took the taxi ...'

'Taxis don't sit outside houses, spying,' Rosie said.

Gwen sighed. 'I suppose so. But the woman might not be there at the same time Ellie and Andrea.'

'When's your free periods?' Ellie asked.

'Tuesday afternoon, Wednesday morning and last lesson on Friday.'

'Morning would be best,' Rosie said. 'If she is a carer, that's when they're most likely to go.'

'I can't do this Wednesday.'

'Oh?'

Andrea turned pinker than she should have been from stuffing bedlinen into a washing machine. 'Mark wants to have another chat about the concert.'

'Really?' Ellie shot a sidelong glance at the blushing face before picking up her mobile phone. 'That's nice.' She clicked through the menus. 'Only a C and B Wednesday week. Mrs Patterson. I'll phone her and see if she'll change.'

'Oo, phones, dear. I forgot for a moment. Mr ... er, Dunes phoned, Ellie. Wanted to speak to you.'

'Dunes, Gwen? I don't know any ... was it Daynes by any chance? The solicitor?'

'It might have been. He sounded solicitorish. Strange. He said he wanted to speak to you about the news.'

Ellie looked at her watch. 'Five fifty. He might still be there.' She hurried out of the room.

Gwen frowned. 'Why would he want to talk to Ellie about the news?'

'Not *the* news,' Rosie said. 'Probably news about her husband's probate.'

'Oh, yes, dear. I'd forgotten about that.'

The washing machine sploshed sounds of swirling water into the silent room. The drum rocked back and forth. The soaked lemon-striped duvet slumped from side to side.

'What if she has to sell?' Virginia said.

Rosie crossed the fingers of both hands. 'Please let's hope not.'

Ellie came back into the kitchen, carrying the cordless phone. 'He's hopeful for probate.' She grinned. 'And I've had an offer on the restaurant.'

Squeals and laughs drowned out the whirling washing. Virginia's face glowed.

'Yeah ... that's great.' Andrea clapped her hands. 'Is it ...I mean, is it enough?'

'Three hundred and forty thousand.'

'Wow.' Rosie leant back in her chair. 'Nice.'

'It would be if it weren't for the mortgage. It'll take almost all of it. By the time I've paid Daynes and the estate agents I'll be lucky to have five thousand left.'

'Oh.' The Virginia's glow extinguished.

'Sorry, Ginnie. You'll have all of it, of course. I just hope it'll be more.'

'D'you think they'd up their offer if you declined?' Rosie said.

'I don't know. I don't know if I dare.'

'Are Quickmove selling it for you, dear?'

Ellie shook her head. 'No. Minchman and Brooke in the city.'

'Ask them what they think,' Rosie said. She frowned. 'Why haven't they been in touch about it?'

Ellie shrugged. 'I don't know ... I can't think straight. I'm not going to phone them now. I'll do it tomorrow.'

'Do it now,' Virginia said. 'Best get it over with.'

Ellie picked up the phone and punched in three of the numbers. A knock sounded on the back door. 'Whoever's that?'

Virginia stood up. 'I'll see.'

A young woman wearing a straight skirt and a short sleeved blouse stood three paces away. A strand of chin-length brown hair blew across her face. She brushed it away. 'Sorry to bother you, but I'm looking for Sweet Spa Therapy. I tried the cottage –' She waved a hand towards the walled garden. 'But there's no-one there.'

'Indeed not,' Virginia said. 'Rosie,' she called. 'There's someone to see you.'

'Oh, my.' Rosie pushed herself up, two-handed from the table. 'I'm so sorry.' She hurried to the door. 'I'd quite missed the time. Are you Miss Barton?'

The woman nodded. 'Celia Barton.'

'Come on then. It's this way.' She stepped outside and closed the door. It opened again. 'Tell me what happens when I'm back.'

Virginia watched through the glass door panel until Rosie and Miss Barton had disappeared. She turned back. 'I didn't know she'd begun accepting clients.'

'I think that's her first one, dear.'

'Hmm. Well, I hope she remembers when the others are coming. We don't want strange people knocking on the door every hour of the day and night.'

'She's making a sign for the path,' Ellie said. She punched more numbers onto the phone and waited. 'Hello?'

'Minchman and Brooke,' said a disembodied female voice.

'I want to speak to Mr Johnstone, please. It's about The Butler's Pantry restaurant'

'Mr Johnstone isn't here at present, madam. Our Mr Richards should be able to help. One moment please.'

The over-familiar strains of Vivaldi drifted across the ether. A male voice broke into Summer.

'Mrs Duncan?'

'Yes. My solicitor tells me there's been an offer on the restaurant. I wondered why I hadn't heard about it from you.'

'Ah. There's a slight problem. We were waiting for the interested parties to get back to us.'

'Problem?' Every head round the kitchen table snapped round. 'What sort of problem?'

'Apparently there's a substantial crack in the rear wall of the kitchen. I assumed you knew.'

'Not at all. It was my husband's restaurant. I hardly ever went there. Does that mean they've withdrawn their offer?'

'No, but if the crack is anything other than cosmetic they will certainly reduce it.'

'But I can't afford to take a lower offer.'

Virginia's eyes narrowed.

'I think you would be very unwise to miss out on this buyer. Assuming they still want it. There aren't many around. It's the recession, you know. I really urge you to consider whatever they offer.'

Ellie bit her lip. 'Let me know what happens as soon as you can.'

'I believe their surveyor is there on Thursday. A Mr Fellowes. I'll telephone as soon as I hear from him.'

'Very well. Thank you.'

Ellie clicked the end call button. No one spoke. Everyone watched her. She sat down.

'There's a crack in a wall. If their surveyor says it's serious, they'll probably reduce their offer. Or withdraw it completely.'

'Are you going to trust their chap?' Andrea said. 'Better get one of your own.'

'Christopher's a surveyor,' Gwen said. 'You do mean houses and things, don't you?'

'Christopher? Your Christopher?'

'Yes, dear.'

Ellie sighed. 'He must be the one they're using.'

'Oh dear. He's always very cautious. The firm he was at before had a big problem with a report so he says he always errs on the side of caution. That's the saying, isn't it?'

Silence again. Nobody felt like moving. Or cooking. Or anything.

Forty minutes later the back door opened. Rosie came in waggling a bottle in her hand. 'I've some elderflower champagne in the cellar. Shall we have some?' She looked at the silent faces. 'What's wrong?'

'There's a structural problem with the restaurant.' Andrea said. 'The buyers might pull out.'

'Oh.' The bottle drooped in her hand. 'I'd better put this in the fridge then, 'til we know.'

'Best thing, dear. My mother always said don't count your chickens.' Gwen smiled up at Rosie. 'How are the chickens?'

CHAPTER TWENTY THREE

The chickens, as it turned out, were well, happy and laying more eggs than anyone knew what to do with. In the furthest, untamed quarter of the walled garden, the Eglu now had company. A chicken house, six feet by four, on low stilts with a ramp up to the door, stood inside a five foot high wire-mesh pen. Half a dozen chickens, with feathers all present and correct, clucked, strutted, pecked and scratched at the ground.

'Where's Clara?' Andrea said, peering through the mesh on Saturday morning.

Rosie scanned the run. 'There.' She pointed at a white chicken pottering around underneath the rear of the shed.

'Ah.' Andrea unhitched the latch on the mesh door and went in. 'Clara. Clara. Chuck, chuck, chuck. Come here.' She dug in the bucket of food pellets and broadcast a handful. The hens bustled towards her.

Rosie closed the mesh door and walked to the chicken house. An extension protruded along one side like some weird, wooden outcrop. The top swung up revealing four cosy nest boxes, each with a single egg on a mixture of hay and shredded paper.

'We're doing well.' Rosie put the eggs gently into her wicker basket. 'That's six today.'

'Good. I'll do cheese soufflé for tea. With salad.' She flung another handful of pellets at the hens' feet. The creatures ruffled and fluffled around her, pecking at the ground and making contented, warbling clucks.

'Oo - lovely.' Rosie lowered the lid over the nesting boxes. 'There's some pick-and-come-again lettuce that's ready. You can have that. No cherry toms though. They haven't done so well, but there's about five baby courgettes if you want them instead.' She shooed a chicken away from her feet and opened the door. 'Shall I pick them?'

'It's OK. I know where they are.' Andrea upended the bucket. The last of the food sprayed onto the ground. 'Baby courgettes in front of the greenhouse. Lettuce beside them.' She lifted her head. 'Was that the doorbell?'

Rosie peered towards the house, shading her eyes against the sun. 'I didn't hear anything. Anyway Ginnie and Gwen are indoors.' She held out the basket. 'If you take this, I'll go and get my room ready. I've another aromatherapy session at five thirty.'

They parted company. Rosie walked to the far exit from the garden and round to the cottage, skirts billowing, sun hat flopping and rising over her forehead. Andrea made for the courgettes. She picked one with its fading pale yellow flower still attached and put it in with the eggs.

'Andrea. Andrea.' Virginia's drifted over the wall. 'Can you come? The lift men are here.'

Andrea abandoned courgettes and garden. She walked onto the terrace. 'I thought they were coming Monday.'

'They were, but apparently today's job finished early.'

Two men stood in the hall. From appearance they were Old Hand and Boy.

'Afternoon,' the old hand said. 'Stairlifts UK.'

'Oh yes,' Andrea said. 'Of course.'

'If we could make a start, we'll be finished by tea time.'

'Indeed.' Virginia folded her hands in her patrician matron fashion. 'Do you need anything?'

'No thanks, ma'am. Just a clear run at it.'

'I leave you to it then, Ginnie. I've still the salad to pick.'

Virginia and Gwen stood in the hall.

'I think I'll fetch a chair,' Gwen said. 'Then I can watch.' She looked at the boy. 'I don't suppose …'

'Let me, madam,' the old hand said. 'Just show me where.'

When Gwen and Virginia were enthroned at a safe, non-interfering distance by the drawing room door the men set to, carrying in long packages, boxes and a tool kit. The first few packages unwrapped to reveal a substantial-looking, straight metal rail and three curved ones in two different sizes.

Virginia leant forward and peered at them. 'They're not all the same.'

'Indeed not, madam.' The older man hefted one end of the straight rail and signalled the boy to pick up the other. 'You've got one two-seven-oh large radius for the main curve of the stairs and two, ninety small bends for the top and bottom. They let you park the seat out of the way.'

The boy let his end of the rail drop onto the pile of cardboard.

'Careful,' Virginia commanded. 'There are antique tiles under that. They'll break.'

Old hand and boy exchanged a quick glance. 'Sorry, madam,' the boy said.

After several intervals of shrieking masonry drill, clanking and screwing, the straight rail and the large curved one were fixed up the stair wall. One sharply-curved rail bent round the lower corner into the hall. The other had disappeared upstairs with the men.

Virginia and Gwen stayed on their chairs, side by side at the drawing room door.

'Dear me,' Gwen said. 'It does look rather … British Rail, doesn't it?'

'I hope it's going to be better when it's finished.'

'I expect we'd soon get used to it, dear.'

The workmen trod down the stairs.

'First part done,' old hand said. 'It's going well.' He pulled out a penknife and slit the gaffer tape around a square box. Multicoloured wires fell out. The boy unrolled the bundle and crawled up the stairs on his knees slotting the wires underneath the rail.

A second set of rails were disrobed from more packaging.

'Do we have to have them on both sides?' Virginia asked. 'I thought it was only one.'

'This is the top rail, ma'am. The one that lets the chair go up and down. That one –' He pointed to the stairs. 'Supports the whole thing.'

'Ah. I see. Thank you. Carry on.'

A look passed between the two men. They fixed the upper rail with more drilling and screwing. Fitting a long chain and a power cable was quieter with only an occasional Marley's-ghost style clank. The boy slit open largest box. He lifted out a chair upholstered in navy linen. Light reflected off its plastic cover.

'Oo, doesn't it look nice, dear?'

'Quite reasonable, I suppose.'

The boy held the chair while the old hand screwed it in place.

'Plug it in,' the older man said. He unwrapped a remote control from a box and slotted some batteries into it. 'Stand back.' He pressed a large green button on the remote. The chair swung round the corner from its resting place and ascended the stairs sedately. It swept round the large curve and disappeared at the top. The man clicked the remote again. The chair completed the return journey.

'Who's going to have first go?'

'Oh, dear me, no.' Gwen clutched her hands together.

'I'd rather someone else did,' Virginia said.

The man nodded at the boy who strapped himself into the chair, flipped the arms down and glided up the stairs like a departing pantomime prince on a magic carpet.

'Would you like to try now?' the old hand said.

'Oh, dear.' Gwen turned to Virginia. 'Do you think Rosie or Andrea would do it?'

Virginia stood up. 'I'll get them.'

Gwen sat in silence until Virginia reappeared with Andrea. 'It's me for the test flight, is it?'

Expressions of relief crossed the faces of both the old hand and the boy. 'If you please, madam,' the old one said.

Andrea allowed herself to be strapped in. The wisdom of keeping her feet on the footrest was emphasised repeatedly. She pressed the remote. The chair swung round and she ascended, waving cheerily at Gwen and Virginia.

Back on terra firma she smiled at Gwen. 'Your turn.'

'Oh, dear,' Gwen said for the third time.

'Come on. It's quite safe. How about I walk up the stairs with you?'

Gwen allowed herself to be led across the hall, settled onto the seat and strapped in. Andrea lifted her feet onto the footrest.

'Be sure to keep them there until it stops at the top.'

Gwen stared at her with enormous eyes. 'Will it be safe?'

'Just think about it like driving your car and you'll be fine.' Andrea caught a significant look passing between the two men. She cast her eyes heavenwards. The old hand grinned.

Gwen clutched the remote with both hands. She pressed the green button. The chair swung round the corner. 'Oh, my,' she squeaked. 'You are coming, dear, aren't you?'

'Of course.' Andrea stopped grinning at the men and trod up the stairs beside the lift.

'Oh my,' Gwen said. 'Oh my,' at the top and 'Oh my,' when she reached the hall tiles again.

'Right. You've done it once. Now do it on your own.'

'Oh, my.' Gwen pressed the remote and, eyes closed, made the treacherous solitary journey. Back down, she opened them again. 'I think that was rather fun.' She pressed the remote again and rose and descended twice more. 'Ginnie you come and try. It's quite good fun.'

Virginia did it unaccompanied, back straight, one hand gripping tightly to an arm, the other holding the remote like some sort of lifeline. She did not think it quite such fun.

The boy stuffed all the packaging into the largest box with as much of the cardboard as it would take

'If you'd just sign, madam, to say we installed it and it worked.' The old hand gave Andrea a clipboard with multiple forms attached to it and a pen. She scribbled. The man ripped of the top copy and gave it to her while the boy swept the hall. 'If you keep it with the instructions and guarantee you'll have the reference number if you ever need it.'

'Thank you.' Andrea said. 'I'll show you out.' She came back to find Gwen sailing upstairs on the lift again. 'At this rate,' she said to Virginia. 'We'll need to bulk buy batteries.'

'How's going?' Rosie came out of the kitchen.

'Yoo hoo. Rosie.' Gwen waved from halfway up the stairs, ascending.

'She's been up and down I don't know how many times,' Virginia said.

'It's good for her.' Andrea smiled. 'Be grateful.'

'She'll be wanting one of those silly little bikes with four fat wheels next'

Rosie frowned.

'I think you mean a quad bike, Ginnie.'

'Now that's an idea,' Rosie said.

'What is?' A veil of anxiety descended on Virginia's face.

'The ride-on mower. The grass is waist high now. At this rate it will take two farmers and their boys to mow it unless we get one soon. I'll google some prices.'

'Google what, dear.' Gwen's magic carpet settled itself at the station round the corner from the bottom step. She pressed the remote. It whined round the corner again.

'A ride-on mower,' Rosie called.

'Oo, I'd like one of them.' Gwen waved. 'Bye, dears.'

'At least it would keep her off the road,' Andrea said. 'She's getting to be a danger to life and limb.'

Rosie rubbed the side of her nose. 'I'd been wondering how to get round to it with her. She frightened me stupid the last time she ran me to Spark's when the car was being MOT'd. She hit the kerb three times.'

'Let's go and see how expensive they are.' Andrea waved at the descending Gwen. 'I think she'll be there for a while.'

'What about the soufflé? Have you made it?'

'Ah. I'll do that first.'

Rosie rubbed her hands. 'I'll make the salad, then. Coming Ginnie?'

Virginia shook her head. 'I'd better stay here and keep an eye on her. She'll either wear it or herself out.'

Rosie and Andrea disappeared into the kitchen.

'Talk about the blind leading the blind,' Rosie said.

'Be grateful for small mercies. At least Ginnie won't be watching our every move and explaining how she'd cut tomatoes.'

She picked an egg off the spiral wire rack and cracked it into a glass mixing bowl. The eggshell landed in the sink before Rosie had picked up the trug now full of small leaves. She flipped through the contents with her finger.

'Where did you get these?'

'What? Which?'

Rosie held up a group of round leaves with slightly rough edges joined at the base. 'These.'

'Where you said. Next to the courgettes.'

'Right or left?'

'Er ... right. Why?'

'Because unless I'm mistaken you've pulled up all the Brussel sprout seedlings I planted out yesterday.'

Andrea stopped breaking eggs. 'Oh. Oops. Sorry.'

Rosie sighed. 'Who was talking about the blind leading the blind?'

Ellie bounced into the kitchen as Andrea lifted an expiring soufflé out of the oven. 'Great news,' she said.

'Bugger,' Andrea said.

Ellie stopped in her tracks. 'Oh.'

The bowl of deflated soufflé slid onto a wooden breadboard. 'Sorry. What's the good news?'

'The crack's not serious. I managed to get the surveyor Ken had in last year. He checked it this afternoon. According to him, it's only a matter of filling and plastering.'

'I thought Gwen's son said it was serious.'

'Apparently what he said was it needed time to prove if it was moving. The buyers sort of *im*proved on that, the bastards. Fancy causing me all that worry.'

'But you haven't had any time,' Andrea said.

Ellie dumped her tote on the table. 'Ah, ha. I didn't need it. The reason Kenneth had him in at all was because he'd been trying to raise a second mortgage and the building society said he'd have to prove it was stable. The strips the chap put across the gap were still there. All he had to do was measure them again. And he did. And they hadn't moved.'

'That's brilliant,' Andrea said. 'What a relief.'

'I know.' She pulled out the nearest chair and sat down. Tears gathered in her eyes.

'What we need,' Andrea said, looking at the flopped soufflé. 'Is a stiff drink.'

CHAPTER TWENTY FOUR

Virginia leant, semi-prone and backwards, against the washbasin in Hairem and stared at the ceiling. Ellie massaged shampoo into her hair. Scents of lemon and vanilla burst from the bubbles.

'Have you heard any more yet?'

'No.' Ellie lowered her voice so Classic FM would smother their voices from Kirsty, the trainee hairdresser, washing Mrs Walker's hair at the basin two feet away. 'Neither Daynes nor Minchman and Brookes have got back to me.' She massaged harder.

Virginia's neck bounced on the foam pad protecting it from the white porcelain. 'That's just the least bit fierce.'

'Oh. Sorry.' She flicked lather off her fingers and pulled the shower handset out of its socket. Warm water trickled into the basin. She sprayed it onto Virginia's thin grey hair until it ran clear. 'I've got a special conditioner that adds a bit more volume.' She squirted a pearlescent trail of pink gloss into her hand and smoothed it onto the hair, combing it through with her fingers.

Virginia pulled the towel closer round her neck. 'They're taking their time.'

'I assume they don't like what my surveyor said.' Ellie hoisted the shower again.

'Well they ought to. He was just as qualified as Gwen's boy.'

The shower drooped. A spray of droplets arched over the basin edge onto the floor. 'Damn. Hang on a minute, Ginnie. I'll have to wipe that up before someone slips.'

Virginia watched, eyes straining sideways to keep her head rigid against the basin. A single droplet ran from her temple down her cheek and inside the towel and gown. She shuddered and patted the towel closer.

'You'd better give them a prod. Phone them.'

'I'm not sure I want to hear what they say.' Ellie bent down, dabbing at the floor with a used towel from the linen bin. 'It might be bad news.'

Virginia eyed the towel and wondered about the one round her neck. 'Not phoning won't make it any better.'

'I suppose not. It just feels as if it would.' She returned to the basin. Satisfied all the conditioner had rinsed off Virginia's hair, she lifted the towel from her neck and patted it round her head. 'Don't say any more,' she whispered. 'I don't want the others to hear.' She wrapped the towel into a turban and guided her to the chair nearest the window. A pile of pink towels sat on a trolley beside it. She whipped the turban off and clipped a fresh towel round Virginia's shoulders. Flicking her fingers through the shoulder-length grey strands, she said, 'How about a change of style?'

'What's wrong with having it just a bit shorter?'

'Nothing. It's just a bit ... severe. And you've had it like this for ages. A shorter style would look prettier. And make your hair look thicker.'

Virginia scowled. 'I don't know.'

'Go on. Be a devil. Give it a go. It'll always grow out if you don't like it.'

Virginia examined herself in the mirror. 'Oh very well. Just don't make me look tarty.'

Ellie looked over the grey head at the reflected face. The chances of making the stick-thin, scowling Virginia look tarty were remote. Human might be best she could hope for.

Twenty-five minutes later Virginia stared at herself. 'Goodness me.' She turned her head from side to side. 'That looks quite nice.'

'I said it would.' Ellie hung the hand-mirror beside the mirror's narrow shelf. She unwrapped the striped gown.

Virginia stood up. She peered short-sightedly at the full-length mirror beside the consol table that served as reception desk. The feathery style softened her features and made the rest of her look less gaunt. 'Lovely. Thank you, Ellie.'

Gwen, fluffy-headed and lacquered, sat on the white painted wrought iron bench beside the desk, clutching Miffy on her lap. 'It looks very nice, dear.'

Virginia patted her hair again. 'I'll put a hairnet on at night. It will keep it tidy.' She clicked open the clasp at the top of her handbag.

Ellie put a hand over hers. 'No, it's still all free.' The bag snapped shut. 'If you come back in on Tuesday I'll wash and blow dry it. Now, I'll run you home.' She helped the only two of her customers who had heard of, let alone used, a hairnet out of the door.

In the car park, Gwen put Miffy onto the back seat of the blue Golf and settled herself beside her. 'When are you going to do your next spying?'

'It was going to be Friday afternoon when Andrea has a free period but she's got another Christmas concert meeting.'

'She's having quite a few of those.' Virginia clicked her seat belt into place.

'Yeah.' Ellie started the car and drove across the back yard behind the shops and onto the road.

'With that deputy head man?' Gwen asked. She lifted Miffy onto her lap. 'He does seems to be taking quite an interest, dear.'

Virginia stopped inspecting her hair in the visor's mirror. 'Who is?'

'That new colleague of Andrea's,' Ellie repeated.

'Oh won't it be nice if she has a new flame?' Gwen said.

Virginia snorted. 'Not if it becomes permanent and she decides to leave us. The way things are going you and Rosie will be the only ones left at home.'

'Oh, don't say that, dear. Perhaps they'd both live with us.'

Another snort. 'Don't be ridiculous. No young couple's going to want to live in a house with geriatrics.'

'Do you mind?' Ellie swung the car out of Chevelling Market onto the main road with a considerable turn of speed. 'I'm not a geriatric.'

Virginia clutched at the armrest. 'Do we know if he's married or anything?'

'She hasn't said.'

'We could always check, dear. On that voting roll.'

'He's only been here a couple of months. He won't be on the electoral register yet,' Ellie said.

'We could if we knew where he came from, dear.'

'We can't go spying on everyone. Ginnie's girl is enough for now.'

'She's not my girl!'

'Sorry.'

'We need to go and look at them again. I'm sure they're not honest.'

'You don't know that, Ginnie. And I don't know when we'll do it. It's going to look suspicious if too many strange people start wandering past the house.'

'Take Miffy,' Gwen patted the dog's head. 'No one looks at you if you're walking a dog. Everyone looks at the dog. Especially a pretty one like Miffy.'

Virginia half turned to look at the back seat. 'There are times when she actually makes sense.'

'She does most of the time. If you listen.'

The turning for the rectory appeared. Ellie indicated and swung into it. 'You're right though. If Andrea and whatshisname do get serious, they'd certainly want to set up together.'

'Let's hope not.' Virginia said. 'Ah, here we are.'

The Golf scrunched along the gravel drive past Rosie weeding round the base of the third cherry tree on the left.

'Are you coming in for coffee, dear?'

'No, thanks. I'd better get back. My next lady's due in twenty minutes.'

Ellie left two of her ladies waving from the front door, tooted as she passed Rosie and drove away, thinking hard about spying, friends and new deputy heads.

Ellie and Andrea took Miffy with them. Andrea drove sedately along the town bypass, headlights on under the darkening rain clouds.

'How are we going to do this?' Ellie sat with Miffy on her lap, more than a little concerned about incontinence in nervous dogs.

'I suppose we park where we can see the door and wait.'

'Until the carer arrives? Then what?'

'Time how long she's in there?'

'And?'

'And when the door opens we'll get out and walk along to her.'

'And?'

'And start some sort of conversation.'

Ellie grabbed at Miffy, stopping her attempt to jump into the footwell. 'I hope the girl's not there. She'll recognise us for sure.'

'I don't think so. She was staring at Ginnie most of the time.'

'But it was you who took the certificate and me she gave her details to.'

'Well we'll just have to hope she's forgotten us. She was a bit worked up.'

'Slow down! That's the turning.'

Andrea rammed her foot on the brake. Miffy slid into the footwell via a brief acquaintance with the glove compartment. She yelped.

'Ye gods. I said slow down, not do an emergency stop.' Ellie hauled the shivering dog onto her knees. 'There, there.' She patted its head. The dog stopped shivering and snuggled into her arms. Ellie wrapped it closer. 'It's not a bad little scrap.' She smoothed her fingernails through its curly white fur. 'More like a short lamb than a dog.' Miffy waved her plumed tail.

Andrea parked several houses away from number fifty-one. She looked at her watch. 'Eleven thirty. I hope we're not too early.'

'Or too late.' Miffy began to fidget. 'I'd better let her out for a minute. Just in case.'

The dog jumped down as soon as the door opened. Ellie grabbed for its lead. The dog shot across the paving slabs and squatted beside the nearest gate post. The lead pulled tight.

Ellie struggled out of the car. Two rain drops pattered onto her head. 'If I get soaked because of this ...' she muttered. She waited until Miffy assumed her normal posture then walked her a few step along the pavement.

'Where are you going?' Andrea ducked to peer across the passenger seat and out of the window.

'She might want to do more. Dogs pee up every post and lamp-post they see.'

'Precisely. Dogs do. *Dogs*. They mark, bitches don't.'

'Ah.' Ellie picked Miffy up and got back into the car.

They waited.

Eventually Ellie said, 'How did the concert meeting go?'

'Oh, fine. It was fine.'

'What's he like, this deputy head?'

'He's fine.'

'Right.' Ellie lifted Miffy's front paws off her chest and settled the dog down on her lap. 'Married?'

Andrea turned faintly pink. 'I don't know. How would I know?'

'Staffroom gossip?'

'Well, I don't know,' Andrea said, still pink.

Miffy shuffled around on Ellie's lap. Her back paws slipped between the legs of her jeans. The dog rearranged itself. Silence filled the car.

A woman cycled along the road. She stopped outside number fifty-one.

Andrea sat up. 'Look.'

Ellie stopped fiddling with Miffy's fur. 'That can't be her. Rosie said she was in a car.'

'Well, it's five past twelve. It must be her. Perhaps her car's broken down or something.'

The woman wheeled her bike behind the low wall into the narrow, paved space that separated house from pavement. She pulled a length of blue tubing from the basket on the front and bent down.

Andrea peered through the windscreen. 'She's locking it. Must mean she'll be there for a while.'

After a glance at the sky, the woman fitted an orange carrier bag over the saddle and tied its handles underneath. The front door opened and the woman went inside.

Minutes ticked past.

Minutes became half an hour. Half an hour became an hour. The grey clouds parted and joined in a sort of heavenly pavane.

At ten past one, the door opened. The woman emerged.

'Quick.' Andrea nudged Ellie. 'Get out.'

Ellie clambered out, trying to stop Miffy from wrapping the lead round her ankles.

The woman waved to someone inside and unlocked her bike. She wheeled it out and pedalled up the road.

Carrying Miffy under her arm, Ellie hurried across the street and walked towards the house. Half a dozen paces away from the pedalling woman she fumbled and dropped the dog onto the pavement. Miffy squeaked.

The woman braked, hopping along with one foot on the ground until the bike stopped moving. 'Oh dear. Poor little thing.'

Ellie rescued Miffy. She patted her head. 'I'm not used to dogs. I'm walking it for a friend who can't get out.'

The woman bent sideways from the handlebars. She reached down and stroked Miffy's back. 'Pretty thing. Dogs are such good company for the housebound. Quite a few of my ladies have them.'

'Your ladies?'

'I'm a travelling hairdresser. It'd be a pity if ladies couldn't look nice just because they can't get out.'

'What a coincidence,' Ellie said. 'I'm a hairdresser too. I've a salon though. I don't travel. Have you been doing someone here?'

'Mrs Swinton, the poor dear.'

'Aw. Not well, is she?'

'No, poor lamb. And her so young too.' She eased her bottom back onto the saddle. 'I must be off. Two more perms before tea. Bye.' She bore down on the highest pedal and the bike moved forwards. It wobbled erratically until she picked speed. The net curtain moved behind Ellie. Miffy's ears lifted. Ellie lowered her to the ground and trotted back to the Peugeot. The dog's legs flashed to keep up. Its feathered tail flailed from side to side.

'Well?'

'She isn't a carer, she's a hairdresser.' Ellie got herself and Miffy into the car. 'Doing a perm, I think. Definite perming solution aroma.'

'Why doesn't Mrs Thing go out?'

'Can't, apparently. I don't know what's wrong but she referred to her as 'poor lamb' and 'so young'.'

'I wonder what's up with her.'

'No idea.' Ellie struggled with the seat belt, dog and lead.

'Hurry up. I need to get back to school a s a p.'

'More Christmas practising?'

'Year seven's next attempt at playing all the notes of O, Little Town of Bethlehem in something approaching the right order.'

'Rather you than me. Of course you could spend the afternoon with perming solution drifting up your nose.' She looked at her watch. 'There isn't time to drop Miffy off at home. I'll have to take her to the salon.'

'Give her a perm. Should make an interesting promo for your salon. Ready?'

'Just for that you can explain to Ginnie what we've found out.' Dog and lead arranged to the creature's satisfaction, Ellie sat back. 'Oh my God. Don't look.'

'What?' Andrea snatched her hand off the ignition key.

Ellie shrank down in her seat. 'It's the girl. Don't look.'

Andrea looked.

George's daughter was walking along the pavement to her home, digging in the fringed shoulder bag she was carrying. Two blue and white striped Tesco plastic bags dangled from the crook of her arm. She paused at the entrance to the minute front garden and looked up. The shoulder bag digging stopped.

'Oh God, she's seen us.' Andrea ducked over the steering wheel, shielding her face loosely with a hand.

The girl crossed the road. She banged on the car window, scowling.

Andrea half turned the key in the ignition. The window slid down.

'What the hell are you doing here?'

'Er ... nothing.'

'Bollocks. You must be. You're spying on us, aren't you?'

Ellie leant forwards. 'Well, what do you expect? Of course we want to see where you live.'

'You can mind your own bloody business.'

'It is our business,' Andrea said. 'You can't go around demanding money and not expect to be investigated.'

'Investigated? You make me sound like some sort of scrounger.' The girl flushed.

'You very well might be. How do we know you are who you say you are? You could be anyone.'

'With a birth certificate?'

'You could have stolen it,' Andrea's face turned as pink as the girl's had done.

'A thief as well as a cheat?' The girl's eyes flashed. 'Lovely. Anything else you want to accuse me of?'

'Possibly,' Ellie said. 'And we'll be wanting a DNA test too.'

The girl straightened up. 'Bugger off. I know who I am. I don't have to prove it to you.'

'You'll have to prove it to someone.'

She grinned unpleasantly. 'I already have.' She turned away, dashing across the road as the rain finally arrived.

Ellie and Andrea watched her go into her home.

'What did that mean?' Ellie said.

'No idea.'

Ellie's phone tinkled. She grasped Miffy with one hand and flipped open the mobile with the other. 'Text from the salon.' A moment's silence, then. 'My C and B's cancelled. Can you drop me off at home instead? It's on the way to school.'

'If you want. You can tell them about that pleasant little exchange.'

When they arrived home, Virginia was not particularly interested in the exchange, pleasant or otherwise. She was sitting in the drawing room staring at the empty fireplace. An official-looking letter lay in her lap.

'What is it?' Andrea whispered to Rosie who was hovering in the hall.

'It's official. The girl's filed a claim on George's estate.'

CHAPTER TWENTY FIVE

'Oh, God. That's what she meant.' Ellie unclipped Miffy's lead and shut the front door quickly against the sudden rain shower. The dog scampered across the tiles to Rosie, leaving a trail of damp paw-prints across behind her.

'Who did?'

'The girl,' Andrea said. 'She caught us watching on her house.' 'Foul-mouthed little madam she was too.'

Miffy shook herself. Her body wobbled from head to tail-end and back again. Rosie scooped her into her arms. Raindrops trans-ferred from dog to all-embracing cardigan of indeterminate shape. She ruffled the feathery ears. 'What did she say?'

'That she'd already proved who she was. Presumably to who-ever's sent that.' She wafted her hand towards the silent Virginia.

'Can she do that?' Andrea asked. 'Isn't it too late? I can't remem-ber what you said.'

'It's supposed to be within six months. I checked on-line again, just to be sure, and it is ... unless -'

'Unless what?' Ellie said.

'Unless there were special circumstances. Or if he'd made any promises to her he didn't keep.'

'Would the mother needing a carer count as a special circum-stance?' Ellie asked.

Rosie shrugged. 'I don't know.' Miffy struggled. Rosie lowered her to the floor. The dog scurried into the drawing room.

'But why do it now?' Andrea said. 'Why not when he died? He's been gone two years now. Two and a half.'

'Perhaps the mother wasn't ill then. If she is ill.' Rosie shrugged again. The silver threads in her green scarf glittered.

'Perhaps the girl wants money to go to uni,' Andrea said. 'Who knows?'

'Someone does,' Ellie said. 'Doesn't it say in the letter?'

Rosie shook her head. 'It just said she's claiming via the Treasury solicitors.'

Gwen tip-tapped out of the drawing room with Miffy pattering along behind. 'Where did we put the brandy?'

Rosie turned. 'It's in the kitchen. In the cupboard beside the fridge. Does Ginnie want some?'

'No. I do. I'm feeling a bit wobbly.' Gwen went in search of the medicinal pick-me-up with a hopeful Miffy trotting behind her.

'What Ginnie needs is a good solicitor,' Andrea said.

'Not Minchman and Brooke, then,' Ellie said. 'Daynes isn't bad. He's a bit of a pain but I don't think much gets past him.'

'She'd probably do better to have the one that did the probate in the first place,' Rosie said.

'But mightn't she want to sue them? If they didn't do a proper job?' Andrea bit her lip.

'How –' Ellie stopped.

Virginia walked into the hall. 'I think I'll lie down for a moment or two.' She continued across the tiles and up the stairs.

'She looks awful,' Ellie said.

'Yes.' Andrea stared at the grandfather clock in the curve of the stairs. 'Oh my God, look at the time. I'll be late.'

She ran out of the door.

'More Christmas concert?' Rosie said.

'I suppose so,' Ellie replied. 'I don't know about Gwen but I need a drink too. Tea will do.'

They went into the kitchen. Gwen was standing by the sink with a cut glass tumbler in her hand. The swirling liquid in it glowed darkly.

'Goodness, Gwen, how much have you had?' Rosie marched forward and took hold of the tumbler.

'Just a little tot, dear. No more than I have for taking my sleeping pills.'

Ellie put a hand to her head. 'You know, sometimes I'm amazed you're still with us.'

'Don't worry, dear. I've been taking them that way ever since Arthur died.' Miffy jumped up at her wool skirt. 'Get down, darling. You can't have any.' The dog subsided onto the floor. 'Come along. I think we'll have a little forty winks too.' She set off towards the hall.

'Don't bother going into the garden room,' Rosie called after her. 'The rain's hammering on the roof and there's a puddle near the door.' She waited until Gwen was out of earshot, if not out of sight, then said, 'I think we'd better have chat.' She pulled out a chair and sat down.

'What about?'

'Ginnie and Andrea. And what we'll do if either of them has to move.'

'You'd better add me in as well.'

'Don't be negative. Negative emotions have a bad effect on the digestion.'

'Reduced offers on restaurants have a negative effect on bank balances.'

'Don't pre-judge. You might be surprised at what's in store.'

Ellie gave up. 'What was it you wanted to say?'

Rosie settled herself onto the chair with a green and blue patchwork cushion on the seat. 'If Ginnie has to sell to pay this girl – and it's a big if – and Andrea wants to move in with her new fella, we need a plan.'

'But you've just said not to pre-judge things.'

'I know, but the point is, how do we manage to stay here if they do leave?' She clasped her hands on the table. 'I've had a few ideas.'

'Like what?'

'We could turn it into a health retreat. You could have your extra salon here. I could do my therapy and potions. Your junior could do nails and stuff.'

'People expect swimming pools at a spa. Jacuzzis. Hot tubs. We haven't got any.'

'Ah ha.' Rosie raised a finger. It caught on the edge of her scarf. 'I've thought of that.' She dragged the fine material away. 'The garden room's enormous. We could put a hot tub in there.'

Ellie propped an elbow on the table and her cheek on her raised fist. 'All of this presupposes we can buy the others out. I can't even begin to think of doing that.'

'We don't. We borrow from the bank.' She dragged a fold of paper out of the deep pocket in her skirt. 'I've drawn up a business plan. I reckon we could break even in two and a half years.'

Ellie held up her hand. 'Steady on. You'd better wait until I know what I get for the restaurant. You never know, it might all be down to you and Gwen.'

A loud rapping on the door knocker echoed into the room.

'I'll go,' Ellie said.

Christopher stood outside, a tartan golf umbrella held over his head. 'I'd like to see mum, please.'

Ellie stood aside. 'She said she was going for a little nap. She might be in the drawing room. Come in.'

He flapped his umbrella twice and closed it. 'Where ...?'

Ellie pointed at the black wrought iron stand behind the door. Christopher slotted the umbrella into it and followed her across the tiles. Virginia was alone, sitting on the sofa and staring at the fireplace, unmoving.

Christopher stopped. 'The garden room perhaps?'

'Tiptoe,' Ellie said.

The sixty-year-old man tiptoed behind the sofa.

Gwen lay in her favourite chintz armchair, eyes closed, feet up on the large pouffe with Miffy curled on her lap like a ball of cotton wool. Rain hammered on the roof.

Christopher tiptoed towards her. 'Mum,' he whispered.

Gwen opened her eyes. She struggled upright. Miffy jumped onto the floor. 'Darling. How nice.'

Christopher dropped a kiss on her forehead. 'How are you?'

'I'm fine dear.'

'I'll leave you to it,' Ellie said.

'Oh, no. Don't go, dear.' Gwen lifted her feet off the pouffe. 'Darling, what about this crack in Ellie's restaurant?'

'Restaurant?' Christopher looked from Gwen to Ellie.

Ellie flushed. 'My late husband owned The Butler's Pantry.'

'Oh. Ah. I gather there'd already been an investigation into it.'

'That's right.' Ellie clasped her hands together.

'And it's been shown to be an historic crack, not a new one? No new expansion discovered. Or expected.'

'So I'm told.'

'Excellent. No worries then.'

Ellie's hands unclenched. 'Oh, I am glad you agree.' She smiled. 'Can I make you some tea or something?'

'No thanks. I just wanted a word with mum about these windows.' He pointed to the window beside the French doors. 'I see they are leaking after all. I thought they would. That's why the plaster's cracked. Water's got in behind it.'

Rosie walked into the room. 'Behind what?'

'Ah, Mrs ... er, Reynolds -'

'Rosie.'

'Rosie. Thank you.' He pointed to the French window. 'There. See.'

Rosie walked to the doors. She looked from the top of the window to the puddle on the floor. 'I know.' She picked up a damp towel from the nearest windowsill and dropped it into the puddle. 'It's worse today though.'

Christopher stood beside her. 'Don't worry too much. I don't think it's serious. Probably nothing worse than perished sealant.' He reached for the handle. 'May I?'

'Do.' Ellie gestured towards the drawing room. 'Do you want your umbrella?'

He shook his head. 'It'll only take a second or two.'

He ducked outside.

Rosie shut the door and watched him run his fingers down the side of the window frame. Ellie took a step towards them. Gwen laid a hand gently on her arm. Ellie's eyebrows shot up. Gwen smiled.

Christopher looked up and down the opposite side then opened the door and ducked back in, his grey hair dark with rain. 'Just as I thought. The sealant's gone. All it needs is being replaced.' He cleared his throat. 'I could do it for you in no time.'

'That's sweet of you, dear.'

'Won't ... er ... your sister ... um ...' Rosie stopped speaking.

Christopher drew a deep breath through his nostrils. 'Yes, well. What Caroline doesn't know, won't hurt her.'

Rosie grinned. 'Would you like some coffee? And cake?'

'Wonderful. Thanks.'

'Dear Rosie's a wonderful cook,' his mother said.

Tea made and drunk, Rosie and Ellie left Christopher and Gwen alone. Rosie peered at the sky.

'The rain's just about stopped. I'm going to have a go at the grass. See how well the mower cuts when it's damp.' She disappeared round to the garage.

Half an hour later, she opened the French doors. Her hair was plastered to her head. Rain dripped off her nose onto her cardigan.

Christopher stood up. 'What in God's name have you been doing?'

Rosie slammed the door behind her. The glass panes shook. 'I thought I'd have a little try at the Honda.'

'In the rain, dear?'

'It was easing off. At least I thought it was. I got as far as the river then the heavens opened.'

Christopher frowned. 'You were driving your car in the garden?'

Rosie shook her head. 'It's our ride-on mower. We've got three acres. Too much to manage without one.'

'I hadn't realised it was that big,' Christopher said. 'No wonder Michael wanted to bring his football.'

'Oh, dear.' Gwen's eyes teared up.

'Don't upset yourself, mum.' Christopher took hold of her hand. 'It's only Caroline having another of her flashes. She'll come round.'

Gwen looked up at him. 'Do you think so?'

'I'm sure she will. You know what she's like. Hot and cold and hot again, all in five minutes.'

Gwen clung to his hand. There was no trace of her smile.

Rosie wrung water out of the corner of her cardigan. 'I wonder if you could give me a little advice, Mr Fellowes.'

'Christopher, please. If you're Rosie, I'm Christopher.'

'Christopher, then. Do you think it would be possible to put a hot tub in here?'

Christopher let go of Gwen's hand. He stood back, looking from end to end of the room. 'Well you could of course. There's plenty of space but what would you do about changing?'

'Changing?' Ellie arrived from the drawing room. 'Changing what?'

He smiled. 'People in hot tubs get wet. If you had one in here, everyone would have to run through the drawing room. Or go outside and in through the ... kitchen, isn't it?'

'Ah,' Rosie said. 'I hadn't thought of that.'

'Rosie specialises in ideas,' Ellie said. 'Brilliant, most of them. Sometimes she misses the blindingly obvious.'

'Well, it's better than stagnating.'

Gwen looked at the narrow ring of water dripping round Rosie's feet. 'You'd better change, dear. Or you'll be rotting, not stagnating.'

Rosie stared out of the window. The last few drops of rain pattered onto the roof. 'I suppose I'd better brave it and go via the kitchen.' She opened the door.

'Where've you left the mower, dear?'

'Under the carport. It's quite safe.' Rosie stepped outside.

'Thank goodness for that,' Gwen said. 'We don't want our mower going rusty.'

'This mower?' Christopher sat on the pouffee beside Gwen's armchair. 'It's yours?'

'Ours, dear. We all paid a little for it. Well – Rosie and Ginnie and I did.'

Christopher glanced at Ellie.

'I'll be paying my share when the restaurant's sold.'

Gwen reached for his hand. 'You won't tell Caroline, will you?'

'I'll tell you what, mum. I won't tell her about the mower if you don't tell her about me repairing the windows.' He held his hand out, palm upwards. 'Deal?'

Gwen clapped her hand down on his. 'Deal.' She laughed. 'When you smile like that, you look just like you're six again, not grown-up at all.'

'Good.' Christopher looked out of the window at Rosie hurrying across the terrace in the rain.

CHAPTER TWENTY SIX

Mr Daynes studied the three women ranged on the other side of his partner's desk. The tall, thin one in the middle, eighty if she was a day judging by the lined face and a jaw line that wasn't so much drooping as drooped, was dressed in clothing of the type his wife criticised as too aging for her elderly aunt. The only smart thing about her was the way the grey hair framed her face. Whatever the problem was, it was causing her to grip the A4 envelope in her lap rather too tightly.

The short, plumper one on the right looked about the same age but was a totally different type. She had a slightly bemused expression on her face. One he'd seen before on his neighbour's teenage son when the angry father had persuaded him to visit the police station over the matter of a small but significant stash of cannabis. Mr Daynes considered cannabis an unlikely cause in this case. Squirming on her lap was a bundle of fur that might have been an automated muff but was actually a dog.

The third woman was a generation younger, fifty perhaps, possibly approaching sixty. Wide, round-faced and faintly bohemian looking with a selection of scarves and flounces, she had introduced herself as Rosie. The name whisked Daynes back to school and passages from *Cider With Rosie*. Images of a woman in a long cotton frock and pinafore and a thatched cottage surrounded by hollyhocks and daisies had bounced unreasonably into his mind.

He rested his forearms on the desk and steepled his fingers. 'How may I help you, ladies?'

Virginia unclasped her hands and held out the envelope. 'A late claim is being made against my husband's estate. I wish to contest it.'

'I see.' Daynes reached for the envelope. 'And this is?'

'His will, the grant of probate, his tax document and death certificate.' Virginia swallowed. 'And the letter from the ... person's solicitor.'

Daynes took the envelope. He inserted a finger under the unsealed flap and eased out the documents. 'And the person is?'

Silence.

Rosie leant forward. 'It appears Ginnie's husband had an illegitimate child. She lives with her mother in a house he bought for them.'

'Ah,' Daynes said. 'I see. A somewhat delicate matter then.'

'You could say that.' Rosie sat back.

'And this was unknown to you, Mrs Lesage?'

Virginia's face turned vaguely puce. 'It was.'

The women sat in silence while Daynes flipped through the document from Olivia Lesage's solicitor. Gwen shuffled in her seat. Miffy shuffled on her lap. Virginia did not so much as flicker a pale eyelash.

'Hmm,' Daynes said.

Rosie twisted the long fringe on her scarf round her fingers until a strand broke.

Daynes turned over a page. 'Hmm.'

The long-case clock in the corner ticked and tocked.

Daynes looked up. 'It is as you say, a very late claim. I am unaware of the mother's condition but –'

'Condition?' An electric shock could not have made Virginia's body jerk more violently. 'She's made a condition?'

Daynes's eyebrows rose. 'I mean her health condition. The complaint that's given rise to the claim.' He produced a soothing smile. 'I will ask for details of course. And appropriate, reliable medical proof.'

'So she is ill, then.' Rosie said. 'We weren't sure.'

'Not that I care,' Virginia snorted. 'We all have our problems. I can't be expected to pay for her health treatment just because she was my husband's ... lightskirt.'

Gwen squeaked. She stared wide-eyed at Virginia. 'Oh dear.'

Lightskirt was not a word that had previously entered Mr Daynes's vocabulary. 'Quite. But I think perhaps a more moderate description would be appropriate.'

'I can think of several descriptions that would be more appropriate.' Virginia's face hardened. 'None of them moderate. Going with a man for money and a house is not a respectable occupation.'

'Quite,' Daynes repeated. He settled his fingers into their customary point. 'If you would like me to proceed in this matter, I am happy to do so.'

'So I should hope,' Virginia said. She stood up. 'Keep me informed.'

Daynes rose. 'Of course, Mrs Lesage.' He nodded to Rosie and Gwen. 'Ladies.' He advanced round his desk and shepherded them towards the door. He opened it. 'Ladies.'

The ladies departed.

'Oh dear,' Gwen said, lowering Miffy onto the pavement and straightening the lead. 'What will Ellie and Andrea say?'

Neither Ellie nor Andrea was thinking of Virginia or George's daughter.

Ellie held the salon phone to one ear and flattened her hand over the other.

'Well tell them it's not enough. My surveyor's report says quite clearly that there has been no further movement. If they don't like that I suggest they speak to their own surveyor again.'

'They have appointed a second surveyor,' the disembodied vice of Minchman and Brooke, Estate Agents' most junior employee told her. 'Apparently the first one's mother lives with you.'

'Are you suggesting some sort of collusion?'

'On no, I'm sure we don't think that, madam. No ... um, not at all.' Overtones of panic coloured the girl's voice.

'Good. Because I'm sure Mr Fellowes would have something to say about it. I certainly would.'

Joanne edged round Ellie, reaching for the appointments book on the table. 'Sorry,' she whispered.

'Tell these people I'm losing patience. They can improve their offer or not as they choose. I'm not accepting the current one. And you can tell them I am completely satisfied with my surveyor's report.'

She slammed the phone down. The heads of Joanne and her recently-dyed client snapped round. Ellie pasted a smile on her face. 'Estate agents, eh?' she said. 'Excuse me for a moment, please, Mrs Harvey.' Her own client nodded. Ellie dashed into the staff room, took aim and kicked the linen basket across the floor.

Andrea stood at the focal point of year seven's recorder class. She tapped the music stand in front of her with a slim baton and raised both hands. Fourteen pairs of ten- and eleven-year-old eyes and a pair of forty-two-year-old ones watched her.

'One, two, three. And ...' She flicked the baton. Several approximations of D G G G A burst into the room. At the back of the room, a suppressed smile tensed Mark Western's face. It stayed there until the final G of the first verse faded up to the ceiling.

'Well done,' Andrea said. 'That's all for today. Now remember to practice at home. Thirty minutes at least. Off you go.'

Plastic-tipped chair legs scraped, shoes scuffed, bags dragged. Year seven recorder class tumbled its way out of the door and into freedom.

'Not bad,' Mark Western said, advancing from the back of the hall. 'They should be OK by Christmas.'

'Which year though?' Andrea closed her music stand. Mark took it from her. They walked towards the cupboard together.

'So what about tonight?'

Andrea sighed. 'I'm not sure.'

'Oh come on. Be a devil. I'm not a predatory carnivore you know.'

'I know, but … oh, all right. Where do you want to go?'

He smiled and dug in his pocket. 'Where did I think you'd like to go?' Two tickets appeared in his hand. 'Here.'

Andrea took the tickets. *Barton Youth Music Theatre* presents *WHISTLE DOWN THE WIND* was printed across the top. Andrea squeaked. 'Mark - that's marvellous. I'd tried to get one but they'd all gone.' A smile filled her eyes. 'How did you manage it?'

'Sheer force of personality,' Mark said. 'And an enormous phone bill.'

Andrea laughed. 'You win. I'd love to go.'

'Right. I'll pick you up at six thirty.'

They walked out of the hall. Two year tens passed them in the corridor, skirt hems considerably above the school uniform's standard. 'Looks like old Cappy's got herself a date,' the blonde one said.

Her friend looked back over her shoulder. 'About time.'

Mark drove up the gravelled drive to the front door of Langston Rectory at six thirty-five. He leapt out of the car and pounded the front door knocker.

Ellie opened it and smiled. 'You must be Mark.' She pulled the door wider. 'You're late. Come in.'

Mark eased past her into the hall. 'I know. I know. I missed the turning.'

'No satnav, then?'

'None at all. I use that old-fashioned thing called a map. Is -'

'Hello.' Andrea crossed the hall. 'I thought you'd forgotten.'

'No, ma'am. Only gotten lost.'

'You're American.' Ellie said. 'I thought you were the new deputy head.'

Mark grimaced. 'Sorry. It was my idea of a joke.'

'Ah.' Ellie shot a quick look at Andrea. The short, slightly crumpled black jacket she usually wore had been replaced by a red velour coat.

Andrea saw Ellie scanning it. 'I thought it might turn chilly.'

'Very sensible,' Ellie said, straight faced. 'September evenings can be lethal.'

Andrea turned to Mark. 'Let's go. I don't want to miss the start.'

Ellie closed the door behind the pair. 'Hmm. Fair-haired, blue-eyed and attentive. Good for Andrea.' She wandered into the kitchen. 'A cup of tea, I think.'

She stood by the sink, waiting for the kettle to boil and watching Rosie driving the lawn mower with her skirt tucked into her wellingtons, appear and disappear beyond the walled garden, working her way down the vast lawn towards the river. Beyond her the sun blazed its low beams across the water, turning it to molten gold. The red mower appeared, cutting a dark silhouette into the amber scene. The kettle bubbled and switched itself off. Rosie disappeared. Ellie dropped a tea bag from the rose-patterned caddy into a mug and poured water over it. Rosie reappeared. Ellie prodded the tea bag with a spoon. Swirls of tan liquid surged into the clear water. Rosie disappeared. Ellie lifted the plastic milk bottle from the fridge and tipped a glug into the mug. The lawn remained Rosie-free.

Ellie watched.

She picked up the mug.

She waited.

Rosie failed to reappear.

Ellie opened the back door. 'Rosie?'

The mower reappeared. Riderless.

'Christ.'

The mug shattered into flowery fragments on the paved terrace.

Ellie leapt down the four steps and ran towards the river. The mower chugged its happy way towards the bank of tall rhododendrons edging the sweep of lawn. She reached it, skip-jogging sideways to catch the key jingling in the ignition. She turned it. The mower sighed into inactivity. The last of its momentum buried its nose under a rhododendron branch as thick as Ellie's wrist.

She spun round. Rosie was lurching to her knees beside the river. Ellie sprinted across the grass.

'What happened? Did you fall off?'

Rosie straightened up, hand pressed to the small of her back. 'Looks like it.'

'Well, yes. Sorry. Are you hurt?'

Rosie flexed her shoulders, her hips and waggled her feet in turn. 'I don't think so.' She cupped an elbow in her hand. 'I've bumped my arm, though.'

'It's not broken, is it?'

Fingers wriggled. 'I don't think so.'

Ellie put her arm round Rosie's waist and helped her towards the house. Gwen and Virginia walked onto the terrace.

Virginia looked down at the broken mug, up at the mower and then at the pair making their way slowly up the lawn. She gasped and hurried awkwardly down the steps to Rosie's other side. 'What happened? Why's the mower in the bushes?'

'Rosie took a tumble off it.'

'Are you alright?'

'I'll be fine. I'll put some arnica gel on my elbow.'

'How did it happen?' Virginia ignored Ellie's warning look.

'I got a bit too close to where the bank rises up near the river.'

'Just as well,' Virginia said. 'Or you and the mower would be in the water by now.'

'The wheels slipped on the grass.'

Ellie glanced down. A thin film of moisture covered her shoes. 'It must be dew. It's made the grass damp.'

'You'll have to make sure you don't mow in the evening,' Virginia said. 'I always thought …' She caught sight of Ellie's face above Rosie's head. She reconsidered. 'Thought we might need driving lessons for that thing.'

Miffy arrived to help and succeeded in getting under everyone's feet.

'Come here, sweetie,' Gwen called. She scooped the dog into her arms. 'I'll make some tea,' she said. 'With a good dollop of brandy.'

'I think we'll have to get a new supply of brandy soon,' Rosie said. 'What with one thing and another.'

CHAPTER TWENTY SEVEN

Gwen emptied the last of the brandy into a cup.

'Here, dear. You finish this off.'

Rosie took the cup and downed its contents in a single gulp. She blinked and coughed, making her frilled blouse shudder. 'Gosh, that's fierce.' Her face turned pink.

'I think there's some rum if you'd like that too, dear.'

'No thanks. Half a cup of brandy was quite enough.'

Gwen toddled across to the kettle, her stick tip-tapping on the tiled floor. Across the hall, the knocker tip-banged on the front door.

'Are we expecting anyone?' Virginia asked.

'I'm not, dear.'

'Perhaps Andrea's forgotten something. I'll go and see.' Virginia headed for the hall.

'Wouldn't Andrea just come in, dear?'

A man's voice echoed from the hall.

'That's your Christopher, isn't it?' Ellie said, leaning her back against the sink.

'Oh dear. I'd forgotten.' Gwen put the empty kettle down and switched it on.

Ellie snatched it up. The kettle obligingly switched itself off.

Christopher followed Virginia into the room. A B&Q carrier bag dangled from his arm. 'Hello mum.' He crossed towards her and hugged his arms round her. Gwen's head disappeared in his ballooning anorak sleeves.

'I'd forgotten you were coming, dear.'

'Never mind. I've a present for you.' He pulled a sealant gun from the bag.

The women stared at it.

'What is it, dear?'

'A sealant gun,' Rosie said. 'Brilliant.'

'Well done, that lady.' He looked at the empty brandy bottle. He frowned.

'It's all right.' Rosie grinned. 'Your mother isn't sharing a house with a bunch of dipsomaniacs. I fell off the mower.'

'Ah. Sorry.' He scanned Rosie. 'Are you OK? No damage done?'

'Only to my pride.' Her eyes widened. 'Oh. The mower. It's still stuck in the rhododendrons.' She turned for the door.

'Here, let me.' Christopher shoved the sealant gun at Virginia who blinked at it then at him. He caught up with Rosie at the edge of the terrace. 'Life's certainly never dull here, is it?'

'Not so's you'd notice.'

'I think it's rather a good idea. We know mum's safe. She happy. Much more than she'd have been at Barton Court.'

'She's certainly good at ladling brandy into people.'

'Ah. Yes. We tried to stop here taking her pills with it.'

'You weren't very successful.' Rosie stopped. Her skirt swished to a standstill round her wellingtons. 'Er ... I thought you were keen on the sheltered place.' She flushed. 'Sorry. I didn't mean to pry.'

'Not at all. It was Caro's idea really. I thought mum could manage quite well with carers and a cook. It's not as if she's ill. Only a touch of arthritis.'

Rosie looked him up and down.

He smiled. 'Re-assessing?'

'Sorry. That was rude.' She started walking again. 'I think I'm turning into one of those old battleaxes you see in television soaps.'

'I'll let you off and no you aren't. I'll bet you're younger than me and I don't think I'm old.'

'I thought you were retiring soon?'

'Retiring early. There's a difference. I want time to do what I want, not what I've had to do to keep a roof over my head.'

'A man after my own heart,' Rosie joked.

'Indeed.' Christopher smiled then stopped.

They stood stock still for two heart beats.

Rosie cleared her throat. 'There's the mower,' she said, unnecessarily.

The Honda sat silently six feet away, half-buried in the biggest of the rhododendron bushes that lined the boundary down to the river. Bunching her flowing skirt in one hand, Rosie pushed the nearest branch aside. Christopher held it away and she ducked underneath two more.

'Here, let me. You'll never manage.'

Half onto the mower, Rosie looked round. 'Oh. Thank you.' She stepped back out of the mound of dark green leaves.

Christopher burrowed his way in and edged onto the mower's seat. The engine hiccoughed into life. Rosie dragged the large branch aside, spraying herself with raindrops. The mower inched backwards into freedom.

'It doesn't seem to have suffered. Not as much as you, anyway. Every time I see you, you're wet.'

'I like being outdoors. Gardening. It's my passion.'

Christopher swung the mower round until it faced up the lawn. 'Mine too. Where would you like this thing?'

'Under the carport, please.'

'Right.' He drove the mower forward then stopped. 'Ah, sorry. Would you like to drive?'

Rosie shook her head. 'No thanks. You carry on.'

They moved side by side across the grass.

Elli watched from the kitchen window. 'He looks a nice chap, Gwen.'

'Oh, he is. So sweet. He worked so hard to qualify too.' She sighed.

'You've never mentioned if he had a family.'

Virginia shot her a sharp look.

'He was married,' Gwen said. 'Such a shame.'

'What ... er ...?' Ellie started.

'She ran off with her boss.'

'Ah.'

'Really?' Virginia said. 'Not terribly imaginative of her.'

'Angela always had an eye for the main chance. I never liked her. Not since she said my first Bichon looked like a permed rat.'

Virginia felt a stab of sympathy for the departed Angela. The back door opened. 'How's the mower thing?' she said.

Christopher ushered Rosie in. 'No damage as far as we can see.' He smiled at Rosie. 'Is there?'

'There's a scratch down the side but that's all.'

'Thank goodness for that,' Ellie said.

'Indeed. Now, where's the sealant?' Christopher scanned the kitchen.

'There.' Virginia pointed to the sink. The gun lay in it like an object of uncertain pedigree and disposition.

'Right. Mum if you'll take me into the conservatory, I'll see about the window.'

'Why don't you take him, Rosie?' Ellie said. 'Gwen looks a bit tired.'

Gwen looked far from tired. 'Oh, yes, dear. Please, if you wouldn't mind.'

When the pair had left the kitchen, Virginia hissed at Ellie. 'What do you think you're doing?'

'Just giving them a little hand. He's a nice man and just Rosie's age. She deserves someone nice after all this time.'

Virginia waited until Gwen had resumed her attempt to boil the kettle. 'What on earth makes you think you've any right to interfere?'

'Why not? If something comes of it, so much the better. Otherwise, no harm done.'

'No harm done? At this rate there'll be no-one left here. And what if Rosie doesn't want a 'nice man'?'

'Tea?' Gwen said.

'Yes please,' Ellie said. 'Rosie made a lemon drizzle yesterday. Would you like some?'

'Oo, yes please.' Gwen pottered about collecting cups, plates spoons, pastry forks and a large, Royal Albert roses and gilt teapot. She put them all on the table, pulled out a chair and sat down. 'I won't bother Christopher and dear Rosie,' she said. 'They can have some together later.' She smiled. 'Christopher likes gardening.'

Three quarters of an hour after the Christmas concert rehearsal finished the next day, the front door banged. Andrea rushed into the kitchen.

'It's that girl again. She's cycling up the road.'

'What?' The colour sank from Virginia's face into her high-necked blouse.

'That girl. Your George's daughter.'

'She's not his daughter. How many times must I say it? She's a confidence trickster.'

Andrea dumped her music bag on the table. 'Have it your way but that birth certificate looked pretty real to me.'

'So you're an expert on forgeries are you?'

Andrea's eyes flared. 'I don't –'

'Girls, girls,' Rosie said. 'Let's not start getting on at each other. We've more chance of facing her down if we do it together.'

Andrea breathed out slowly. She closed her eyes briefly. 'Sorry, Ginnie. It's just … well, I don't know what it is.'

'Recorders can be very piercing,' Gwen said. 'Even when they hit the right notes. Caroline never could.'

Three women stared at Gwen. The front door knocker rattled into the silence.

Virginia drew a deep breath. She rose and walked into the hall.

'We'd better stay out of sight,' Rosie said.

The three of them hovered near the kitchen door.

The front door swung open.

Virginia looked down her nose at the dishevelled figure on the doorstep. The black hair devoid of shine spread round her head in a tousled halo. Under the black fleece a grey T-shirt with *Get It Out* in sliver glitter hung off one shoulder showing what was presumably a bra strap.

'Yes?'

'I want to talk to you.'

'So I assume.'

'Can I come in?'

'No.'

The blue eyes heavily edged with kohl flashed. 'Ok. I want my money now.'

Virginia started to shut the door. A biker boot shot out from under the ruby and black patterned skirt Virginia considered too short to be decent and stuck onto the threshold. 'You'd better listen. The solicitors say I'm almost certain to get half of what he left. Give me some now and we'll call it quits.'

'You must be mad.'

The girl's face crumpled. She clamped her lips together and screwed her eyes shut until Virginia thought the creature's head would explode.

'It's not much. Not as much as I would get.'

'Definitely not.' Virginia leant on the door.

Little claws tickled across the hall tiles. Miffy's head poked round the edge of the front door. Behind her, Ellie tip-toed into view, hissing, 'Miffy, come here.'

The girl pushed the door aside. She looked from Miffy to Ellie. 'Have you been back spying on us again?' She glared at Virginia. 'You'd better stop them.'

'Nonsense,' Virginia said. 'We haven't been spying on anyone.'

'It's not nonsense. I know what I saw. And I definitely saw her.' She pointed at Ellie. 'And that.' Miffy cowered behind Virginia. 'It's harassment, that's what it is. I'm going to report you to the police. You can't go harassing mum like that.'

Ellie peered round Virginia. 'I told you, we were only checking on you where lived. We didn't go near your mother.'

'How did you find us?'

'I ... um,' Ellie said. 'We checked on-line.'

The girl's eyes narrowed. 'How?'

'Gwen remembered where you'd been born. Your mother's on the electoral roll.'

'No, she's not. We ticked the box to keep her off.'

'It was an old entry on 192.com. Two thousand and four, I think.'

'It is completely immaterial how we found out where you lived. I'm not giving you any money so you can go.'

'I only want nine thousand, seven hundred and sixty three pounds.' The girl drew herself up. 'Take it or leave it.'

'I'll leave it.' Virginia swung the door halfway shut.

Ellie grabbed the edge. 'Wait. That's a very specific amount.'

'So what?'

'So what's it for?'

'Mind your own bloody business.'

'There is absolutely no call for obscenities. Be off. And don't come again.'

The girl transferred her anger to Virginia. 'Don't tell me to be off like I'm some beggar.'

'That's exactly what you are.'

'No, I'm not. And I'm not having you spying on us.' She flung round and stomped down the steps. 'I'll be back. And I'll have the police with me. See if I don't. Depriving a poor invalid of her rights.' She grunted. 'That'll look good in the local rag, won't it? Posh, rich woman condemns poor, sick woman to ill health by refusing to let her get the right treatment. Ha! That'll sort you.'

She grabbed her bike away from the pillar by the door. Her skirt shot even higher up her thighs as she hitched her bottom onto the saddle. She peddled down the drive without a backward glance.

'That is a very unusual sight,' Ellie said.

'What is?'

'The bike.'

Virginia watched the girl peddling. 'What's unusual about it? It's a bike?'

'It's a Mary Poppins sort of bike. Old bone-shakers like that haven't been on sale for decades. Centuries probably.'

'Never mind the bicycle, what about the press? What's she going to do about that?'

CHAPTER TWENTY EIGHT

'Is there a problem?' Christopher walked into the middle of the hall.

'No there is not.' Virginia slammed the front door. 'Not at all.'

Christopher looked from her to Ellie and back again. 'Quite. Sorry.'

'Have you finished, Ginnie, dear?' Gwen stood at the kitchen door. 'Come and have some tea and drizzle cake.'

Virginia drew a loud breath in through her teeth. 'Is tea and drizzle cake going to help?'

'I think there's still some rum if you'd rather?'

Virginia rubbed her hand across her mouth. Her chest expanded to its utmost with another indrawn breath.

Ellie put a hand on her arm. 'I wonder why she got so anti when I mentioned checking her mother online.' She frowned.

'I noticed that too,' Rosie said. Virginia stared at her. The faintest of flushes coloured Rosie's cheeks. 'We were listening in case you needed help.'

'I don't need any help to deal with the likes of her.'

'No, of course not, dear. Now, you why don't you go upstairs and google something about her and let Rosie and Chris have their cake in peace after all their work.'

Virginia's body did not move. Her mouth, though, fell open.

'Oh, come on,' Andrea said. 'I've got an idea.' She led the way with Ellie following. Virginia brought up a very reluctant rear.

Gwen smiled at Rosie and Christopher. 'Come along, dears. Tea and cake.'

Upstairs, Ellie's fingers hovered over the keyboard of Rosie's laptop. 'What was her name?'

'The girl's or the mother's?' Andrea said.

'The girl's'.

'I don't know. Ginnie?'

'Linnie. Livvie. Something like that.'

'Livvie,' Andrea said. 'Olivia.'

Ellie typed *facebook* into the address line. She clicked on the link to the homepage.

Virginia peered over her shoulder. 'What are you doing?'

'Searching for her.'

'She wasn't on facebook,' Andrea said. 'I remember.'

'Damn.' Ellie googled *Olivia Lesage*. A page of links appeared with *About 2,140,000 results (0.77 seconds)* at the top. 'Ah.' She added *Mansfield* to the parameter. 'Ah ha! She has a blog'. A few more taps and a prettily coloured page filled the screen. Three heads leaned closer.

Seconds passed.

'Oh,' Ellie said.

'Oh dear,' Andrea said. 'That's sad.'

Virginia straightened up.

No one spoke.

After a minute, Andrea said, 'Is it fatal?'

Ellie paged down the blog. 'Doesn't say.' She right clicked on a word and asked google to search for it. Wikipedia listed every known type of Lupus by its Latin name. 'Good grief.' She clicked again and found a support site that was distinctly less intimidating.

'Well that explains why she needs the money,' Andrea said.

Ellie scowled. 'If NICE had approved that drug she wouldn't need to get her mother to America.' She clicked on the red Xs at the top right hand corner. Successive browser windows shut down. The screen saver picture of the RHS Wisley herb garden appeared. She sat back in the swivel chair. Feet still, she swung her knees from side to side. The chair squeaked and swivelled.

Andrea caught the side of her bottom lip between her teeth.

Virginia folded her arms across her chest.

'Right,' Andrea said. 'I think I want a cup of tea.'

'Me too.' Ellie swung the chair through a hundred and eighty degrees to avoid Virginia's legs and followed Andrea out of the room.

Virginia stood where she was, staring out of the window at the herb garden. A tall terracotta vase over-filled with vivid geraniums stood on the central paved circle, edged all about with multi-coloured thymes.

Silence hung round Andrea's oak-topped kitchen table. The four women and single man seated at it avoided each other's eyes.

At last Christopher said, 'What exactly is Lupus?'

'Some sort of auto-immune thing,' Ellie said. 'The body attacks itself.'

'Oh.'

'Lots of pain and it makes you very tired,' she added. 'In fact you name it, and it causes it.

Christopher ploughed on. 'And there's a drug in America you can't get here?'

'So it said on her blog.' Andrea sighed. 'You've got to admire the girl, raising all that money.'

'But why the urgency now?' he asked.

'Something to do with her mother's kidneys getting worse,' Ellie said. 'Apparently they're trialling some stem cell treatment in America. She pinning her hopes on that and wants this drug to delay the effects until that's available.'

'God,' he said. 'No wonder she wants the money.'

'Raising five thousand and whatever couldn't have been easy,' Rosie said. 'Not these days.'

'I wonder what your friend will do now,' Christopher said.

'Perhaps she'll be generous, dear.'

'Would you be, mum? If you hadn't has us and then found out dad had had a daughter?'

'Not to mention a long-term arrangement that had kept you short of money in your old age,' Rosie added.

'Perhaps I'll go and have a word.' Gwen reached for her stick.

Christopher put his hand on her arm. 'Leave it, mum.' He glanced at his watch. 'I've got to go.' He stood up. Four faces stared up at him. He only looked at one. 'I'll ... er ... come and check on the window tomorrow, shall I?'

Gwen's eyes strayed from Rosie to Christopher. 'You do that, dear. Do you mind me not showing you out? My knee's a little stiff.'

'I'll do it,' Rosie's chair shot backwards on the tiled floor.

Ellie watched the pair walk out of the kitchen. 'Gwen Fellowes, you're a wicked schemer.'

Gwen smiled in her usual abstracted way. 'I'm sure I don't know what you mean, dear.'

In the hall, Rosie opened the front door.

'Well then,' Christopher said. 'I hope your friend will be ... well ...'

'I don't know what she'll do. If anything. Why should she?'

'Indeed.' He hovered on the step. 'Mum's lots happier here.'

Rosie smiled. 'She's a sweet thing. A bit confused, perhaps.'

'Sweet? Confused?' A joyful laugh that belied his years burst out of him. 'She's about as sweet and confused as a hooded cobra.'

'Oh.'

'I don't mean she's nasty ... far from it. Just don't you be deceived by the helpless pose.' He leaned against the door post. 'She has this way of getting you to do what she wants without you ever noticing how she does it. Until his dying day I'm sure dad didn't know it happened, bless him.'

'But your sister? She's so ...'

The humour left his face. 'Caro found it very hard when dad got Alzheimer's. She took over managing their affairs. It was her way of coping. She's a bit of a control freak at the best of times. She couldn't control dad's condition but she could control the bills and things.' He shrugged. 'Mum let her. Wanting mum in that sheltered place was just more of the same.'

'Oh, I'm sorry. I didn't know it had happened to your dad too.' Her face saddened.

'Too?'

'My Malcolm had it.'

'I'm sorry.' He paused. 'He must have been very young.'

'Barely fifty. He was older than me, of course, but it was still young.'

'I'm sorry,' he repeated.

'Oh, never mind. It just makes me sad to see people at odds when you never know what tomorrow might bring. It's best not to waste time.'

'Indeed.'

A small silence developed.

At last Rosie said, 'It's a shame she's at odds with your mum.'

Christopher's smile returned. 'She'll come round. I'm working on it.'

Rosie smiled up at him. 'I'm glad. I like your mum.'

'I quite like her too.' He looked down. 'Well ...' He rummaged in his pocket for his car keys. 'I'd better let you get on. See you tomorrow.' He hesitated, then stuck out his hand.

Rosie shook it. 'See you.'

He dashed down the three steps, flicking the key fob. The BMW's side lights flashed a welcome. He waved and climbed in. The car door whispered shut.

Rosie waved back and went inside, clicking the front door shut. She leant against it, listening to the engine fire then recede down the drive, almost drowned by the scrunch of tyres on gravel.

She heaved her shoulders off the door and wandered into the kitchen. Gwen looked up. She smiled. Rosie couldn't quite see the cobra effect. She was the only one who could not.

The four sat there picking at crumbs of lemon drizzle cake and speaking not at all until Virginia appeared.

'Tea?' Ellie said.

'With a little brandy, dear?'

Virginia sat down. 'You said we've run out of brandy.'

'Rum then, dear.'

'No.'

The room sank into silence again. Miffy pattered across the floor to her water bowl. Slurping noises lapped into the hush. Thirst satisfied, she pattered back to Gwen leaving a trail of droplets across the floor. Gwen picked her up and settled her onto her lap. The dog balanced her chin on the edge of the table. Two small brown eyes stared at Virginia from the fluff of white fur.

'I'm not going to give her any money.'

'If you say so, dear.'

'Why should I? It's mine. God knows, they had enough of it while George was alive.' Virginia launched herself from the chair. 'How could he? How could he do it?'

'Men are strange, dear.'

'You can say that again,' Ellie said. 'Kenneth didn't have a mistress but the restaurant was as good as one.'

Virginia glared at her. 'At least you don't have a line of little bastard restaurants demanding money from you.'

'She has the Revenue,' Rosie said.

'It's not the same.' Virginia folded her arms tight and paced to the sink and back. 'How could he?' She paced the route again. 'All those years. All those lies.' The seven steps to the sink were not far enough. She changed direction to the massive American fridge and back. Stopping at the edge of the table, she glared at them all. 'It's not my responsibility. It isn't.' She spun round and marched out of the room.

No-one spoke.

Ellie patted her finger on the lemon drizzle crumbs on her plate and lifted them to her mouth.

'We could help a little,' Gwen said.

'I can't. I still haven't sold the restaurant.'

'I don't mean money, dear. We've got three fridges in one of the garages. And four tumble driers, three washing machines and a dishwasher. Not to mention the vacuums. And Arthur's lawnmower.'

'You want us to do a car boot?' Andrea asked. 'They're too heavy for us.'

'No need for that, dear.' Gwen smiled. 'There's an eBay. The girl can sell them there.'

'God,' Andrea said. 'You know more about the internet than I do.'

Rosie was sure a cobra was hissing somewhere.

'We could invite the girl here, dear. See what she thinks.'

'Ginnie wouldn't stand for that,' Andrea said.

Ellie frowned. 'And it wouldn't make much money even if she sold them all. Not nine thousand whatever it was.'

'No, but if she was here, dear, we might get to know her better.'

'So?' Andrea frowned.

'So perhaps she'd stop being so cross and Ginnie might be kinder.'

Andrea put her hand on Gwen's arm. 'I don't think that would help. Personally, if I were in Ginnie's position the last thing I'd want to do would be to get to know my deceitful husband's illegitimate child. Or help his ailing mistress.'

Rosie propped her elbows on the table, laced her fingers and tapped her two thumbnails against her teeth. 'There might be a better way.' She stopped the teeth tapping and rubbed one set of fingers across her mouth. 'It wouldn't be that convenient for me but there might be a way round that.'

'What are you talking about?' Ellie asked.

'The cottage.'

'Sell the cottage?' Andrea stared. 'I'm not going for that.'

'I don't mean sell it. I mean let them live there and rent out their house.'

Andrea, Ellie and Gwen stared at her.

Ellie's eyebrows reached her fringe. 'Why?'

'They'd have much quicker access to some money.'

'And who's going to suggest that to Ginnie?' Andrea said.

Gwen smiled. 'Perhaps I will, dear.'

The cobra hissed again.

CHAPTER TWENTY NINE

'No. No. Absolutely not. That woman is not coming here. No. Not at all. Not ever.'

'But it would mean they'd be able to go to America sooner. And be out of your hair.' Andrea had drawn the short straw of making the initial approach. She watched Virginia pace across the drawing room.

'She was my husband's mistress. I'm not having her here.' Gwen's silk Chinese rug suffered under Virginia angry footsteps. 'And it would not save them money.'

'Why not?'

'Because they'd lose their benefits. They're bound to be on benefits.'

'They might not. Your ... George might have made provision for them.'

Ellie shrank down on the sofa, waiting for the storm.

'Ha!' Virginia wrapped her arms around her waist. 'Even if he did, they'd be on benefits. People like them always are. Dishonest to their last drop of blood.'

'You don't know they're dishonest, dear.' Gwen stroked Miffy's head.

'Of course they are – well, she is. She's lived off another woman's husband. What's that if it's not dishonest?'

Ellie abandoned the idea of mentioning love. 'The girl seems to be doing her best.'

'Her best? I suppose you think she's some sort of angel for doing her duty. Pity her mother didn't do hers. Or George.' The Chinese rug took another pounding.

'She gave up her university course to work at Mason's. And she raises money with sponsored walks and so on.'

Virginia snorted. 'A student. I might have known. What did she do at university? Beauty courses? How to cheat benefits?'

'I think it was art of some sort,' Rosie said.

'There you are then. A load of bohemian rubbish. Dead cows masquerading as art.'

'Whatever it was, she gave it up to save on tuition fees.'

'Took to walking the streets I expect. Not that she'd get much custom looking like that.'

'Ginnie, dear.'

Virginia unwrapped her arms. 'Why are you all ganging up on me?'

'We're not, dear. We're trying to help you.'

'Having that … that person living here won't help me at all.'

'You wouldn't have to see her. The cottage is the other side of the garden walls,' Rosie said. 'That's why I wanted my aromatherapy there. So none of you'd be bothered by clients calling at the house.'

'And what about that? What are you going to do about your clients? Are we to have them trailing through the house after all?'

'No Ginnie, dear, we're not. Rosie can use the snug for a while. It has its own door so it would be quite private.'

Virginia glared at her. 'You've got this all planned, haven't you? How much whispering behind my back did it take?'

'Ginnie. Dear. Why don't we see if they'd be interested? They might not want to be near you any more than you want to be near them.'

Four pairs of eyes watched. The Chinese rug endured two more crossings. Virginia stopped by the fire. Back to the marble carving she looked at the others. 'If you insist. Just don't expect me to meet them.'

'No, dear. We'll ask the girl to come and you can stay upstairs while she's here.'

'Excellent,' Virginia said. 'Banished in my own house.' She marched to the door. 'Do whatever you want.' She opened the door and went out. For only the second time in her life Virginia Henrietta Lesage slammed a door behind her.

Livvie Lesage sat on the edge of the blue linen sofa closest to the door, feet and knees pressed together, hands tight in her lap. The black leather jacket and short skirt remained but the black boots had been unlaced and left, neatly side by side, at the front door. A pair of black and purple striped socks covered her feet.

'We were sorry to learn about your mother's condition, dear.' Gwen, all in pink, leant forwards on the opposite sofa. 'It must be such a trial for you both.'

Livvie's kohl-rimmed eyes flicked towards her. Her hands gripped tighter.

'We saw on your blog that you need to get this drug ... what's it called, dear?'

'Belimumab.' The word forced itself out of a mouth devoid of lipstick. The eyes blinked. And blinked again. She sniffed.

'Ah, yes, that's it. I'm not so good at names any more, dear. What will it do for your mother?'

'We don't know. It's only a trial for people with kidney complications.' The kohl began to run. 'They're recruiting for it now.' The hands gripped tighter. 'If I can't get mum to America ...' She swallowed the rest of the sentence down her throat.

'And you haven't enough money yet to get her there?'

'I can get her there and pay for two month's rent. If they accept her.' Diluted kohl ran down one cheek.

'How long is the trial, dear?'

'Five years.'

'Five years?' Andrea lurched forward on her chair. The pale blue skirt wrinkled. 'You're going to stay there for five years?'

'Fifteen thousand won't cover that, surely,' Rosie said.

'If they let her join the trial I'm hoping they'll let us continue it at home. If we pay for the blood test and things.' She shifted backwards a little on the sofa. 'Even if they don't, we're hoping she'll get a prescription for Belimumab and we can get a regular supply from there.' She looked at the three faces gathered round her. Had it not been for the pastel clothes Gwen had insisted upon they might well have appeared to be members of the hubble bubble sisterhood. 'What do you want? Why did you ask me here?'

'We've had a little idea, Livvie,' Gwen said. 'We thought perhaps we could help.'

'How?' She looked form one to the other. 'The only help I want is some of my father's money.'

Andrea took over. 'It'll take a long time for this claim against Ginnie – Mrs Lesage – to be resolved. Legal things always take ages and ... well, from what we saw on your blog, time is ... an issue for your mother.'

Livvie hands kneaded each other. Another streak of kohl slid over her cheek.

'Now,' Andrea continued. 'We have a cottage here. It's got a downstairs living room with a kitchen at one end and a bedroom at the other. There's a couple of rooms upstairs.'

Livvie blinked but did not speak.

'We thought if you and your mother moved in there you could rent out your house for an income and that would help get ... or keep you in America longer.'

Livvie looked from face to face again.

Gwen gave her a gentle smile. Rosie disentangled her arm from yet another floating scarf. She reached along the sofa and patted the girl's tense hands.

Livvie's face crumpled. Tears wiped the last of the kohl from her lower lids. 'Why?'

'We all know what it's like to lose someone.' Andrea's eyes clouded over. 'For some of us it took a long time for them to go.'

'But it wouldn't make enough. There'd be rent to pay you for.'

'We weren't going to charge any, dear.'

Livvie scrubbed a hand across her face. The edge of her black leather jacket left a red graze on her cheek. 'But Mrs Lesage? She's ... I mean, she can't possibly want us here.'

'Ginnie wouldn't have to see you, dear. Or your mother. The entrance to the cottage is out of sight of the house.'

'But she'd know. She'd know mum was round the corner. And me.'

'We think she'd manage it,' Andrea said. 'Of course once the lawyers get going it might be difficult but perhaps you'd be back in your house by then.'

Livvie bit her lip. She bit her thumbnail. She laced and unlaced her fingers. 'I don't know. Mum might lose all her benefits if she had an income.'

'But not if the rent was paid to you,' Rosie said. 'And any way, Disabled Living Allowance – your mother does get that I assume?'

'Yes. And I get Attendance Allowance too.'

'Excellent.' Rosie practically clapped her hands. 'They aren't means tested so getting rent for your house won't be a problem.'

The dark eyes now pink with smudged edges looked at Rosie. 'You seem to know a lot about it.'

'Rosie's our financial whizz,' Ellie said. 'She'll sort out anything to do with finances.'

The girl's face resumed its previous unhappy expression. 'It's not that easy. Belimumab has to be injected intravenously every four weeks. After the start, that is, and it takes an hour.'

'Done by a nurse I suppose?' Ellie asked.

Livvie nodded.

'That might be tricky,' Andrea said. 'Ginnie was a qualified nurse but I don't expect ...'

'Nor do I,' Rosie added. 'I'm pretty sure she wouldn't do it. But we could get someone from the gp's ... or hire someone suitable. If you were back home.'

Livvie kneaded her hands. 'I don't know. I don't know what mum would say.'

'Perhaps you could persuade her, dear.'

'I don't know. She's always been a bit ...' The tears stared again. 'She's not a bad person. She always said daddy shouldn't spend so much on us.' She sniffed and dug in her pocket. A crumpled tissue emerged. 'Mum doesn't want her money. It's me that ...' Her voice submerged in tears.

Rosie reached over the arm of the sofa and lifted up a box of paper hankies. 'Here.'

Livvie pulled a handful out. She blew her nose twice. 'I expect Mrs Lesage doesn't like us.'

'Not exactly, dear. But I think she'll see this is the best way for us all.'

The young tear-stained eyes looked at the women. 'Would you like to meet mum?'

'I think so, dear.'

Livvie sniffed. 'I'll ask her. I don't know what she'll say.'

CHAPTER THIRTY

Jammed among the arm-thick branches at the heart of the tallest rhododendron, Rosie braced herself with one wellington-booted foot on the ground and the other on a horizontal limb. She wielded the giant bow saw with more enthusiasm than skill. A thirty inch blade of shark-like teeth held between the ends of the saw's arching green handle flashed in a shaft of sunlight. She dragged it backwards across the bark of the condemned branch. Gripping with both hands, she pushed.

The blade skidded, pitching her forwards. The saw slid down the bark, perilously close to her knee.

'Damn thing. Grip, will you.'

'Problem?'

Rosie jumped. Her head hit the branch behind her and her left foot slid off the one she was bracing herself against. The wellington boot squelched into the soft earth.

Beyond the tangle of branches and long evergreen foliage Christopher stood with his hands in the pockets of his sports jacket. Peering at her through the leaves, he said, 'What are you trying to do?'

Rosie extricated herself from the rhododendron's squid-like grip and emerged triumphant, dragging the saw behind her. 'It's too big.'

'The saw or the bush?'

'The bush ... well, both, really.' Freed from the evergreen embrace, she straightened up. 'I decided these three ...' She waved at the last three bushes. 'Are blocking the original view of the church.'

Christopher paced backwards until the spire appeared over the top of the leaves. 'I think you're right.' He came back. 'Shall I have a go?'

'If you like.' Rosie held the saw out. She looked him up and down. 'You look a bit overdressed for it.'

'You're not, I see.'

Rosie bent down to brush dirt off a pair of worn and crinkled jeans that she had stuffed into the top of her wellingtons. The hem of the ancient farmer's smock she was wearing descended to her knees. 'Well ... sort of. It's not as practical as I thought it might be.'

'I'll get my overalls out of the boot and have a go.'

'Overalls in your boot?'

He smiled. 'Good old standby for we wise surveyors. We have to get into some dire spaces at times.'

'Oh. I see. Well, if you don't mind doing it ...'

'Not at all.' He looked along the length of the rhododendron bank. 'There's more than these three need doing. They all look like they haven't been shaped for years.'

'Probably not. I don't know how much gardening the previous lot did. Not much if the state of the greenhouse and walled garden were anything to go by.'

Christopher grabbed one end of the saw. Rosie let it go and he hefted it in his hand until its weight balanced evenly. 'Have you done much to it?'

Rosie started walking towards the house. 'Quite a lot.' She stopped. 'Would you like to see?'

The smile again. It lit up his face and made his eyes shine.

Rosie smiled back. 'Come on then.' She led the way across the lawn.

Christopher looked at the ten foot walls round the kitchen garden. 'Impressive.'

Rosie lifted the latch in the newly-painted gate and pushed it open. She stood back, watching Christopher's face.

He took one step inside, then stopped.

'Good grief.' He looked around the forty foot square garden, from the sparkling greenhouse, across the partitioned vegetable beds to the espalier fruit trees on the west wall. Mixed greens of dark cabbages, broccoli and tightly wrapped balls of cauliflower filled the bed in the farthest quarter. Closer to him ran lines of late salad, feathery celery tops and vivid chard. A few remaining courgette plants spread their palmate leaves across the weed-free soil.

He pointed at the Eglu and chicken house. 'Ha! Mum said you had chickens.'

He marched along the gravel path, past the final quarter of the garden filled to overflowing with rosemary, tall fennel spires, fading parsley and chives. 'This is wonderful.' He peered through the high mesh cage. 'How many have you got?'

'Ten, now.'

'You must get lots of eggs. What do you do with them?'

'Ellie sells the spares in her salon.' Rosie clasped her hands and waited.

He turned round. 'This is ... wonderful. You are so lucky.'

'Gwen said you enjoyed gardening. She was telling me about the pots you grew tomatoes in when you were little.'

He laughed his little-boy laugh. 'That's mothers for you. No sense of shame when it comes to embarrassing their children. You'd think by my age, she'd have got over it.' He stood arms akimbo scanning the garden again. 'I envy you.'

'Don't you have garden then?'

'No. I have an apartment. And very well named it is. Apartments are apart from everything.'

'Why don't you move if you don't like it?'

He shrugged. 'Inertia, I suppose.' His face went quiet. 'When Angela left …' He looked up. 'You've heard about Angela, no doubt.'

Rosie nodded. 'Gwen did say something about her.'

'Nothing good, I'll be bound.' He shrugged again. 'Angela wanted to live in the city. To be near the life and lights, she said. So we got the apartment. When she 'ran off' as mum puts it, I just stayed where I was. Hibernated. Seemed the easiest thing to do.'

'Easiest, but not the best.'

He tilted his head as if the thought had not occurred to him before. 'I think you're right.' He looked around the garden once more. 'But then if I had a garden I wouldn't be thinking of offering to help you out here. There's a lot to do.'

Rosie beamed. 'There is. And I have my aromatherapy too so I don't get as much time as I'd like. I have great plans though. There's so much potential.' She clenched her fists. 'So many possibilities.'

'Big plans, then?'

'Oh, yes.' A wide grin lit her face. 'I've drawn them out. Would …' Her face turned a little pinker than the fresh air usually made it. 'Would you like to see them?'

'I most certainly would.'

'Come on.' She grinned. 'They're in the cottage.'

Ellie found Gwen in the drawing room with the new gas fire humming in the grate. The flames flickered, images of a real log fire leapt chimneywards.

'You on your own? I thought it was Christopher's car in the drive.'

Gwen put down her knitting. 'It is.'

'Where is he? Checking the garden room for more leaks?'

'Oh no, dear. He's in the cottage with Rosie.'

'Rosie?' Ellie looked towards the French windows. She turned back to Gwen. 'You're up to something. What is it?'

'I'm sure I don't know what you mean.'

'Now I know you're up to something. Only Virginia says 'I'm sure I don't know what you mean.' What is it?'

Gwen closed her needles together, folding the half-finished row in two and laid the knitting down. She patted the sofa seat beside her. 'I do have a little plan I mentioned to Ginnie.'

Ellie lifted Miffy off and sat down. 'Tell me.'

'Well, darling Christopher is all alone. And he and Rosie are of an age, so I thought …'

'You'd do a little match-making.'

'Why not, dear? If they could be happy together, why not?'

Ellie folded her arms. 'And what makes you think they would be? They hardly know each other.'

'But they have so much in common. They're both sweet, helpful people. Always thinking of others before themselves. And they both love gardening. Christopher still has loads of gardening books even though he hasn't a garden.'

'Gardening and being sweet. So that's a good basis for marriage, is it?'

'Isn't it, dear?'

Ellie gasped. Surprised tears flooded into her eyes. She swallowed hard.

Gwen rubbed her hand up and down Ellie's back. 'There, there, dear. You've had a bad time of it. Too much disappointment.'

A sob.

'You'll be fine soon. There's bound to be a nice man for you somewhere.'

Ellie shook her head. The short blonde crop bounced. 'No. Not again.'

The back rubbing changed to hand patting. 'You just give it time.'

A watery gurgle escaped Ellie's mouth. 'You're a witch, you know. You've got that girl asking her mother to meet us and you're guarding Andrea like an old-fashioned duenna. I suppose the next thing you'll have is Rosie and Christopher married and setting up home in the cottage.'

'Not quite yet dear. We've Mrs Swinton and Livvie to see to first.'

Ellie hugged her. 'Well, just leave me out of your schemes. I'm alright as I am.'

Gwen hugged her back. 'Yes dear.'

Ellie stood up. 'I'm going to make dinner. Would you like a cuppa first?'

'Yes, please, dear.' Gwen watched Ellie leave the room. When she had gone she said, 'You are alright, dear. For now.'

Livvie Lesage sat on her bed in her red pyjama bottoms and T-shirt, staring at the carpet in the dim light from her bedside lamp and wondering how she was going to persuade her mother to meet the inhabitants of Langston Rectory, let alone agree to move in there.

A shoe box painted with bright flowers stuck out from under the bed. She pulled it out. On top of the forms and envelopes inside it lay a navy blue Nationwide ISA pass book. On top of that was a small, square jeweller's box, a little roughened at the corners. Livvie opened it. On a bed of cotton wool lay a silver christening bangle, engraved with miniature roses. She picked it up. The words *To Olivia with dearest love from daddy* were engraved round the inside. Tears pricked her eyes. She closed her fingers over it. With a long sniff, she released it back into its nest and pulled out the savings book. The final entry read five thousand, three hundred and twelve pounds, twenty-four pence. She'd only managed to raise an extra seventy-five pounds in the past month and that had taken the sale of her last two paintings, including the one she'd done for her mother's birthday two years ago. There wasn't anything else to sell or any more pictures to paint. She'd used all the oils and the only tubes of watercolour she had left were viridian, Payne's grey and lamp black. Not much she could do with them.

She put the book in the box and shoved it back under the bed. A door creaked on the landing.

'Mum?' Livvie pushed her feet into a pair of slippers with rabbit's ears. She hurried out. 'What's the matter?'

Her mother's voice came in short gasps. 'Nothing, sweetie. I only need the loo.'

'I told you to call if you did.'

Margaret Swinton crossed the head of the stairs and stretched out a hand for the banister. She leant heavily on the rail, putting one foot in front of the other until she reached the bathroom. 'You don't have to get up. I keep telling you.'

'I don't like you getting up without me. You might fall down the stairs.'

'Perhaps it would be a blessing.'

'Mum! Don't say that.' Livvie clasped her hands round her mother's waist. 'You mustn't ever think it.' Hot tears started from her eyes. 'Promise me you won't get up at night until you've called me.' She half shook her mother. 'Promise me. Promise.'

Her mother held her close. 'I promise, sweetie. But it's no life for you chasing after me all the time.'

'I'm fine, mum. Fine. I'd rather do that that not have you.' She paused. 'Mum ... there's something I need to talk to you about.'

Margaret Swinton stared at her daughter's face. 'What? Has something happened, Livvie?'

'No ... well, yes.' Livvie smoothed the long sleeves of her mother's nightdress. 'Nothing bad. I think I've found a way to get us to America.'

Her mother's face brightened. 'How.'

Livvie smoothed the brushed cotton even more. 'I'm not sure you'll like it.'

Her mother frowned. 'What have you done, Olivia?'

CHAPTER THIRTY ONE

Rosie drove Gwen and Andrea to Estelle Pankhurst Road. Trees lined the street in front of the terraces of Edwardian houses and cast dappled shadows across the car. She braked to a halt and swung into a space barely four feet longer than the Astra.

'Well,' she said. 'This is it.'

She opened the driver's door, climbed out then helped Gwen lever herself out of the front passenger seat. Gwen's stick clattered to the pavement. Rosie picked it up for her and she walked to the gate. Andrea pushed the seat forward and struggled out of the back.

'Well,' Rosie said again, locking her car. 'Let's get on with it.'

'How do you manage to get us into these things, Gwen?' Andrea asked. 'Is there some evil gremlin that creeps into your mind at two in the morning and says 'This is a good idea'?'

'I just think of other people, dear.' Gwen's stick tapped on the black and red tiled path.

The blue front door opened. Livvie stood on the threshold. She squashed herself against the hall wall, letting the three women walk past her. 'It's the first door on the right.'

The room was quite simple. A three piece suite, a coffee table, a television on a unit holding a Sky box and a DVD player. On the far wall, a carved fireplace with a mirror above it and a watercolour on each side. Apart from the paintings the only decoration was a large ceramic vase of hydrangea flowerheads filling the empty grate.

A woman sat in an armchair facing the television's blank screen. Her hair was thin but permed. Rose pink lipstick covered her pinched mouth. Her eyes must once have been violet. Now they had faded to match the circles beneath them. She had a peach coloured fleece pulled round her shoulders. Its sleeves dangled down.

'Mum, this is Gwen and Rosie and Andrea. Mrs Fellowes, Mrs Reynolds and Mrs Capstowe.' She turned to the three women. 'This is my mum, Margaret Swinton.'

Gwen walked across the plain carpet, leaning heavily on her stick. She held out her hand. 'It's kind of you to see us, Mrs Swinton.'

'It isn't my idea.' Margaret Swinton forced herself upright in her chair. 'Olivia's got it into her head I'm going to agree to some scheme you've dreamt up.' She pulled the fleece tighter round her thin body. 'I don't want any charity from Mrs Lesage. George left me enough. And there's Livvie's trust for her.'

'Her trust?' Rosie looked at the girl. 'You didn't mention a trust.'

'I can't get at it until I'm twenty-five. That's four years from now. It would be too ... difficult.'

Her mother stirred. Every woman in the room knew what Livvie had not said.

'Do you mind if I sit, please?' Gwen asked. 'I'm not as steady as I used to be.'

Margaret Swinton waved her hand at the seat opposite.

Gwen lowered herself gently. 'Thank you.'

'Would you like a coffee?' Livvie said.

'Tea, Livvie. Tea,' her mother told her.

Livvie left the room.

Rosie pointed at the sofa. 'Do you mind?'

'If you want.'

Rosie and Andrea arranged themselves side by side.

'Are they from your garden?' Gwen asked, pointing her stick at the hydrangeas.

Margaret Swinton nodded.

'I always like hydrangeas,' Gwen said. 'What colours are ours, Rosie?'

Rosie blinked twice. 'Er … mostly blue but there are a couple of mauvish ones by the cottage.'

'Ah, yes. I remember. Very pretty. Is gardening a hobby of yours, Mrs Swinton?'

The woman shifted. 'It was.'

'Yes, of course. I'm sorry.' Gwen propped her stick against the side of the armchair. 'I understand your condition makes you very fatigued.'

A small, bitter laugh. 'You could say that.'

'Did George know about it?'

A shake of the head. 'No. It was only diagnosed a few months before he died. I didn't tell him. Wouldn't have told him.'

'I see.'

Rosie and Andrea watched the exchange as if viewing Wimbledon.

'I wonder what he would think of our idea.'

George's long term mistress looked at Gwen. 'That is a low blow.'

'Is it, dear? Wouldn't he be relieved to know we'd found a way to help?'

Livvie nudged the door open with her hip. She put a round plastic tray with five mis-matched mugs on the coffee table. 'Does anyone take sugar?'

'Only me,' Andrea said.

'Oh. I'll go and get it.'

'It's OK. I'll come.' Andrea lurched to her feet. 'Save you bringing it in.' She picked up a yellow and green checked mug.

Livvie led the way into the kitchen. A range of grey-green units lined each side of the narrow room. Every door had a cartoon-like farmyard animal painted in the middle.

'Did you do those?'

'Yeah. I thought it would amuse mum.'

Andrea bent down and stared at a black and white cow. 'They're very good.'

'Yeah.'

'I'm sorry you had to give up your course.'

'I can do it later. They said I could go back when ... I mean, once mum's stable.'

'I take it she wasn't keen on the idea of the cottage.'

Livvie shook her head. 'You could say that. She said she's had enough from daddy.' Colour crept up to her eyes. 'I wish she would go for it.'

'Perhaps she will. Apparently Gwen, Mrs Fellowes that is, has a method of getting her own way that not even her family have sussed out.'

Livvie took the lid off a cream china pot with a chicken on it. She held it out to Andrea.

'Spoon?'

'Sorry.' Livvie put the pot down, took a spoon from the draining board and dried it on a tea towel.

Andrea stirred a small heap of crystals into her mug. 'Let's see how Gwen's getting on.'

The cobra smile greeted them. 'Margaret is going to take a look at the cottage. To see if it would suit Livvie.'

'Suit me?'

'Yes, dear. The garden is beautiful. Lots of autumn colour. It will be such a good place for you to keep on with your art.'

Livvie looked from Gwen to Andrea. 'I see what you mean.' She walked to her mother and kissed her head. 'Thanks, mum.'

'What are they doing now?'

Andrea peered out of the landing window between their bedrooms.

'How can I tell? You're in the way.' Ellie took a hurried bite of the sandwich on her plate.

'I'm going to see.'

They started down the stairs. Virginia was looking out of the first floor landing. They stopped and exchanged looks. Ellie jerked her head backwards. They crept back up to the top of the flight.

'I think,' Andrea said in her best, carrying-over-year-seven's-chatter voice. 'That I could do with a coffee.'

Below them, footsteps crossed the landing. A bedroom door shut quietly.

Ellie and Andrea continued downstairs. On Virginia's landing, Ellie took another bite of prawns, lettuce and bread. 'I wonder what'll happen when they meet,' she mumbled.

'Don't you mean if?'

'You're underestimating Gwen's powers of persuasion.'

'True. I didn't believe you until I saw her in action.' Andrea walked towards the kitchen door. 'Shall we go and see how she's getting on this time?'

'Can't. I've got to get back to the salon. Lord knows how I'll concentrate.' Ellie put her plate on the hall table and grabbed her bag from it. 'Let me know how it goes.' She dashed through the front door to her car.

Margaret Swinton sat on the sofa in the cottage, breathing shallowly.

'I'm sorry you found it such an effort to get here, Margaret,' Rosie said. 'At least you wouldn't have to do it too often.'

After three deeper breaths Margaret Swinton looked round the room. 'It's very nice.'

'I'm pleased you like it, dear,' Gwen said.

'I only said it looked nice. Not that I was agreeing.' A shaky breath. 'It's a ridiculous idea.'

Livvie sat down beside her mother. 'The bedroom's nice. And it's downstairs.'

'But the bathroom's upstairs,' her mother said. 'And the loo. What are the stairs like?'

'A bit steeper than ours.'

'That's no problem, dear. We know a very nice man who does stair lifts. And it wouldn't take much to install a loo down here.' She looked around, frowning. 'Somewhere.'

Livvie smiled. 'I'm beginning to think you have a magic wand, Mrs Fellowes.'

'Call me Gwen, dear. It's much easier.'

'I think I'll paint a picture of you with a pair of fairy wings and a cloud of magic dust.'

'As long as they're fairy wings and not the angel sort, dear.'

'You haven't painted a portrait since daddy went.' Margaret swallowed.

The D-word hung in the room.

'Well,' Gwen said after a moment. 'Shall I lead the way upstairs if you're feeling a little recovered?'

The quartet attempted the stairs. Gwen, walking slowly, led them into the larger room which just happened to have the best view. 'What do you think?'

Andrea and Rosie had almost ruptured themselves converting one end of the studio into a bedroom. They had opened the tall, wide window that filled most of the end wall and hauled the brass bedstead from Rosie's old spare room up through it. Then they had twisted the mattress through the door in the kitchen and up the stairs to join it. A crisp white duvet cover and pillowcases patterned with rosebuds covered the bed. Plaited pink ribbons looped back matching curtains. Close to them stood a white painted desk to serve as a dressing table. An oak wardrobe faced it across white painted floorboards and a bright plaited rag rug.

Rosie pointed to the window. 'There'll be plenty of light for you to paint by.'

Livvie's face brightened. 'What do you think, mum?'

Mrs Swinton lowered herself, breathing rapidly again, onto the bed. She fingered the crocheted spread folded across its foot. 'It'll be fine for you but you're forgetting something, sweetheart.'

'What?'

'I haven't met Mrs Lesage yet.'

'Perhaps we should go and find her,' Gwen said.

'No. Not yet. I don't think I've got the energy. Any sort of energy.'

'I'll tell you what,' Rosie said. 'I'll go and get her.'

Hurried footsteps echoed down the stairs. The outside door opened and banged closed.

Mrs Swinton dragged another breath into her lungs. 'Oh, dear,' she said. 'I'm really not sure about this.'

CHAPTER THIRTY TWO

Ellie ran the tail end of her comb front to back across Laura Downham's scalp.

'No, Ellie. I said the other side.'

'Oh, sorry. I don't know what's the matter with me today.' Ellie combed the hair back and redrew the parting. 'I think I've left my brains at home.'

'I expect it's the restaurant.' Laura settled herself back into the chair, arms folded underneath the cream striped gown. 'Any news yet?'

'Not yet.' Ellie parted a section of hair at the nape and wielded her scissors. An inch of dark brown hair dropped off the gown and onto the floor.

'I expect they'll sort it soon.' Laura peered short-sightedly at the curly-framed mirror in front of her. 'You're not cutting too much off, are you?'

'You said about an inch. It's nearly ten weeks since you were here.'

'I know. I was up with our Suzannah. She had such a bad time of it.'

'Ah, yes. How is she? And the baby?'

The new grandmother shifted in the chair. 'Not so bad now. And the baby's fine, which is a blessing.'

Ellie prepared herself for an excursion through the trials of Caesareans. Kirsty tapped her on the arm.

'There's a call for you, Ellie.'

Scissors hovered in mid air over Laura's right ear. 'It's probably Andrea. Can you take a message, please?'

'It isn't. It's a Mr Johnstone.'

'Oh.' Ellie looked at Laura's face in the mirror. 'Would you mind? It might be news about the restaurant.'

The wet head shook. 'No, not at all.' Laura patted at an escaping droplet. 'You go and see.'

'Mrs Duncan? Excellent. Johnstone here. Minchman and Brooke.'

'Yes Mr Johnstone?'

'The buyers have decided ...' Ellie's heart lurched. 'That the crack in question isn't a problem after all. They're ready to exchange at the price you accepted.'

Ellie's leant a hand on the table. Behind her, Kirsty and Laura Downham exchanged glances.

'That's fine, Mr Johnstone. What would you like me to do?'

'If you could call in at some point we can finalise the details. Would, er ... sometime tomorrow morning suit?'

'Yes ... er, just a moment please.' She flicked the appointment diary open. Mrs Grange was booked for a trim and blow dry at nine-thirty followed by Zara Philbert for another lengthy session of humbug-coloured highlights at ten-fifteen. 'Mr Johnstone? It will have to be midday. Is that all right?'

'Perfectly, Mrs Duncan. I'll see you then.'

Ellie stuck her finger on the end-call button, waited for one breath the lifted it and speed dialled the Rectory.

'Rosie? Great news. They've agreed. I'm going in tomorrow to sort it out. Will you tell Ginnie I'll be able to ...' She saw Laura and Kirsty's faces reflected in the glass door of the products cabinet beside her. 'To sort out that other matter.'

'Well I would,' Rosie said. 'But she's not here.'

'What? I thought she was meeting Mrs Thing and Livvie at the cottage.'

'She was but she's done a bunk. We can't find her.'

Ellie frowned. 'She's not in the garden?'

'No. I've looked.'

'How odd. Wherever she is, she must have walked.'

'I'll get the car out and have a drive around.'

'Good idea. She's a bit of a pain but I'd hate anything to happen to her.' Ellie put the phone down and returned to the pleasures of Laura Downham's nape.

Virginia Lesage was walking along Croft's Lane in a pair of burgundy sheepskin-lined slippers and a beige linen jacket with Rosie's half-finished crochet shawl round her neck. Rosie recognised the shawl before anything else. She swerved gently past Virginia and braked to a halt, angled across the verge.

The car creaked on its hinges as Rosie struggled out. 'What are you doing, Ginnie?'

Virginia stopped walking. Her fingers knotted themselves through the double-crochet loops. 'I'm not meeting that woman.'

'But you agreed.'

'Well I've changed my mind.' The fingers knotted tighter. 'That … that tramp shared my husband's bed. She lured him away from me.' She spun round, pale eyes glaring. 'And he gave her money. There's a word for women like that.' She dragged the shawl tighter. A crochet hook fell onto the ground. 'Prostitute.'

A tractor slowed behind the car. Its driver gesticulated none too kindly.

Rosie rescued the crochet hook and waved back, unkindly. She opened the door. 'Get in. You can't stay here.'

She folded Virginia into the seat and slammed the door. Thirty seconds later the car chugged along the lane, leaving the tractor to turn into a field of stubble. Ahead of them, a small triangle of grass supported a signpost. Rosie did a no-point turn around it, narrowly avoiding the ditches, and headed back home.

Gwen waited at the front door.

'Have they gone?' Rosie asked.

'We put them in a taxi, dear. About five minutes ago.'

'Good.' Virginia stomped across the hall into the drawing room. The muddy sheepskin-lined slippers left a trail of smudged footprints.

Rosie and Gwen looked at each other.

'Leave her to me, dear.' Gwen patted Rosie's hand. 'You go and make us some tea.' Her stick tip-tapped towards the drawing room. 'And bring some cake.'

Much later Gwen slumped back in her Easy-riser armchair. 'I'm exhausted.' Miffy yelped as she was pushed off her lap.

'I'm not surprised. That was quite a tour de force.' Rosie shoved the large footstool towards her with a toe.

Gwen settled her feet onto it. 'I don't think dear Ginnie will back down this time.'

'Nor do I. I think it was saying Livvie might drop her claim that did the trick.'

'Maybe, dear, but if Margaret hadn't been so adamant about not wanting any money we'd have never got Ginnie to agree.' Miffy ventured onto the footstool.

'Well, whoever's genius is was, I'm glad it's sorted.'

Miffy jumped from footstool to Gwen's lap. 'Are you sure you'll be able to manage with your clinic in the snug?'

'It'll be fine. I can easily move the couch in there if we push the piano to the side. Everyone will use the outside door. And there's the loo if they need it. It'll be no bother to anyone.'

Miffy sighed when Gwen tickled her ear. 'It's not as if you'll have to be there long. They'll be off to America as soon as they can.' Gwen settled herself against the cushions. 'I think I might have a little nap.'

When Rosie returned with a cup of tea both dog and mistress were snoring softly. Rosie went back to the kitchen.

Virginia stopped staring out of the kitchen window. 'Asleep?'

'Both of them.' Rosie made herself a cup of pomegranate and raspberry tea. 'Are you all right?'

A shrug. 'I suppose I might be.' She peered at the cup. 'What's that taste like?'

'Lovely. Try it.' She lifted a mug from the draining board and tipped some into it.

Virginia sipped, considered, then said. 'OK, I suppose.' She fished a tea bag from box to mug and poured almost-boiling water over it. 'Do you think I was wrong to fuss?' She dragged out a chair and sat down at the table opposite Rosie.

'Not at all. I've no idea how I'd have behaved if some girl had turned up on my doorstep claiming to be Malcolm's love child.'

'But was she? Is she, I mean? A love child?'

Rosie shrugged. 'I suppose there must have been something. Some occasion when ... well, you know.'

'That's just it, I don't know. I don't know how long it lasted. How often he ... Anything.'

'All I know is the little Margaret's let slip. Perhaps it was fairly short-lived. I gather she was a stenographer or suchlike at some conference or other.' The last of the tea disappeared down Rosie's throat. 'Did he go to many?'

'A few. He wasn't very interested in them.' Virginia fished the teabag out with a spoon. 'If she'd been a girl at the golf club I'd have understood it. He was always going up there.'

Rosie hoped that Virginia never discovered that Margaret had transferred her stenographic abilities from conferences to golf clubs.

A knock pounded on the front door.

Miffy yelped, jumped off Gwen's lap and ran into the hall determined to tell any invader they were not wanted.

'What now?' Rosie drained her topped-up cup.

Caroline stood on the doorstep looking rather pink. 'I've come to see mother.'

'Of course you have.' Rosie stood aside for Caroline to enter. 'She's dozing in the drawing room. It's been something of a day.'

'So I gather. I hear there's another pair going to sponge off her now.'

'What?'

'That couple - mother and daughter - moving into the cottage. Rent free.'

'How did you hear that?'

'From Christopher. Not that it's any of your business.' She turned her back and marched into the drawing room, dragging her horseshoe-patterned scarf from round her neck.

Rosie shut the front door and hovered in the hall. Memories of her conversation with Christopher crossed her mind.

'Darling.' Gwen put her feet on the rug and struggled upright among the squashy cushions. 'This is a lovely surprise.'

'I want to talk to you, mother.'

'Oh.' The brightness faded from Gwen's eyes. 'What about?'

'About these other people you're letting live off you.' Caroline towered over her mother. 'What were you thinking of?'

'Sit down dear and I'll explain.'

Caroline settled her middle-aged rear on the footstool. She stared at her mother throughout the tale without speaking.

'So you see,' Gwen finished. 'It's the only thing to do.'

'No, it isn't mother. It's being taken advantage of. I don't like to see people taking advantage of you. All this,' she waved her hand round the room. 'You didn't have to do this. You could have come to live with me if you'd wanted company.'

'Sweetheart.' Gwen reached for Caroline's hands. 'I know I could. But Grandma came to live with us when I was your age.'

'I know. It was lovely.'

'It was for you but she was such a ... a decided person that it wasn't quite so lovely for me. Truth to tell, after six months I wished Grandma was in sheltered housing somewhere - not that they had sheltered housing in those days, only convalescent homes. I don't want you to feel as guilty as I did.'

'I wouldn't be like that.' Caroline's eyes filled with tears. 'But doing this.' She waved her hand again. 'It feels like -' She folded her lips, squashing the words back. They burst out anyway. 'It feels like you like them better than me.'

'Oh, sweetheart. I like no-one better than you and Christopher. Daddy used to say he always felt third in line when you were little.'

Caroline fingers searched up her sleeve. A man's handkerchief appeared. She blew her nose loudly.

Rosie stopped hovering and tiptoed into the kitchen. 'Put the kettle on, Ginnie. We need tea and cake. Gwen's having another counselling session.'

'Who with?'

'Caroline. Mother and daughter stuff.'

Virginia grabbed the kettle rather smartly. 'Not something I'd know about.' The tap gushed too fast, flared up out of the kettle and soaked Virginia's new Pringle twinset. 'Damn,' she said.

CHAPTER THIRTY THREE

'And there too, please, Mrs Duncan.' Mr Johnstone pointed to a pencilled cross on the contract.

Ellie scrawled her signature.

'Excellent. That completes the legalities.' He smiled. 'You can leave it to us now. We'll exchange as soon as is possible.'

'Excellent,' Ellie repeated.

'May I say what a pleasure it's been to handle your business?' He reached out his hand. 'And if we can be of further help just let me know.'

Ellie stood up from the snazzy client's chair in front of his desk and shook the extended fingers. Excitement bubbled up inside her despite her best efforts to suppress it. 'Thank you Mr Johnstone.'

She collected her bag, slung the turquoise looped scarf Rosie had made for her birthday round her neck and hurried out of the office. The Golf was parked in the furthest corner of Minchman and Brooke's triangular carpark. The small space was wedged in between the back of their building and the rear of Beautilicious boutique whose clothes Ellie could never afford. Perhaps I'll treat myself, she thought. On Monday. It took a tight five-point turn to have the car facing the exit.

'I think we deserve some champagne,' she said out loud. 'I'll call in at Tesco's.'

She slipped into the evening traffic and headed out of town towards the small trading estate, a full half of which was occupied by the ubiquitous supermarket. Some champagne was on offer. Some was not. She blanched at the Non Vintage Bollinger for thirty-one pounds ninety-nine and settled for the Non Vintage De Vallois Brut at fourteen quid instead.

'Ta da,' she announced standing at the kitchen door and waggling the champagne bottle above her head. 'Guess who's signed the contract?'

'Oh, dear, bless you. That's marvellous.' Gwen heaved herself out of the chair and kissed Ellie's cheek, or tried to. She only managed to reach her jaw.

Ellie bent down and gave her a one-armed hug. 'Where is everyone?'

'Ginnie's upstairs lying down with a headache. Andrea's not back yet and Rosie's scraping up the leaves on the lawn. Apparently quite a few are falling already.'

Ellie dumped her bag on the table as usual. 'Well it is October so I suppose they are.' The contents of the utensil drawer clanked as she clattered around in it searching for the bottle opener.

'What are you doing, dear?'

'Bottle opener.'

'Ellie, dear, champagne doesn't need a bottle opener. The cork pops off.'

Ellie's arm drooped. 'I must be going senile. Of course it does.'

Gwen patted the drooping arm. 'No you're not, dear. It's all the stress. It stops your mind from working properly.'

'Let's hope so.'

The back door opened. 'Hi,' Rosie said. 'Home for the weekend?' She saw the bottle. 'Oh ho. What's that for?'

'I signed the contract today. It's all going through.'

A wide smile split Rosie's face. 'Hooray. No more sleepless nights. And ...' She levered her feet out of the gardening clogs and stuffed them into a pair of tartan slippers that had, judging by their downtrodden backs, seen years of service but were actually quite new. 'Ginnie will have something to be pleased about.' She shuffled across the floor and opened the display cabinet. Glasses chinked as she lined them up on the worktop.

'Yes, she will, the poor dear,' Gwen said. 'Why don't you pop up and tell her. Take her a glass of champagne. It might be just the thing to help her headache.'

'You know, your idea of a remedy for everything is a snifter of something alcoholic.'

'Well, it does help, dear. When I was feeding Caroline the mid-wife told me to have a small sherry a little before her last evening feed. Said it would help to settle her down.'

Ellie stared at her.

'And it did. We hardly ever had a sleepless night after the first few weeks.'

Ellie looked from Gwen to Rosie and back again. 'I think I'll go and see if Ginnie's awake.'

Virginia was asleep. The bedroom door creaked when Ellie opened it and woke her.

'Hi. I hear you've got a headache.'

Virginia rolled onto her side. 'More or less.'

'Would a glass of champagne make it less?'

'Why would I want a glass of champagne?'

The carpet cushioned the sound of Ellie's footsteps. 'Because I signed the contract on the restaurant today.'

Virginia lifted herself up onto one elbow. 'Really?'

'Really. So I can pay you back now.'

'There's no rush.'

'Yes there is.' Ellie perched sideways on the bed. 'I can't tell you how grateful I am that you helped me out.'

Virginia patted her hand. 'It's been worth it. Living here is so much better than I'd thought.' She sat up. 'Apart from that woman.'

Ellie moved so Virginia could swing her feet down and into her flat house shoes. 'I hear you've agreed to meet her. And Livvie.'

Virginia drooped. 'I know. Gwen said it might stop them carrying on with their claim.'

Ellie sat down beside her on the elaborate eiderdown. 'It might. I don't suppose it will be very easy for you.'

'That is something of an understatement.' Virginia rubbed two fingers across her forehead. 'I can't say I'm looking forward to it.'

'I imagine not.'

'The more I think about it, the more I can't believe George did it.' She looked round at Ellie. 'I mean why? Why did he have such a long-time thing with another woman?'

Ellie shook her head. There wasn't much she could think of to say that did not involve mentioning that Margaret was thirty years younger than Virginia. 'Some men are just like that, I think. No one woman, however perfect, is ever enough.'

Silence. Then, 'I don't think I was very perfect.'

'No-one is. I'm not. Kenneth certainly wasn't.' She stood up and held the glass out. 'Come on. Drink up then we'll go down for some more.'

The four of them stood in the kitchen, toasting The Butler's Pantry restaurant and vowing never, ever to set foot in it.

'Shall we leave some for Andrea?' Ellie asked.

'I think it will be flat by the time she gets home, dear.'

'Why? Where is she?'

'Out with her beau.'

'Her what?' Ellie said.

'Little Miss Southern Belle here means the new deputy head.' Rosie swigged the last of her champagne, tipping her head back to drain the final drops from the narrow flute.

'She's seeing a lot of him, isn't she?' Virginia said.

'All to the good, dear.' Gwen lifted the bottle. 'It'll stop her looking backwards.'

'She was rather gloomy about Anthony when we first met,' Ellie said.

'She was more than gloomy,' Virginia held her glass out to Gwen. 'She was bordering on alcoholic.'

Gwen tipped up the bottle as the front door slammed. 'Ah, that must be her now.'

Andrea's footsteps trailed across the floor. Her face was distinctly more gloomy than happy. 'What's this?' she said in a voice devoid of interest.

'We're celebrating. I sold the restaurant.'

Gwen tipped the last of the bubbles into her empty glass and held it out. 'Here you are dear. Toast the future.'

'Ha!' Andrea took the glass and raised it silently to Ellie.

'We were going to finish it off so you're only just in time, dear. I thought you said you were going to be later than this.'

'I was.' She turned her glass in her fingers.

'So?' Gwen's voice was soft.

'Oh, I don't know. I was going to dinner with Mark but ...' She shrugged. 'I don't know. It didn't feel right somehow.'

'What's not -' Ellie started.

Gwen put her hand on her arm. 'It's best to come home if you're not comfortable, dear. Rushing things is never a good idea. Taking it slowly is best.'

Three others stared at her.

Andrea drained her glass. 'I think I'll have an early night.' She put the glass down. 'Congrats and all that, Ellie. It's been a nightmare for you. I'm glad it's over.'

She walked out of the room, leaving the rest looking after her.

Ellie turned to Gwen. 'What were you on about? You just said ...'

'Hmm ... yes. It seems that young man is keener than she is after all. Perhaps she needs a little space to sort her mind out.'

'She certainly needs to find where she's at,' Rosie said. 'And centre herself. We don't want her getting into something she'll regret.' She put down her glass. 'I'll go and get her some Silicea. It's good for feeling overwhelmed with anxiety and indecision.'

'Well bring me some too,' Virginia said.

Ellie sat in Margaret Swinton's sitting room among the boxes and plastic carrier bags. Livvie perched on the arm of the sofa.

'Are you nervous about taking your mum to meet Ginnie?'

Livvie shrugged. 'A bit, I suppose. Always assuming she's going to be there this time.'

'Yes ... well. I think she will be.' Ellie looked at the black hair, the black sweatshirt over a black t-shirt. The black tights and the heavy black boots with chains on them. 'Mind if I make a suggestion?'

Another shrug.

'Ginnie's a bit old-fashioned. It might be an idea if you sort of modified your appearance a little. Sort of.'

'What d'you mean?'

'Have you got a frock?'

'A frock? I haven't had a frock since I was six.'

'Well, a skirt then. And a top. In something other than black.'

'What's wrong with black? It's cool.'

'It might be but it's rather ... aggressive.'

Margaret Swinton staggered into the room. 'What are you talking about?'

Livvie leapt up to help her mother slump into her chair. 'Ellie was saying I should dress differently to meet Mrs Lesage.'

'I just thought it would be one less thing Ginnie could ... er, find fault with.'

Margaret's voice came on an exhausted sigh. 'You're right.' The tired eyes looked up at her daughter. 'You could wear that skirt of that little suit I had for your christening. George always liked it. That's why I kept it.'

'Mum, it's years old. Older than me.'

'I know. But it's such a petty shade of blue. Blue always suited you.'

'Why don't you try it on, Livvie? Where is it, Margaret?'

'In the case on top of my wardrobe.'

Ellie looked hopefully at Livvie.

'And there's the little jumper in there that I got to go with it.'

Livvie sighed and disappeared. Her boots thumped up the stairs. A door opened, a suitcase dragged against the wardrobe top. Minutes later she returned clothed in a very creased A-line skirt. The jumper had a peach rose embroidered on one shoulder. Livvie sighed. Ellie looked at the black, chain-decorated boots. And sighed.

Virginia stood in front of the triple mirror on her walnut dressing table. Her new pleated wool skirt fell to mid-calf. She brushed the sleeve of her cardigan. The beige twinset hadn't pilled as yet and it toned rather nicely with the brown over-check tweed. Her mother's narrow strand of pearls lay on the glass tray on the dressing table. She lifted them with care and clicked the clasp behind her head. One hand patted her hair. Ellie had done a good job that morning. The grey curls marched across her head in neat feathers. She pushed her feet into the newly-polished Hotter low-heeled courts.

The gold watch on her wrist said five past one. Four hours to go. Four hours.

Virginia walked out of her bedroom on legs that were not completely steady.

CHAPTER THIRTY FOUR

'I think dear Andrea is getting anxious about that chap.'

Caroline paused from guiding her mother into the customer lift at John Lewis's. 'What?'

'Andrea, dear. I think this new chap is fretting her.'

'What chap, mother?' Caroline jabbed the close door button. The doors hissed shut. 'Is someone stalking her?'

'No, of course not. Andrea's not the sort of person to be stalked.' The lift gave the tiniest shudder and started its ascent to Womenswear. 'I just think this new teacher she's been seeing is going a little too fast.'

The lift arrived at the first floor. The doors slid open. Caroline guided her mother out.

'From what I've seen of her, she's well able to take care of herself.'

'I don't think so, dear. She's very -'

Caroline looked round the fashion floor. 'Now, where do you want to start?'

Gwen sighed and consigned her concerns about Andrea to a corner of her mind for later consideration. 'I thought perhaps a new skirt or two.'

'Oh, no, mother. You'll need an evening dress. And a cocktail one.'

A tiny smile spread across Gwen's mouth. Caroline was back on form. Gwen suppressed the smile and allowed her daughter to weave them through the new season's stock now occupying the various concessions towards Evening and Party Wear.

Twenty minutes later a most helpful assistant had shut them in the changing cubicle reserved for disabled shoppers. Four long gowns and as many cocktail dresses hung on the coat hooks. Caroline persuaded Gwen out of her Brettles French neck thermal vest.

'It'll show, mother, and spoil the effect.' The vest slipped up over Gwen's head. 'And anyway, those ships are quite warm. You won't need a vest to go round the Canaries for a week.'

'Twelve nights, dear.'

Caroline picked a fuchsia satin dress off the hanger. 'I'm not sure about this colour, mother. Surely a nice black would be better.'

'I don't like black, dear. I want something nice and bright.' Gwen struggled into the dress. Four inches of satin skirt settled onto the changing room floor around her feet.'

'It's far too long.' Caroline lifted the ticket. 'It comes in lavender too. That would be nicer.'

Gwen pulled up the zip under the arm. 'No thank you, dear. Too much like that film.' She adjusted the wrap-over skirt. 'Do you think they could put a few stitches in this, dear? Just to make sure it didn't unwrap when I sit down?'

Caroline checked the ticket again. 'For that price, I'm sure they'd sew up the entire front if you asked them.'

Gwen postured between the two angled, full-length mirrors. 'I rather like this.'

'Let's try the navy one, mother. It's less noticeable.'

'No, dear. This one.' She untangled a second hanger from the hooks and peered at the ribbon label stitched across the back of the dress. 'Fenn Wright Manson. They sound like solicitors, dear. Not dressmakers.'

'They're very well known.'

Gwen held the dress against her and stared in the mirror. 'Hmm.'

'Hmm what?'

'A bit young.' She twisted the dress. The skirt floated away from her knees. 'No, dear, I don't think so.'

Twenty dishevelled minutes later they emerged from the changing room. Caroline sallied to the sales desk with Chesca's velvet devorée dress in walnut and rose, plus matching bolero, and their Cinderella spot dress and shrug in periwinkle draped over one arm. She held the fuchsia Ghost Taya lace and satin dress ahead of her. The seamstress followed behind them.

Gwen parted with her credit card and the sales girl clicked through the process, adding the alteration charge at the end.

'A coffee now I think, dear.'

'Don't you want to see about shoes for them?'

Gwen shook her head. 'I need a little sit down first. Do you do Irish coffee here, dear?'

The salesgirl shook her head. 'I'm sorry, madam. I'm afraid I don't know. If you ask at the restaurant, I'm sure they'll be able to help you.'

Caroline sighed. 'All right. Coffee first and then shoes and day clothes.'

Afterwards the sales girl was not quite sure but she rather thought the elder of the two ladies winked at her.

Gwen and Caroline arrived home when Virginia was checking her watch for the thirty-seventh time. One hour to go. The sight of multiple carrier bags and shoe boxes diverted her momentarily. The driver stood them in the hall beside the front door.

'Good heavens, Gwen. Have you bought the shop?'

'Not quite, dear, but Caroline's advice has been very helpful.'

The taxi driver opened the boot. He dragged out a hard-shell suitcase whose stunning scarlet would have shamed the most rigorous colour sergeant in the Brigade of Guards.

'Over there, please, driver.' Caroline pointed to the side of the hall. She clicked open her handbag and produce a ten pound note.

Her hand remained open while the driver, with a certain amount of bad grace, counted all of the change into it. 'Thank you. I'll phone when I need collecting.'

The driver looked as if he hoped someone else would answer that particular summons. He nodded to Gwen and left.

Caroline began to collect the bags from the floor.

'Oo.' Rosie emerged from the kitchen, wearing items that had never seen a fashion floor. She clapped her hands. 'Buying. Lots of buying.' She picked up two of the smart paper carrier bags. 'Are we going to have a fashion show?'

'Gwen looks rather too tired for that,' Virginia said. 'And besides ...' She twisted her watch.

'Oh, yes. I'd forgotten.'

'Forgotten what, dear?'

'Margaret.'

'Margaret?' Caroline's head whipped round. 'Isn't that the woman who ... I mean ... the one that's coming to live here?'

'Oh, yes,' Gwen said. 'I'd forgotten it's tonight.'

'I'll stay, mother.'

'There's no need, dear.'

'Yes there is. I'll stay.'

'But I think -'

'I think that is an excellent idea, Mrs Thackary.' Virginia stopped twisting her watch. 'Perhaps you would care for some tea?'

Rosie and Gwen looked from Virginia to Caroline and then at each other. Rosie gave the smallest of shrugs.

'That would be very welcome, Mrs Lesage.'

'Call me Virginia. If you take your mother into the drawing room, I'll put the kettle on.'

As tea parties went it was about as comfortable and relaxing as one on a sinking Titanic. Tea was poured. It was drunk in careful sips.

Biscuits were handed round. Napkins were placed across knees. Crumbs fell from the occasional mouthful.

'Tell me how your grandchildren are getting alone, Caroline,' Virginia said. 'I can't remember their names.'

'Michael and Felicity.'

'Ah, yes. Pretty name, Felicity.'

'Thank you. We all thought so. And of course she's Gwendolyn too.'

'Of course.'

If Rosie had been wearing anything as old fashioned as stays she couldn't have felt more unreal.

'And are they at school?'

'Greenham's.'

'Excellent. Though the fees must be quite a challenge for your son.'

'Indeed. They are quite high but we're paying. Bradley and I think it's well worth it.'

'I'm sure you're right. A good education and contacts will see them onto the right path.'

Rosie stood up somewhat quickly. 'More tea anyone?'

Virginia glanced at her watch. She swallowed. 'I'm not sure there will be time.'

'Yes there is,' Rosie said without looking at the clock on the marble mantelpiece. 'I'll go and make it.' She looked at the relaxed figure on the sofa near the fire. 'Bless her, she won't be wanting any.'

Right on cue, Gwen snored softly. Her hand on Miffy's back moved.

Rosie fled to the kitchen. The left-hand cupboard of the dresser contained the new bottle of St Remy Napoleon brandy. She twisted the top. The seal cracked and split. The top spun onto the floor. Rosie took a hefty swig straight from the bottle. She coughed and took a second.

'Saints and little sinners,' she said to the window. 'I hope it doesn't get any worse.'

Ellie pulled away from fifty-one Estelle Pankhurst Road. Margaret Swinton sat beside her. The hands clenched in her lap knotted and unknotted repeatedly.

Livvie leant forward from the back seat. The pale blue skirt slid up her thighs. 'It'll be OK, mum. Really it will.' She squeezed her mother's shoulder.

Margaret stopped torturing her fingers for a moment and reached up to pat her daughter's hand. 'I'll be fine. Don't worry about me.'

Livvie sat back. She tugged the skirt down, smoothed the matching jumper over it and wrapped her black duffle coat more tightly around her.

Ellie negotiated the T-junction. The lights of the rush hour traffic reflected on the wet road, sending multiple flashes across the windscreen. With a deep breath, she settled into the nose-to-tail line of cars.

'How long will it take to get there?' Margaret's voice barely sounded above the noise of the tyres splashing through the puddles.

'About twenty minutes. Maybe a bit longer if the traffic stays this bad.'

Silence.

Successive street lights flicked orange bands across the car.

'Um ...' Ellie tried again. 'We'll be quicker once we get onto Deerton Road.'

Silence.

'We've made a few changes since you were there last time.' She braked to a halt at a red traffic light. 'The path's a lot easier now.'

Silence.

Ellie gave up.

Virginia pulled a curtain aside. The line of small lights down the drive glowed faintly.

'They won't get here any quicker, dear, for looking out there.' The damask curtain swung back into place.

'I thought I heard a dog,' Virginia said.

'Caroline, dear, are you sure the children will be all right?'

'Yes, mother. I phoned Leanna Creighton. She collected them for me. They're staying with her two until Bradley gets home.'

Gwen sighed. 'How very well organised of you, dear.'

Caroline put down her fourth cup of tea. 'I really expected the shopping to take longer than it did, mother. I must say, you surprised me. Such bright colours.'

'Bright colours are by far the best. They cheer you up no end.' Rosie hiccoughed. 'Pardon me.' She looked at the empty cups. 'More tea?'

'Not for me, dear, but you have one if you want.' Gwen smiled.

'I might just do that.' Rosie left the room. In the kitchen the St Remy suffered another onslaught.

Ellie turned onto Rectory Lane. 'Almost there.'

Silence.

Livvie leant forward again and put her hand on her mother's shoulder and squeezed it through the padded coat. Margaret's hand crept up. She held on to her daughter's fingers while Ellie drove up the drive.

'Is that the car?' Virginia said.

'I think so, dear.'

Caroline stood up.

Virginia walked to the fireplace. She positioned herself centrally before it beside an upright chair by the fireplace that had not been there that morning.

Gwen lifted Miffy onto her lap. The dog shivered.

Ellie stopped as close to the front door as she could manage.

'It's only a few steps. You won't really get wet.' She slid the gear lever into neutral and switched the engine off.

Margaret tugged at her seat belt clasp.

'Here, let me.' Ellie unclipped it. She climbed out of the car and ran round to open the passenger door. In the back seat, Livvie waited until Ellie had helped her mother out then pushed the seat forward. The blue skirt stretched across her thighs as she climbed out.

Virginia gripped her hands together. Caroline walked three paces towards the fireplace.

Rosie opened the front door. Leaning on her daughter and Ellie, Margaret Swinton made her painful way up the three steps and into the hall.

'Come into the warm,' Rosie said. She stood aside until the slow progress into the hall was completed. The front door slammed.

Virginia heard the noise. Her hands clenched tighter. She turned to face the door.

Margaret Swinton reached the drawing room's double doors.

Rosie pushed them open.

Margaret Swinton took two slow steps.

She stopped on the threshold.

Virginia Lesage and her husband's mistress stared at each other.

CHAPTER THIRTY FIVE

Miffy jumped from Gwen's lap and chased across the carpet, yapping wildly. She jumped her front paws onto Margaret's knees. Margaret wobbled.

Ellie scooped up the dog. Livvie grabbed at her mother's arm with one hand and slung her other arm round her back. Her fingers gripped into the padded jacket.

'Oh, Miffy' Gwen called. 'You naughty girl.' She beckoned with one flapping hand. 'Bring her here, Ellie, dear. I don't know why she did that. She never jumps up at people.'

After a quick glance at Margaret, Ellie carried the yapping Miffy to Gwen and dropped her on her lap.

In front of the fireplace, Virginia was not looking at the dog. Every one of her facial muscles was rigid. Caroline moved closer beside her.

'Well,' Rosie said. 'Shall we all sit down?'

Andrea looked from Rosie to Virginia and Caroline at the fireplace, to Livvie and Margaret at the door and finally to Ellie marooned midway between them. 'Good idea.' She seated herself beside Gwen.

Ellie continued to the newcomers and helped Livvie with her mother's slow progress to the nearest sofa. The movements were painful to watch. With each difficult step, Virginia's tense mouth relaxed fractionally. Margaret flopped down onto the corner of the sofa. Her daughter propped cushions around her then sat close beside her, holding her hand. Virginia seated herself on the dining chair. She folded her hands in her lap.

'Shall we have some tea?' Rosie asked.

'I think introductions first would be better, dear.'

'Right.' Ellie walked to the centre of the room. 'Everyone, you know Livvie but this is Margaret. Her mother.' She looked at the surrounding faces. One by one she made the introductions. 'Margaret, you know Gwen and Rosie and Andrea but this is Caroline, Gwen's daughter.' She drew a breath. 'And this is Virginia.'

Margaret Swinton's face coloured. 'Good evening Mrs Lesage.'

Virginia inclined her head. 'Good evening, Mrs Swinton.'

'Right,' Rosie said. 'That's done. Now for some tea.' She disappeared rather too quickly out of the door.

Caroline advanced across the carpet. 'How do you do, Mrs Swinton?' She held out her hand.

Margaret took it by the fingertips. 'How do you do?'

'Do you live here too?' Livvie asked.

'No. I live with my … er, family on the other side of town.' She looked at the pair. 'I can get here quite quickly of course if there's a problem for mother.'

'I don't have problems, dear. Now come and sit down.' She patted the sofa cushion.

'Um …' Andrea rubbed her mouth. 'How are the arrangements for renting the house going?'

'We've sign the agreement thing with the management lot,' Livvie said. 'They want us to leave everything and let it furnished. Mum's not too sure.' She held her mother's hand between both of hers. 'Are you, mum?'

'It's my home. With my things. I don't want anyone else using them.'

'I can totally understand that.' Virginia's voice cut across the room. 'I feel exactly the same about people using things I thought were mine.'

'Ginnie, dear. That isn't helping.'

'Helping? Why -'

'Look, Mrs Lesage.' Margaret's weaker voice broke into Virginia's. 'If this is going to work - and I'm not sure it is - we really need to clear the air between us. We. Us two. By ourselves.' The outburst left her panting a little.

'I'm not leaving you, mum. Not with her.'

'I'll be fine. Don't fret. You go and have some tea - or coffee with these ladies. Mrs Lesage and I will have it out.'

Livvie stared at Virginia. 'Don't you bully her. She's not well.'

'I've no intention of bullying anyone. And it that's the tone you're going to take then perhaps your mother's right. She and I should do this on our own.'

Gwen pushed Miffy off her lap. 'Come along, dear. The sooner it's started the sooner it will be finished and we can all relax.' She struggled up and led the way into the hall.

With a final glare at Virginia, Livvie dropped a kiss on her mother's head and followed them out.

Gwen's voice echoed back into the room. 'Close the door, Livvie dear.'

Margaret eased herself back into the sofa. Virginia stared at her.

'My voice isn't very good today. Do you think you could move your chair a little closer?'

Virginia stood. She grabbed the dining chair by its back, then released it. As upright as a fence post she walked to the adjacent sofa and sat at the end nearest her rival.

'Thank you. Now, what do you want to know about me?'

'I think an apology might be the first thing to start with.'

'Why?'

'You stole my husband.'

'No I didn't.'

Virginia snorted. 'What else was it then?'

'Love. Companionship.'

Another snort. 'I was his wife. That was what he shared with me.'

'I know. He was just ... just too much for any one woman. You must have known that.'

'I didn't know anything of the sort.' Virginia's voice faded. Memories of the way George flirted with any attractive woman he met edged into her mind.

'He was such a handsome man when he was younger,' Margaret said.

Virginia sighed. 'He was.' Her ramrod spine slackened. 'He was still handsome when he died.' She looked at Margaret. 'Were you ... you and he still ...?'

'Oh no. It was over long before that. We were more like brother and sister.'

'Oh. I'm not sure that's any better. I'd assumed you were still ...'

Margaret shook her head. 'No. Not since I got pregnant. He only kept in touch because of Livvie. He didn't want her to suffer because we weren't married.' She shot a quick look at Virginia. 'He didn't want you to suffer by knowing about us.'

Virginia's spine stiffened again.

'Or about the others.'

'Others? What others?'

Margaret shook her head. 'There was always someone. Someone new.'

'You must be mistaken.'

'I'm not.' She paused. 'I'm sorry.'

Virginia stared at her. She put the backs of her bent fingers across her lips and pressed. No breath came. 'Oh, God,' she gasped at last. 'I must have been a laughing stock.' She moved her hand to her forehead.

'You weren't. He was always very discreet.'

Virginia's head jerked up. 'Not so discreet that you didn't know about them.'

'He told me. Every time.'

A pause. 'That couldn't have been easy for you.'

'It wasn't. Particularly.' She coughed and drew three shallow breaths. Her voice came weakly. 'The thing to remember is that he always came home to you. Stayed married to you.'

Virginia slumped back in the sofa, arms clasped across her chest. 'Why?'

'You were his wife. He loved you.'

A sharp retort rose to Virginia's lips. It died there. Silence, then, 'That's something, I suppose.'

'It is.' The voice regained a little of its strength. 'He was kind to you, wasn't he?'

Virginia shrugged. 'I suppose so. Apart from the pension. That wasn't kind.' Her eyes hardened.

'I'm sorry about that. I didn't want him to do anything for me, only Livvie.' Another shallow breath. 'He insisted. And I was so angry when I found out what Livvie had done. Coming here, demanding money from you.'

'Oh, you can't blame the child. It was very dutiful of her. You're her mother. She's bound to want to do whatever she can for you.'

'It's good of you to see it like that.' A trembling smile. 'She's a good girl, you know. So talented. I didn't want her to give up her studies.'

'Gwen said there were lots of things she could paint here.'

Another smile. 'Mrs Fellowes is capable of the most unsuspected, unsurpassed deviousness I have ever seen.'

'Why do you say that?'

'She seems to get everyone doing what she wants without them realising it.'

'I hadn't -' Virginia broke off and sat buried in thought for quite a time. 'Now you mention it, I think you're right.'

'I know I am. She persuaded me to come here with that comment about Livvie's art.' She smiled at Virginia. 'Livvie doesn't paint much. She wants to be a potter.'

Virginia flopped back against the cushions, laughing. 'The minx. The wicked minx.' She stopped laughing. 'If he's looking down on us I suppose the old devil would find this amusing.'

'I think he'd be relieved.'

'How so?'

'You were on your own. No family, I'm sorry to say. Perhaps he thinks we could be a little bit of ... well, company for each other.'

Virginia looked her up and down. 'You're quite a lot younger than me.'

'So's Rosie. And Ellie and Andrea. You all get on all right with them, don't you?'

Virginia re-folded her arms. 'I suppose I do.'

'Well, perhaps we'll get on all right too. If you could stop hating me.'

'I don't hate you ... I think. I'm more inclined to hate George.'

Margaret smiled. 'You can't hate George. Not with those eyes of his.'

Virginia smiled softly. 'They were something, weren't they? Especially when he was young.' She pulled a long breath into her lungs then released it in a single gush. 'Well ... if you'd like to ... I suppose it's ... manageable'

CHAPTER THIRTY SIX

Virginia stood on the threshold of the front door, feet together, hands folded. Beyond the long oval lawn down to the gates, the late October sun flickered low through the elm tree's skeletal branches. The tail lights of the taxi heading down the drive glowed in the fading light.

Caroline leant against the door jamb, watching Michael and Felicity chasing after it, waving and shouting, 'Bye Gran-gran. Bye.'

'How exactly did mother get Andrea onto the cruise?'

'Something to do with the cocktail pianist breaking a leg. Or some such thing. There was a letter explaining there wouldn't be one after all and as she had single occupancy of her stateroom … well, it just fitted. I'm surprised Andrea went though. I wouldn't have thought cruising was her sort of thing.'

'I suppose that's why mother mention the pianist bit. It's just like her to come up with a scheme.' She pushed herself upright. 'Felicity. Michael.' She pointed at the bicycles abandoned on the grass. 'Pick those up and take them round the back.'

The women watched the children wheel the two bicycles round the corner of the house.

Virginia shut the door. 'She was sure Andrea needed a breathing space from this man. She thinks he's courting her a little too quickly.'

'Courting.' Caroline snorted. 'People don't court any more.'

'You mother thinks they do.'

'How did Andrea get the time off from school? Half term's only a week.'

'It's only a twelve day cruise. The two weekends means she only needs an extra three days.'

The children erupted into the hall. 'Can we have some cake?'

'I beg your pardon?' Caroline frowned.

'Sorry, Grannie.' Felicity slid her hand into her grandmother's. 'Please may we have some of Mrs Rosie's cake?'

'It's chocolate this time,' Michael said.

'You'll have to ask Mrs Rosie.'

'We did.' Michael grabbed the other hand. 'She said to ask you.'

'Who's she?' Virginia said. 'The cat's aunt?'

'We don't say she, do we?' Caroline swung her hands, making the children laugh.

'Mrs Rosie, then.' Felicity tugged Caroline's hand again. 'Pleeeease.'

'Very well. Where is Mrs Rosie?'

'In the kitchen with Uncle Christopher.' Felicity skipped over the tiles.

'They're holding hands and looking soppy.' Michael shuddered. 'Yuk.'

'When you cease to be eight, young man,' Virginia said. 'And are a few years older, you will understand about holding hands and being soppy.'

'If I can't be Mrs Andrea's bridesmaid, can I be Mrs Rosie's?'

Caroline dragged her hand free. 'That's enough. Stop talking this nonsense.'

The six-year-old face fell. 'Michael bet me his Christmas sweets they'd be engaged by then.'

The matriarchal grandmother frowned. 'In that case he had better not have any this year.'

'Ratfink,' Michael called from the kitchen door.

'And any more of that sort of talk and there won't be any Christmas for you at all.'

Virginia and Caroline proceeded into the kitchen where Rosie and Christopher were holding hands.

'Chocolate cake?' Rosie asked.

'Only small pieces, please,' Caroline said. 'And you two, wash your hands first.'

'The place will feel quite empty now mother and Andrea have gone too,' Christopher said.

'Oh yes.' Caroline sat down. 'Have you heard from Margaret?'

'Livvie emailed yesterday.' Rosie cut four sizeable chunks of cake and lifted them onto plates. 'Margaret managed the journey quite well but they're letting her rest for a couple of days, just to be sure she isn't too exhausted.'

'Poor woman,' Caroline said.

'Are you talking about the funny lady who lives in the cottage?' Michael asked.

'Don't be so rude,' Caroline said. 'She's not funny. She's just not very well.'

Christopher caught Rosie's eye. 'Do you fancy a stroll down to the river before it's absolutely dark?'

'If you like. We can shut the chickens in on the way back up.'

The pair left the room. The back door had barely closed when Michael said in a loud stage whisper. 'Do you think they're going for a snog?'

Felicity spluttered chocolate crumbs across the table. 'They're old. They don't snog.'

'Michael, if I have to speak to you again, I'll tell mummy you aren't allowed to come for a month.'

Virginia looked from the children, to their grandmother, to Christopher and Rosie disappearing across the terrace. All in all, she decided, Rosie's idea hadn't turned out so badly after all. There was company, lots of it, and sometimes very noisy. The house was large and warm. That was better than living alone in a mausoleum she couldn't afford to heat. And of course, the bills were considerably lower too.

She turned to Caroline. 'Would you like some tea, dear?'

THE END

Printed in Great
Britain
by Amazon

32279557R00163